A
DEAD MAN'S
EYES

A
DEAD MAN'S
EYES

A Lisa Jamison Mystery

Lori Duffy Foster

LeVel
BEST BOOKS

First published by Level Best Books 2021

This novel is entirely a work of fiction. The names, characters and incidents portrayed in it are the work of the author's imagination. Any resemblance to actual persons, living or dead, events or localities is entirely coincidental.

Lori Duffy Foster asserts the moral right to be identified as the author of this work.

AUTHOR PHOTO CREDIT: TSF Photography

First edition

ISBN: 978-1-953789-25-9

Cover art by Level Best Designs

This book was professionally typeset on Reedsy.
Find out more at reedsy.com

For Tom, my rock.

Praise for A DEAD MAN'S EYES

"Only a skilled and experienced reporter could craft such an authentically gripping story. Duffy Foster is the real deal—emotional depth and honest story-telling make this a terrific debut!" —Hank Phillippi Ryan/ *USA Today* Bestselling Author of *The First to Lie*

"A fine debut, packed with action and intrigue. We see in *A Dead Man's Eyes* what it truly means to be family, and sometimes what it takes to protect the ones we love. Lori Duffy Foster has given crime fiction a wonderful new protagonist: a journalist with the curiosity and heart to get her into trouble, the smarts and bravery to get her out of it, and the humanity for us to care deeply that she succeeds. Duffy Foster skillfully kicks off with a grim puzzle, then hurls us into a deadly game of cat-and-mouse, keeping the tension high, and the stakes higher. We can only hope this will be the first of many adventures with protagonist Lisa Jamison." —Mark Pryor, author of the Hugo Marston series

Chapter One

It pays to be friends with the medical examiner.

It was two a.m. when Lisa called the direct line to the morgue and, sure enough, Alex answered and agreed to let her in. She knew he would be there. He liked working at night. He got the bodies when they were fresh, and the evidence was still intact. And he liked to talk. All he required of Lisa was that she honor their deal: that anything he ever told her stayed between them. She could use the information to push buttons and get other sources talking, but she could never allow the trail to lead back to him.

And he never, ever wanted to see his name in the newspaper.

"This isn't for a story, Alex. You know that," Lisa said as he reached for the zipper on the black body bag that filled the table between them. Black bags for homicides. White for naturals, accidents, suicides, and unknowns. She couldn't bring herself to watch as he exposed the face. She wanted to see him all at once. So, she focused on the blue-gray of Alex's veins bulging beneath the latex gloves and on his slightly chubby fingers. Anything to distract herself from what she was about to see.

"I just have to know if it's him."

"This case was next on my list. You sure you can handle this? They don't look so good when they've been dead for almost twenty-four hours." Alex looked up at her through bangs that desperately needed a trim. Stubble, a good day's worth, pushed through his pale skin. His eyes were webbed with red. He had not likely been home since sunrise. He was like that, always working day and night. He was a good reminder to Lisa of just how much her

1

daughter grounded her. Alex had no pressing reason to leave, no children to disappoint.

"I'm sure I've seen worse." Lisa sighed. "I know I have. Remember the kid who hit the tree at one-hundred and ten miles per hour down by Mount James last spring? The suicide? I still see him sometimes. At strange times—in the shower, when I'm out for a run, while I'm watching my daughter's soccer games. His skin was just shredded. All of it. Like hamburger. This was a gunshot wound. It can't be that bad."

"Yeah, but you've never known the dead guy before. It's a whole lot different when you knew the body as a person. Your call, though." His hand rested on the zipper, and he stared at her, waiting for an answer.

In her hurry, Lisa had forgotten to rub Vick's ointment beneath her nose. Death, with its unmistakable odor, freely infiltrated her nostrils and spread through her lungs. She knew she would take it with her when she left—that musty, rotten smell, like sweaty socks and decaying meat—and that it would take multiple washings to get it out of her clothes if it came out at all. She needed to get this over with, to quit over-thinking it, to get out of there and go home.

"Just go ahead, please?"

Lisa held her breath as the zipper parted to reveal a face that was still familiar after sixteen years. His skin was gray and undamaged. His brown eyes, with their amber halos, were open, but they were empty. His thick, dark hair was disheveled and matted with dried blood. He was already rigid. Cold and empty. One arm pushed against the side of the bag, the muscles frozen in the position of death. It didn't scare Lisa. Dead bodies never scared her. Instead, they gave her faith there might really be some kind of afterlife. They were empty. Hollow, like discarded shells. Whatever had made Marty human was gone. But it was him.

It was definitely him.

Lisa couldn't look anymore. Not like this. But as she shifted her gaze, a glint of silver on his chest caught her eye. She reached for it, not thinking about whether that was allowed, whether she was tainting evidence or breaking some kind of rule that would forever sever her from possibly her best official source. Her fingers followed the chain around his neck to the pendant that hung from it. It was a Native American Kokopelli, hunched over and playing his flute, the necklace she had given Marty just months before they last saw each other. The chain was new—brighter silver, cleaner, and more expensive than the original—but the pendant was the same.

"Had enough?" Alex asked, gently removing her fingers from the pendant. It dropped back onto Marty's neck, resting in the hollow between his collar bones. Lisa hoped his family would think to leave it there, that they would sense somehow that it had meaning for him. She couldn't imagine he had ever told them where it had come from.

"Yeah," she said in little more than a whisper. "Thanks."

She hadn't thought about how she might feel. Her heart had quickened. Her palms were slick with sweat. Her body—though long, lean, and fit—suddenly felt small and weak, inadequate to handle the emotions that weighed her down. But she wasn't sad, and she wasn't frightened. Well, not frightened in the usual way. It was a different kind of fear. A surprisingly selfish fear. The kind that white-collar criminals must feel when they realize how much they've risked and that the consequences are real, that their whole world might just crash down around them, that their neighbors might learn some ugly truth that will isolate them from the suburban illusion forever. A fear possessed by liars.

But Lisa had never hidden from Marty, and she had never lied to him. There was no reason to feel this way. She had refused to see him when he emailed her last month. That was true. But his note was unexpected, and she wasn't ready. All she had asked for was time. A few months. And he had agreed. She couldn't have known this would happen.

She pulled up a stool and tried to take it all in. Her hair, long and smooth, was falling out of her pony tail and sticking to her neck and face. The make-up she had applied nineteen hours earlier had been washed away by the stress of deadlines. Her clothes carried the sweat and smells of a full day in the newsroom, in the courthouse, on the streets and, now, in the morgue. She needed a long shower. She threw her head back and drew a deep breath, closing her eyes long enough to relieve some of the sting. This was too much.

Alex tugged the zipper closed, and just like that, Marty's face was gone. Then he grabbed a pole that held up a plastic replica of a human skeleton and rolled it over, explaining that whoever hit Marty either got lucky or was an excellent shot. The bullet went straight through the subclavian artery just below his shoulder, he said, causing a massive bleed. He died just after he arrived at the hospital.

"A shot in the shoulder usually does some damage, but not like this," he said. "This one hit the artery just right. The drugs were apparently in his jacket pocket. Not much. Just a couple quarter grams of methamphetamine. Nothing worth killing over. The hit was too clean and came from too far away, though, to be some strung-out druggie who couldn't afford a high. This was a professional hit, probably his supplier making an example out of him. He must have had a beef with the big guy."

"I just don't see it, Alex," Lisa said, watching him as he peeled off his gloves and scrubbed his hands clean in the stainless-steel sink. He scrubbed hard and fast, paying close attention to his fingernails and cuticles. He rinsed and dried them just as thoroughly with a paper towel. She waited until he turned to face her again. What she wanted to tell him was that she knew Marty's core. That part of people that doesn't change. Alex was wrong. The police were wrong. They had to be. "I know it's been a long time since I saw him last, but I knew him, and people don't change that much. He wasn't the type. Marty wasn't a drug dealer. I don't get it. Why would anyone want to kill Marty?"

"You're a reporter. You know that we don't always know people like we think we do. How many times have you quoted someone after a homicide saying that this kind of stuff doesn't happen in 'her' neighborhood, or that 'he was such a nice guy...he would never do anything like this'?" Alex rested against the sink with his arms folded across his chest and watched her for a moment.

"I'm very sorry, Lisa," he said in a quiet voice. "I know this is hard, but you've got to give stuff like this a chance to sink in. Go home and take a hot bath and then maybe take a sleep aid or something. You could use the rest. Things will look different tomorrow."

Alex smiled, a subtle, reassuring smile, the kind Lisa needed at that moment. But his expression quickly faded when a loud beep sounded, indicating someone had entered through the morgue's back door. He stood up straight, and Lisa stood as well, grabbing the leather jacket she had carried in with her and slipping her arms through it, hoping it would appear that she had just arrived and was just about to leave. No matter who it was, she knew it wouldn't look good for Alex to be chatting it up with a reporter in the middle of the night in the morgue.

The swinging door to the autopsy room flew open, but the assistant medical examiner stopped its motion with her hand when she saw Lisa and Alex. Her tanned skin, polished nails, and smooth, sun-bleached hair seemed too upbeat, too relaxed, for the hour and the place. But Lisa had learned long ago never to underestimate Anita Ulman. Her pronounced cheekbones gave her a certain kind of strength along with her large, ice-blue eyes that never seemed to miss a movement and her tight, thin lips that responded with smiles only when accompanied by sarcasm.

Anita had never been kind to Lisa, and she was barely even polite most of the time, yet Lisa couldn't deny that she had a bit of respect for her. Anita had moved up high in a largely male-dominated field, one in which any expression of sympathy, fear, or revulsion could easily knock her down a few notches. Lisa understood her need for hardness. She didn't like it, but she understood it, and she saw how it made Alex, Anita's boss, jump to attention. Even he was afraid of her.

"What brings you in?" Alex asked a little too cheerfully.

"If you had checked the schedule, you'd see that I am on call. A phone call to let me know you had it covered would have been nice, especially at this hour, but I see you were distracted by your company." Anita looked Lisa up and down, the way a man might check out a woman in a sleazy gym, the kind with a bar in the lobby. It was an interesting technique for making anyone, male or female, highly uncomfortable. Lisa was used to her after all these years and wasn't terribly intimidated. Still, she found herself smoothing her pants with her hands, glad that she'd worn her new black slacks that day instead of jeans, and subtly checking her leather boots to be sure the toes

5

had no scuff marks, mud, or dust on them.

"I was just leaving," Lisa said, pulling her jacket more tightly around her body. "The victim was an old friend, a good friend, and Alex was kind enough to let me confirm that it was him. Thank you, Alex. I won't keep you two from your work any longer."

The late September moon was hazy and low in the sky when Lisa stepped out into the parking lot. The air was cool but thick with moisture, most likely pulled from Lake Ontario. Seneca Springs, like the rest of Central New York, was preparing for another long winter with its wet, heavy, lake-effect snow, the kind that quickly melted to slush and then froze, making the roads treacherous twice over. In another month, Lisa would have to trade her leather jacket for her down one and her all-season tires for snow tires. Rudy, the night janitor, was having a smoke beside his car before leaving for the night, probably headed to another job. He stared at her as she crossed the wide lot to visitor parking, so she waved in his direction, and he nodded in return.

In just a few hours, the sky would be bright, and people would be reading the news with their coffee, swiping from story to story on their smartphones in Starbucks or Dunkin Donuts, or flipping the physical pages in the few print copies that were still thrown from car windows onto doorsteps, and folding them just so. Lisa thought about the blurb that would appear in the left-hand column of page B2 of the print edition, the blurb that was already available online. Six inches. Long for a brief. Just another drug killing. The case would go to two investigators who would work on it here and there for a day or two, knowing that they weren't going to get any answers and that there would be no public pressure to make an arrest.

Years later, maybe they'd have somebody in custody for some other crime, and he'd confess, or he'd rat on a friend in hopes of getting a break. But more likely, no one would ever pay for Marty's death. To the cops and the readers, he was just a street-level drug dealer. That was all. But he was more than that to Lisa.

He was the father of her daughter.

Bridget would be asleep when Lisa got home. She would find her as she always did, snuggling with her comforter in the fetal position with her fingers entwined in her mahogany waves. Bridget's hair was a gift from her father, far deeper and fuller than Lisa's own dull brown and the envy of anyone who passed her by. She had Marty's skin tone, too—light olive and quick to tan. And those eyes—much like Marty's but with a hint of green. Not a trace of the steel gray Lisa had inherited from her own mother. But Bridget was tall and slender like Lisa, and quick-tempered. They shared a cynicism and a dry sense of humor that only the two of them seemed to appreciate. She was beautiful, inside and out, but Marty would never know that. Lisa felt a chill and picked up her pace.

Despite the late hour, she knew Dorothy would still be awake, watching over Bridget and worrying over Lisa. Watching after a long day of painting. Bright, colorful scenes with earth tones cleverly hidden in the layers in a way that somehow left Lisa feeling uplifted and grounded at the same time. Dorothy's stamina amazed Lisa. She was thirty-one years older than Lisa and her best friend. They'd met when Bridget was eight years old. Lisa was hiding her swollen eyes in a magazine while Bridget played on the monkey bars with a classmate, but Dorothy sat beside her on the bench and wouldn't let her be. Dorothy's husband had passed away three years before, and she was lonely. She often came to the park, Lisa later learned, hoping to make friends. She poked and prodded. She was relentless.

Lisa told her everything that day, how she had gotten pregnant at fifteen, but still managed to graduate high school and college, only to find herself faced with giving up the career she'd worked so hard for. She had been with the newspaper for a year and had already been through five child care providers. She could rarely say with certainty what time she'd be done work, and she couldn't find anyone who could be that flexible. Journalists can't work nine-to-five, she told Dorothy. She'd just have to forget about it and find something else.

The next thing she knew, Dorothy was sleeping on the futon in the living room of her two-bedroom apartment, staying with Bridget when Lisa worked late. Over time, she became "Grandma Dorothy," and when Lisa finally bought a house on the city's east side, Dorothy moved with them, paints, easel, brushes, canvases, and all. Bridget no longer needed a babysitter at sixteen years old, but Lisa felt better knowing she was never home alone, especially whenever she thought about herself at that age. Bridget was one year older than Lisa was when she gave birth. That was hard to comprehend. She wasn't perfect, and they'd had their rocky moments—lately, it seemed the rocks were more jagged than usual and harder to climb over—but she was an honors student, a sweet girl and a starter on the high school soccer team. She was everything Lisa had hoped she would be.

She searched her purse for her car keys and pushed the button to unlock the doors. The beep seemed exceptionally loud in the empty parking lot. The janitor was gone, and she was alone. Lisa suddenly felt exposed. Vulnerable. Marty's face came back to her, his blank expression. The smell of the morgue still clung to her clothing. She couldn't escape it. He'd been murdered. Someone killed him intentionally, and his lifeless body was right there, just a few yards away. She quickly got in her car and locked the doors. As she pulled out of the lot, she wondered what Marty knew about Bridget—when he learned her name and that she was a girl. She hadn't heard from him in sixteen years until that email last month. They were just kids when she got pregnant, and she'd been taken into the system, lost within the physical and psychological void of bureaucracy.

It was a short email, an apology for not having come forward sooner. And it was a request. Marty wanted to meet his daughter. He needed to know her, he wrote. But Lisa wasn't ready. She needed time to explain things to Bridget, and, most importantly, she needed to figure things out for herself. How could she tell her daughter that all this time her father had been just a few miles away, that she could have contacted him, that she had no good reasons to avoid him or to keep her from him, but that she'd done it, anyway? And now? How could she tell Bridget her father, who had been so accessible all that time, was dead? That he had wanted to meet her, but that Lisa had put it off, believing there would always be time? Did Marty know this was coming? Was that why he wrote her?

Her response was just as short.

"I'll call you when we're ready. Maybe this fall. I need time."

Lisa stopped for a traffic light and dropped her head onto the steering wheel. She couldn't leave it like this. She couldn't tell her daughter Marty was a no-good drug dealer who'd been killed over a few baggies of meth. That wasn't the Marty she knew. She needed to learn more about Marty. She owed it to both of them. A car horn sounded, startling Lisa from her thoughts. She hit the gas and accelerated through the intersection. She gripped the wheel tightly and drove too fast, too recklessly, the rest of the way home.

Chapter Two

The newsroom was just waking up when Lisa set her messenger bag under her desk. She was used to coming in around mid-afternoon when most reporters were hidden behind their cubicle walls working on stories, and the editors were all in meetings. The county reporter who occupied the next desk over had already come and gone, off to see the highway commissioner about a controversial road project. The intern who made the morning cop calls was arguing with an editor over the length of a brief. She wouldn't last long with that attitude. A few reporters were updating stories online or working on blogs. But most people were nursing coffee, and chatting over their cubicle walls, checking email, or pairing up to head down to the cafeteria for coffee or a bagel or a doughnut.

In the old days, the newsroom was void of reporters at this hour. That was at the cusp of the technology boom when human contact with sources was considered crucial. The good reporters got started early, trying to catch people before they entered their offices or between meetings or after they sent their kids off to school. When she first started at the newspaper, editors scoffed at email interviews, reminding reporters of the value of reading faces and hearing intonations in voices. Email was for those last-minute facts, like time and dates of events, or budget numbers, or correct spellings of names.

But these days, email interviews were common practice, especially for the newer reporters, fresh out of college with courses in digital reporting. Lisa rarely gave in to the temptation, not even for the profiles that appeared on the weekly suburban pages. The most valuable information came when people were comfortable with reporters, when she could shift the conversation according to the interviewee's reaction or tone, when she could let them lead a little, exploring tangents that might reveal more critical information. Why would anyone give up off-the-record or personal information to a reporter on the receiving end of a computer? She couldn't understand how reporters got pleasure from creating stories researched online and through email. For her, the people were the best part. She enjoyed stepping into people's lives, experiencing another world and then slipping out.

Lisa checked her messages and her email and then sneaked over to her editor's desk and snagged a copy of the local section. She still preferred the real thing over the online edition, though the online stories were more up-to-date. It should have been easy to find a copy of the paper in a newsroom, but it wasn't. Only a few assignment editors got print copies, and they guarded them with their lives. But her editor wasn't in yet, and Lisa would slip it back before she got there. It all seemed so surreal, seeing everyone doing the same things they did every day, even though Marty was dead. Part of Lisa was still numb when she looked at the front page and saw one of her stories above the fold, the premium position. She waited for that familiar thrill, but it didn't come. "Rouge Justice Loses Bench: Illegally Jailed Man Free," the headline shouted. The photo showed Clyde Oliver grinning and waving as he walked out of the jail building with no cuffs and a plastic bag full of his few belongings in his other hand.

He was such a sweetheart, Lisa thought as she studied the picture on the way to her desk. The poor guy was mentally disabled and had been living with his mother. He slipped through the cracks and became homeless when she died, and a ticket for loitering landed him in court. When Oliver told the justice he couldn't pay the fine because he had no job, the justice said there were plenty of openings in the county jail and sentenced him to a year. The fact that he skipped the required presentencing investigation, which would have identified Oliver as the victim he was, only came up when Oliver became eligible for early release, four months after he'd been jailed. Oliver would be in good hands now with the help of social services.

"I guess I owe you congratulations."

Standing at Lisa's cubicle with his elbow resting on its edge was Jacob, the daytime crime reporter. He was the last person Lisa wanted to see. Jacob was a wanna-be police investigator, and he was obvious about it. He tried to walk like them, talk like them and even dress like them with his button-up shirt and loosened tie. He brought bagels to the guys in the Criminal Investigations Division at least once a week, and he frequented the bars where the cops hung out. They got a kick out of him. He was like their mascot.

"Another poor, helpless citizen saved by Lisa Jamison, huh?"

Lisa usually ignored Jacob, but his smirk was too much for her this morning, especially after the night she'd been through. Jacob was the kind of guy who liked to draw a thick line between himself and criminals, believing that line would protect him from himself. No matter how much he had in common with the burglar who was just looking for a place to sleep or the woman who got hooked on drugs at thirteen, or the seventeen-year-old who was driving too fast and plowed down the runner on the side of the road, he honestly believed he was better than them because he stood on the other side of the line.

What he didn't know was that society ignores lines we draw ourselves. To the rest of the world, his line was drawn in invisible ink. One night, he might just drive home drunk from that bar and hurt somebody. Or he might get caught cheating on his wife with the new intern, the one with the manicured nails, the straight, silky hair, and the hands that were always on his shoulders, or forearms, or the small of his back. Or maybe he'd lose his job when they found out he'd been tweaking stories to please his cop friends. If that ever happened, he could point at that line all he wanted, but no one else would see it. It would be meaningless.

"Please go away," Lisa said with a sigh. She grabbed coins from her drawer for a cup of coffee and kept her back to him. "I'm here early to get some work done, and I really need you to leave me alone today."

But Jacob wasn't ready to give up. He stayed at her shoulder as she walked down the hall, past the conference rooms, the bathrooms, and the window that provided a view of the two-story-tall press that had become a relic now that their printing was all done digitally. She could feel his breath on her neck. He didn't seem to grasp the concept of personal space. He was so close, he could have spooned her while she poured her coffee. She could easily make a quick turn, spill hot coffee all over his starched, white shirt and call it an accident. But she wasn't like that. Besides, there was a part of her that actually felt sorry for him. The fact that she was a different kind of crime reporter bothered him, and she knew that, but she had no intentions of changing.

"The guys at the station tell me you were asking a lot of questions last night about that drug homicide," he said, rocking on the heels of his leather shoes beside her when she stopped to fill a Styrofoam cup. She tried to focus instead on the aroma of the hot, black liquid, but Jacob made it impossible. He was the last person she wanted to talk to about Marty. "You know, Lisa, they don't like it when you do that. The cops don't trust bleeding hearts."

"If you read the brief, you'll see that it was his heart that was bleeding," Lisa said without turning her attention to him. "I don't tell you how to do your job. You don't tell me how to do mine. Why do you feel the need to harass me?"

"I'm just saying—"

"I'm just saying go away. Now."

Lisa pushed past him, dropped her change in the cashier's hand, and charged back to her desk. Hot coffee spilled over her fingers, and she'd forgotten to add sugar, but she didn't care. She knew she'd been more short-tempered with Jacob than usual, but she didn't have the tolerance for him just now. He'd have to find another player for his semantic games. She set her coffee on a coaster and sucked on the burned fingers, which were already bright red, and cursed under her breath.

Aside from the fact that the dead guy was the father of her daughter, something else bothered Lisa. The Marty she dated when they were fifteen was smart. Smart and motivated. And, from what she had learned since his letter, he ran two convenience stores—one near his apartment in the city and one in Mohawk County about thirty miles away. For a guy with no family to support, he was doing well. Alex had told her there were no obvious physical signs Marty was a user. So why was he on a corner selling

13

petty drugs? He wouldn't have made much money, and it didn't seem he needed it. If the clean hit was more than luck, why would an experienced marksman risk arrest on someone like him? Shooters like that work for big money. No ring would send out their best for a street-level dealer. If he wasn't selling drugs, if this was a set-up, why did someone want him dead? And why did he want to see his daughter now, after sixteen years? Did he know someone was trying to kill him?

She flipped through the newspaper. Then she woke her laptop and started browsing through the folders. Within minutes, she found what she was looking for: the obituary. It wasn't in the paper yet, but it was in the system. It was scheduled to run tomorrow. Martin Joseph Delano would be buried on Thursday. Calling hours were Wednesday from two to four p.m. and seven to nine p.m. He had an associate's degree from IroquoisCommunity College. He most recently worked as a regional manager for the One-Stop convenience store chain. He was survived by his mother, two brothers and a sister, and several nieces and nephews. But no children. Not officially.

Lisa reached under the desk and pulled her messenger bag onto her lap. She riffled through documents, press releases, print-outs, and clips, searching more frantically the second and third times through. Then she pulled it all out, laid the contents on her desk, and went through them again, paper by paper. It was gone. The printout of the email from Marty that she'd been carrying around since the day it arrived was missing. So was the notebook she'd used last night. She had always returned the letter to the bag, knowing Bridget wouldn't stumble across it there, and she remembered clearly tossing her notebook in with it. She had not touched it since. Has someone taken them? But who? Who would even care? She hadn't looked at her notes since deadline last night. She took her bag into the morgue with her and left it in her car overnight. She lived on a dead-end street. She never locked her car at home. That would have been the only opportunity—while she was sleeping.

The guys in CID told Jacob Lisa was looking into Marty's death. There was plenty of activity at the station when she was interviewing the lead detective last night. Anyone could have heard their conversation and witnessed her surprise when she read Marty's name and birthdate on the report. She mentioned that she'd known a guy by the same name and birthdate when she was a kid. That was all. But maybe somebody knew she'd be curious and didn't want her to look further. Maybe this was a message. Well, that was a mistake. Lisa loved a challenge, especially a forbidden one. She grabbed a fresh notebook and headed for the door. She'd need to see that report again.

Chapter Three

T he creek was cold, but Bridget pulled off her sneakers and socks, rolled up her jeans, and stood in it anyway. She walked to the middle, ignoring the pain as her feet slipped on the smooth, uneven rocks, twisting her ankles in unnatural directions. Her presence changed the path of the current, forcing the water to flow around her. She felt strong, powerful, in control, and the coldness of the water revived her.

It was ten-thirty, and she should have been in math class, but she didn't feel like going. She was tired, and she just wanted to get out of there. Bridget wasn't a skipper. She'd never done it before, but it was easier and more satisfying than she had imagined. It was an impulsive thing, and it felt good to do something without thinking for once. It felt good to just turn around and walk away. Walk away from everybody and everything.

The creek ran through the woods behind the school, where students liked to sneak off for a smoke or a few guzzles from a flask, but those kids didn't come this far downstream. Bridget couldn't even see the school from where she stood. It was peaceful and quiet. Nothing like the crowded hallways she'd left behind filled with screeching, squealing, hooting, and childish chattering between classes, and the smells of sweat and urine when classes were in session. And, most important, there was no Mandy out here. No one to annoy her.

Bridget stared into the clear, rushing water that surrounded her. She'd been standing still so long that a crayfish came out of hiding and crawled along the creek floor close to her toes. She was mesmerized by the motion of its little legs, by the way it held its claws to the side and out of the way so effortlessly. She leaned over slowly, trying to keep her feet motionless in hopes of touching the little creature. Her fingers were almost there when she was startled by a loud snap. The crayfish skittered under a rock as she wiggled her toes to maintain her balance.

Bridget stood up straight and looked around. It had come from the clusters of maples, pines, and birches on the other side of the creek. But everything was still. Nothing, and no one moved, the only sounds a few birds in the trees, the muffled sounds of a car or two in the distance and the water. Bridget shivered with the feeling that someone was watching her.

"Is anyone there?" she shouted.

She waited, but no one answered. Then a flash of gray caught her eye, and she smiled. It was a squirrel sprinting and hopping across the long grass and up a tree, its mouth bulging with its winter stash. The solitude was making her paranoid, that and the fact that she'd skipped out of school. The squirrel had probably hopped on a dead branch, causing it to break. How cool would it be to live like a squirrel, she thought. No friends, no family, no emotions, really. Just an instinct to survive season after season, to have babies and send them off on their own and then survive again until either a couple more babies came along or she died. Simple.

But her life was not simple, not anymore.

Mandy was her best friend, or rather she had been for years. She was different from Bridget in every way—shorter, curvier, and with straight, blonde hair that rested precisely at her shoulders. While Bridget usually preferred as few words as possible, Mandy was chatty. Always chatty, even when she was depressed. Today was no exception, but today Bridget could have used someone to talk to and, listening to Mandy, she realized she had no one.

"Come on. Let's take the long way past Benjamin's class," Mandy had said, tugging at Bridget's arm as she tried to balance her math and English books, along with notebooks and her pencil case. "He's always there early. I want him to see me, and I want to make sure that new chick from Boston sees me, too. She'd better not touch him."

Mandy never really looked at Bridget. She didn't ask Bridget what was wrong. She didn't ask why Bridget seemed so down, so tired, so unmotivated. It had to show. Bridget was sure of it because it was all so overwhelming. So heavy. Her mother had come home late last night and was still sleeping when she left for school. Bridget had pretended to be asleep when her mother checked in on her at three a.m., whispering her name, because she didn't have the energy for conversation. Not the kind that her mother always seemed ready to launch into lately. Her mother exhausted her. Every day, all day, it seemed Bridget had to reassure her she would make it another day, another month, another year without getting pregnant. It wasn't fair, and it drained her. She couldn't handle Mandy. Not today. And she really didn't want to see Benjamin.

"I have to use the bathroom," Bridget said. "You go ahead. Look, there's Helen. She'll walk with you."

And Mandy left. Just like that. She was gone in an instant, unconcerned and unbothered, and Helen, a cheerleader who had little else going for her, was clearly thrilled by her company. It hurt a little, but it felt right to let them go. It was a relief. Bridget was outgrowing Mandy anyway, and she knew it. Mandy had the depth of a toddler pool, and though they'd been great together as kids, Bridget was finding less and less to talk with her about.

That hadn't always mattered. Bridget hadn't cared whether Mandy ever listened when they were in elementary school or junior high. Her mother had always been her best friend and confidante, and she didn't need that from anyone else. Mandy was fun. She made her laugh, and Bridget honestly believed no one else had it so lucky. She didn't have a father like Mandy, but she didn't have to share her mother with anyone, either. Grandma Dorothy was good to her and kept her fed and entertained, but when Bridget's mother came home, her body filled up with the kind of warmth that came with a cup of hot chocolate on a cold, rainy day. She knew she would have her full attention from that moment until work or school tore them apart again. She craved that and relished it.

But now, for the past two years, she found herself cringing when her mother entered a room, finding somewhere else to be, homework to be done, or a reason to go to bed early. It wasn't that she didn't love her, or that she loved her any less. She just couldn't stand to be around her so much, to be under that constant scrutiny. She knew this happened to mothers and teen-aged daughters, this division that stemmed from a need for independence. She'd read about it in one of the many self-help books she'd picked up at the library, hoping to understand what was happening and make everything better. But this was different. Her mother did not simply annoy her. It was the way her mother looked at her, pretending her concern was all about Bridget. That was what bothered her most.

Her mother didn't even know who Bridget was anymore. She didn't see her. Bridget knew that, instead, when her mother looked at her, she saw herself at that same age, and she feared it. She feared her own daughter, and the only thought in her head was whether Bridget was pregnant on that particular day. Even when she asked how things were going in school, when the soccer game was, how Mandy was, that other question was there, pushing to get through right behind the rest, suppressed only by her mother's irrational fear of the answer. That question was boiling within her mother when the whole Benjamin thing blew up a few months ago, and Bridget knew it. In that case, her mother was at least right about something. She didn't love Benjamin. She couldn't have because she felt nothing whatsoever when they broke up. No joy. No anger. Nothing. She clearly didn't know what love was or how to be in love.

But the other stuff—Bridget had no idea how to tell her mother that, how to talk about it, how to make her mother understand and open her eyes. No book out there could help her with this. If her own mother no longer knew her, then who did? Definitely not Mandy. Bridget was alone for the first time in her life, and she was struggling to remain strong. It was tiring. Completely exhausting.

If she was going to be alone in her head, she wanted to be alone physically, too. So Bridget just did it. She turned her back on Mandy and Helen, threw her books into her locker, and left. She pushed right through all those other kids who seemed to know exactly where they were going and why, who got excited about parties and dates and upcoming vacations. Right past them and out the front door. No one tried to stop her. No one did anything at all.

Would they even miss her, she thought, if she never came back?

And then she heard it: another snap.

This time, when Bridget looked, she was sure she'd seen something, and it was not a squirrel. She'd caught a glimpse of color within the trees. Blue—too bright for any animal—and it had moved behind a thick trunk. She could still see a thin edge of the color. The comfort she'd felt alone in the woods was gone. No one knew where she was. Anything could happen. She had to get back, but she was stuck in the stream, in the middle of it, with her sneakers and socks in her hands. The rocks were slippery. It would take time to navigate to the bank without falling. She'd never make it, not if the person in blue had a gun or shoes with good treads. She couldn't move, not even when she heard it for a third time, not even when she saw that streak of blue again, moving closer. Not even when the color came into focus, and she saw that it was a man in a blue plaid shirt with jeans and that he was pointing something at her, something that reflected the sunlight. Her chest ached, and she couldn't make her feet go or utter any words. She couldn't even scream.

"Bridget!"

The voice came from the other direction, from the other side of the creek along the path she'd taken from school, and it was familiar.

"Bridget Jamison, get over here now."

It was the dean of students himself walking down the path in his usual black suit and tie with a very angry look on his face. When she turned back toward the other bank where the snapping sound had come from, Bridget clearly saw a man's silhouette running away, dodging through the trees, disappearing as quickly as he had appeared. Something in his hand caught the sun again, but at least he was headed the other way. She was in trouble, and she knew it. She'd had to walk past the dean's office to leave the building, and he'd probably seen her. The smokers were at least careful. They left through side doors or windows. But she didn't care. Someone did notice that she was missing, and, at this moment, she was grateful. Very grateful.

Chapter Four

There was nothing good about working the crime beat in the mornings. It was a whole different shift in the Public Safety Building, and most of these people didn't know Lisa. Instead of getting waved past the metal detector, she had to empty out her pockets, take off her belt and give them her purse to search. Most cops took this shift so they could be home with their families at night. The sense of adventure had been drained from them by years of working days. The morning employees in records, where she was headed, had to worry about supervisors looking over their shoulders. She didn't have a rapport with this crew, which meant that she would have to persuade whoever was working behind the counter of the merits of her request, and then, even if they didn't make her go through the whole Freedom-Of-Information-Act process, they would charge her copying or printing fees. She wasn't good at that kind of bullshit.

Lisa got into the graffiti-covered elevator with a young, scrawny-looking assistant DA and a couple of cops in uniform. They all got off on the third floor, where the investigators work. She resisted the urge to hold the door open, to get off and burst into Criminal Investigations Division, demanding to see Marty's files. Somewhere in those offices, there were interviews with strangers who saw him go down or who found his body. There were descriptions and pictures of the pattern his blood made on the sidewalk, the way his body was splayed out, the expression on his face when he died. They had the phone numbers of his mother, his sister, his brothers. His life was being scrutinized in a way that made Lisa angry, angry because she knew they believed he had brought on his own death. That, maybe, he even

21

deserved to die.

The elevator opened on the fourth floor, and Lisa forced herself to refocus. She had to be careful to keep this professional. A journalist could get almost anything. An ex-girlfriend could not. The corridor was empty. She'd once thought it was the night that made this place so unbearable. But even during the day, it was dark and dingy, and the air was stale up in records. The halls were a nauseating shade of dark beige. The counter was around the corner and then straight ahead. No one else was waiting.

The clerk was a large, black woman in uniform. Probably in her late forties. She was someone Lisa had never met before, so she wasn't surprised when the woman asked to see her ID. Lisa wondered whether anyone ever asked for this job or whether it was some kind of punishment. Why would any cop choose to spend eight hours a day up here? Maybe they were injured. Maybe they were unfit for duty. But when she thought about the night shift, she realized that one of the clerks was a Black man and the other was a woman, and that it had always been that way—white women, Hispanics or blacks. No white males up here. Lisa smelled a story, but it would have to wait a few days. She pulled her press card from her pants pocket and gave it to the clerk, who took a quick glance and returned it. The clerk slid the clipboard full of arrest summaries across the counter.

"We already had someone from the *Sun Times* come by here this morning. Don't you people have anything better to do?" the clerk asked as she picked up a thick pile of folders and started sorting through papers, pushing them through a scanner.

"My God, people really do work in here," Lisa said. Something about this woman told her she might have a sense of humor. "You wouldn't know that from the night shift."

"Don't get me going on the night shift."

"Actually, I came in early to do some research on a story I'm doing on methamphetamine," Lisa said as she flipped through the previous night's arrests. "There was a guy killed just before midnight day before yesterday who was selling. I was hoping to get some more of the reports. Got a daughter who just turned sixteen a few months ago. This stuff scares the heck out of me. I was kind of hoping its hey-day would be over before she hit her teens."

The woman stopped what she was doing and took a good, hard look at Lisa.

"You've got a sixteen-year-old? My oldest is fourteen. You barely look half my age."

"Well, I was an idiot, but something good came out of it." Lisa put down the clipboard, pulled out her purse, and slipped a school photo out of her wallet. "Her name is Bridget. She made the Honor Society this year. Can't say I ever did that."

"Beautiful girl," the clerk said with a smile. "My boy is the oldest. Got two daughters younger than him. What's the name you're looking for? I'll see what I've got, but I'm going to have to charge you for the printouts."

"Martin J. Delano. Thanks. I appreciate it."

Lisa flipped through the summaries on the clipboard and found a few things that would make good briefs if Jacob hadn't already gotten them: a woman who was arrested after she threw a pan of chicken wings at her husband, a felony assault, a break-in at the library. A few minutes later, the clerk pushed twenty-one sheets of paper across the counter. Lisa extended her hand to the woman.

"Name's Lisa, by the way."

"Marie," the clerk said, shaking Lisa's hand with a strength in her grip that surprised her. "But don't be getting any ideas. This is a onetime deal. I don't make friends with reporters. And that'll be two dollars."

Lisa gave her the money and thanked her again. She liked Marie. She guessed that her kids got away with very little.

Back in the newsroom, Lisa pored over the reports. Two of them were from the first cops on the scene. The third, and the longest, was from the lead investigator on the case. A rap sheet was attached. Marty had been arrested once for driving while under the influence of drugs just outside Port Edison in Mohawk County, where Lisa went to college. That was four years ago, and there was no conviction. At least none in these files. The rest was traffic violations: one conviction for speeding and another for running a red light.

She could believe Marty might have smoked pot. He smoked now and then when they were young, and some guys never grow up. But the rest—what happened last night—still didn't make sense. He knew how she felt about drugs, the hard stuff, when they were teenagers. He knew about her parents and never had the desire to touch the stuff as far as she knew, or she wouldn't have dated him. That was part of what had attracted her to him. He had a good job. No record to speak of. He didn't even have a family to support. Why would he sell? And why meth? If it's true, if his death was drug-related, then he must have been strictly selling, not smoking because, if he'd been an addict, there would have been more arrests. He probably would have lost his job. He would have been sickly and pale when he died. Not strong and toned with a bit of extra beef on his bones like the Marty she saw in the morgue. No, there would have been more physical evidence because nobody does meth without becoming an addict. But he had no reason to sell. Not that she could see.

It would probably be easier to tell Bridget her father was a drug dealer, a dangerous man she could not allow into their lives. Maybe he was. Maybe she should let it go. She hadn't even seen the guy in sixteen years. She owed him nothing. But it wasn't just about Bridget. Something bugged Lisa about this case, and her journalistic instinct was kicking in. She'd been thinking about the email and the notebook in her bag. She could justify losing one, but both? She couldn't remember having the notebook and the email out at the same time, so how could she have lost them both in one night? She was sure now someone took them. Someone had a reason. Lisa had asked more questions than usual last night. She had not kept quiet about the fact that she knew the victim. Was someone afraid she would ask more? What were they afraid she would find? What was going on in Marty's life?

She needed to learn more about that arrest in Mohawk County. And maybe she would stop by the calling hours. She'd never met his family, so they wouldn't recognize her. She was a runaway when she and Marty met. She wasn't the kind of girl you brought home to mom. She'd just say she knew him a long time ago and leave it at that. But first, she needed more coffee. She should have taken Alex's advice and gotten some sleep last night, but she couldn't. Her mind was too busy, too full. She had taken only a few steps away from her desk when the phone rang. She was tempted to ignore it, but curiosity won.

"Got something interesting for you," the caller said.

Lisa was startled to recognize Alex's voice. Alex was a friend, but he was a work-friend. He rarely called her with offers of information. She usually had to pull it out of him. He knew what this meant to her, though. He was the only one she'd told about her relationship with Marty, about her past. She supposed medical examiners were allowed to show a little sympathy once in a while.

"I've been getting a few calls from the Mohawk County sheriff's office about your friend. They're asking when I'm going to close this up. They're not saying much, but he had a drug-related arrest there a few years back. I'm guessing maybe he turned informant. Got himself in trouble."

He paused.

"Maybe you should leave this alone, Lisa. I know you. Let the cops do their job. Let me do my job. Someday we'll solve this, but these things take time. You know the drill. You arrest somebody who knows somebody who bragged about something. Eventually, they confess. They tell someone because they are proud of what they did and they are criminals. And criminals are mostly stupid."

There it was, that word "criminal." The way Alex said it made her nauseous, and she couldn't even imagine the impact it would have on Bridget. This was Bridget's father. Lisa was wrong to think it might be easier to tell her Marty was a dangerous criminal. Bridget had been so moody and distant lately. Unreachable. News like this would only push her further away. Telling her nothing wasn't an option. If Bridget ever found out her father died and that Lisa hid it from her, the barrier between them would become insurmountable. She needed to follow her instincts as a mother and as a journalist and make that trip to Mohawk County, especially if someone there was in a rush to close this case.

"Come on, Alex," she said. "I'm just a journalist, and they're cops. They get all sorts of fun tools in their investigations. They can tap phones, do surveillance, all that stuff. All I've got is my pen, my paper, a cell phone, and Google. How big a threat can I be?"

"Listen." Alex cleared his throat and softened his tone. "I'm telling you this because you're a good person and a good reporter. I'd hate to see anything happen to you. Just promise me you won't do anything stupid. People who kill informants usually aren't very nice."

"I can't promise that I won't make a call or two, but I can promise I'll let you know if my pen happens to stumble onto anything." Lisa never made promises she knew she couldn't keep, and she couldn't bring herself to lie to Alex. He risked his job every time he talked to her. She appreciated that.

"Just be careful," he said. "I really don't want you coming in here through the back door." A loud beep in the background interrupted their conversation.

"Looks like I've got another customer coming," Alex said. "I'd better get a bed ready."

"Alex?" Lisa's voice grew low and serious.

"What is it?"

"Thanks."

"Just remember, you've got a daughter who needs you," he said. "Sometimes, it's not worth it."

Chapter Five

O kay, so maybe Alex was right. It was a stretch, but maybe Marty was an informant. Lisa could make herself believe that, she thought as she pulled her car onto the highway. She just needed to see the report from that one arrest. To understand, at least a little bit, how he'd gotten involved in all this. Why he'd died. How he could have possibly been so valuable to the police and such a threat to some criminal. It didn't make sense. The charge was driving while under the influence of drugs, not possession or sale. There had to be something more.

Lisa tried to focus on the road, on the thirty-five-minute drive from Seneca Springs to the Mohawk County Sheriff's Department. She kept both hands on the wheel and her eyes on the pavement and tried to think about how she would get the deputy working the desk to cooperate without involving the city desk or her editor or the newspaper's lawyers. The Mohawk County Sheriff's Department was not known for its cooperation. She tried to think about other reporters who had tried to break barriers with these guys and failed, and how she could do better.

But the four-lane highway was flat and empty and void of exits for the next fifteen miles. She couldn't do it. She couldn't concentrate. Her head was too full of Marty, and the last time she saw him when they were partying, and Brian Prentice put a bullet in his brain, and the cops came and Social Services took her away.

She was six months pregnant, big enough for the cops to notice. That's why they didn't let her go like the rest of them. Everybody else just gave statements, told the cops how Dugan had found the gun in an alley a few hours earlier and had brought it to the abandoned house on Market Street, where they all liked to hang out and party sometimes. They told the cops how they all started making bets about whether it was loaded, how they all held and examined it. Everybody except Lisa. Lisa was the only girl there, and she didn't mind being a coward about it. Guns terrified her, plus the baby was kicking like crazy, and she was uncomfortable.

They were all sure it was empty, but they weren't sure enough to try the trigger. The more beer they drank and the more joints they passed, the more obsessed they became with that gun. They held it some more and pointed it around the room, and tried to guess what caliber it was, even though nobody knew anything about guns. Marty was sober that day, thank God. Completely sober. He was never much of a drinker anyway, but ever since he'd learned Lisa was pregnant, he'd been good about that. She knew he'd had a beer or two when she wasn't there now and then, but he didn't touch pot anymore, and he never drank in front of her.

Nobody was sure who started it, but the next thing they knew, the guys were daring each other to hold the gun to their own heads and pull the trigger. Marty told them they were crazy, and he passed, but the other guys were drunk and high and stupid. Each time someone pulled the trigger and nothing happened, they got more confident. They laughed more and less nervously and urged each other on. On the fourth turn, they taunted Marty—two guys, Abe and Tyler. They called him a coward and tried to push the gun into his hands. Lisa didn't know Abe and Tyler well, but she didn't like them. Most of the guys in the group were in the midst of growing up, experimenting with rebellion in the way so many aimless kids do. But these guys were rougher around the edges than the others, more dangerous. That night, they couldn't stand the fact that Marty wouldn't participate. They got in his face and accused him of thinking he was better than them. Just when Lisa was about to intervene, when she was sure they were going to pull the trigger for him, Brian grabbed the gun from Tyler. He lifted it to his temple and made a goofy face. Then he was gone. In an instant, Brian was dead, and the room was quiet.

Too quiet.

So that's what everybody else told the cops. Then they got to go home. Or not go home. Nobody cared. But everybody's a sucker for a pregnant teenager. When they found out she'd left home four months earlier and that her parents were okay with that, they decided to find her a better home. They found her the farm here in Mohawk County, across a narrow road from the shore of Lake Ontario, with four other pregnant girls and Winnie and Leo, a wonderful couple who let her stay with them long after she gave birth and until she graduated college.

The farm had seemed so far away then. She was a teenager without a car, out in the country, stuck in a new school back in the same grade she'd started a year earlier, changing diapers when she needed a break from homework. Everything seemed far away. It never occurred to her to find Marty, to call his house or write him a letter or send him an email. And when it did, when she had a job and was on her own and Bridget was starting second grade, it didn't feel right. Too much time had passed.

It had started to rain, and Lisa could see larger, darker clouds rolling toward her from the direction of Lake Ontario. The drops were heavy and loud, and the road was getting slick. The wind picked up, urging her car slightly to the right. This was a good thing. The storm forced her to focus on something else, anything else. She thought about the rain and the storm and staying on the road until finally, she pulled into a visitor's space in the sheriff's department parking lot. When she stepped out, she was surprised to find the rain carried with it the lake's scent, the fishy, earthy smell that had brought her so much comfort on the worst of her college days, on those days when sleep seemed impossible, papers and exams mounted, and so did the bills for tuition, diapers and occasional antibiotics.

Those were the days when she would simply walk away from all of it, leaving the dull, rectangular, brick buildings and the concrete sidewalks and the throngs of ordinary students—those who lived on their parents' dimes with homes to go back to for Thanksgiving and Christmas and summer break—all behind. Lisa would cross the road that circled the campus and step sideways down the steep, grassy slope to the smooth, rounded rocks that lined the lakeshore below. At her feet, small, black spiders crawled in, out, and over the rocks with a furious sense of purpose, reminding Lisa that, for most creatures, life was always this way. Perhaps luxury time was unnatural, a human creation that had developed into an unhealthy need.

Lisa would keep moving until she found just the right spot. There, she would lift her face to the spray from the waves that crashed endlessly against the rocks, drowning out the sounds and thoughts of the reality just a few yards away. For just a few minutes—she dared not waste more—Lisa would give herself to the immenseness of that lake with its invisible shores and green-tea water. She would toss her worries, her stresses, all of her troubles into its currents and watch as they sank further and further to the unexplored bottom where she was sure they would be weighed down by all the sunken ships, empty whiskey bottles, and the old tires that had come before her. Then she would turn her back to the lake and leave. And she would feel lighter, just light enough to get through that day and the next day and the next and the next.

She had just turned off her engine when her cell phone rang. It was the dean of students. Bridget had skipped math class, and he'd found her walking through the creek in the woods behind the building. She wouldn't say why she skipped, he said, but she seemed pretty shook up when he caught her.

"I don't think she'll do it again, Ms. Jamison, but you'll want to get to the bottom of this," he said. "That's not like her. I talked with her teachers, and there has been no change in her academic performance, so I'm hoping you'll find out what motivated her now before she starts down a more destructive path."

Damn. Lisa didn't need this. She thanked the dean for calling, assured him she would talk to her, and checked her messages. Bridget had sent three texts in a row, and her words sounded desperate. It was obvious she was trying to reach her before the dean did.

Mom, call me back.

I need to talk to you now.

Please. It's really important.

Well, let her sweat. Let her panic and let her get carried away, imagining the potential consequences. It would be good for her. She'd talk to her

30

tonight when she got home. This was not going to happen to Bridget. She was not going to become one of those kids. She slipped the phone into her back pocket and took a deep breath of the heavy, moist air, drawing that old feeling into her lungs. It felt good, especially now.

Lisa grabbed her notepad, a pen, and the folder with the Freedom of Information request inside and raced through the rain for the doors. She hoped she wouldn't have to take the legal route. She didn't want to have to tell her editor what she was up to, especially since she was stepping out of her territory. The Mohawk County bureau reporters would be upset. And how would she explain herself without letting on that this was personal? But, usually, the letter was enough. They'd see that and see the hassle that lay ahead and just give up the information. They might make her wait a few days, but it would happen. They were legally obligated to give her that report, and they would know it. It'd be a waste of time and money to fight.

The building was old with large, rounded pillars and a decorative, concrete archway. But the original double doors had clearly been replaced by smaller metal-framed ones, probably for security reasons. The architects had filled in the gaps between the old and the new with ordinary steel and glass designs. Inside, the sheriff's department had that musty smell, like an old cinder-block elementary school in the middle of the summer. The floors were coated with that same gold-trimmed granite tile that she'd seen in so many courthouses and city halls and police departments before. But these floors were scratched and dull. Uncared for. She shook out her dampened hair, smoothed her shirt and pants, and walked down the hall, past the jail entrance and toward the signs that said "Sheriff's Office." The deputy who stood behind the counter was nice enough. He greeted her warmly, wrote down the name, and turned toward a wall of filing cabinets on his right. It was the lieutenant who was the problem. He came barreling out of an office behind the front desk and ordered the deputy to go get some coffee.

Then he turned on Lisa.

"You're not wasting my deputy's time digging up reports on an arrest that took place God-knows how long ago," he said. "We're not the city here. Our system is new, and we don't have all that money lying around to scan all our old files and just pop them up on a computer screen whenever we feel like it. Who do you people think you are? Take your pretty little notebook and get out. Just get out of here. Goddamn bullshit."

His badge said Hildebrandt. He was large in every direction, with pock-marked drooping jowls for cheeks. His hair was silver, but greasy silver, and he was the kind of guy who slicked a slab of it across his forehead to cover his receding hairline. He worked so hard to be intimidating that Lisa almost laughed out loud. Instead, she cleared her throat and smiled.

"You know, in some departments, the cops invite me back while they're pulling the paper files and their filing systems look a lot like yours right there. Organized first by year, then by month, and then alphabetically," Lisa said, pointing to the filing cabinets. "I could pull the file myself in a few seconds. So I really can't see how I'm wasting anyone's time.

"So there are two ways we can do this. You can walk over there, get the file and make a copy. And I'll pay you the standard fee per page, and I'll be gone. Or…" She pulled a typed letter from the folder in her hand. "I can give you this Freedom of Information request, our lawyers can contact your lawyers, who will spend a lot of county money telling you to give me the damn thing, and you can start looking over your shoulder when your contract is up while your elected boss contemplates whether he really needs a lieutenant here anymore."

The lieutenant's face reddened quickly and easily. Lisa worried he might have a heart attack right then and there. He leaned over the counter, bringing his face so close to her that she could smell tuna on his breath. But she didn't move. Not an inch. She had learned long ago that men are intimidated when women are not. Just as he started to speak, a rough hand clamped on his shoulder and pulled him back slightly. Behind Lt. Hildebrandt stood a tall, broad-shouldered man in his late fifties, who gave Lisa a polite and practiced smile.

"Give the lady the report," Sheriff Weidenfeld told the deputy, who had just returned to the desk with coffee and was standing behind the two of them. "It's not like she's asking for a play-by-play of the arrest, right, Lieutenant?"

Lt. Hildebrandt backed away from the counter as the sheriff removed his hand from his shoulder and gave him a loud pat on the back. He said nothing, and he didn't turn to look at his boss as he took his coffee from the deputy and retreated to his office. Lisa thought she heard him mumble something under his breath just before he slammed his door shut, but she couldn't quite make out the words.

"Lt. Hildebrandt here likes to play the tough guy now and then. We don't get to do that much in this county," the sheriff said, still grinning. "You just put that letter away. We don't do business that way in MohawkCounty. Leave your card with the deputy. I do like to know who is poking around in our files."

With that, he left Lisa alone with the deputy, a guy named Donlin, according to his tag. He was about Lisa's age and only slighter taller, with hair shaved almost down to his scalp, military-style. The hair didn't quite go with his dimples. For the first time, Lisa noticed that he limped and used a cane.

"Sorry about all that," the deputy said with a slight smirk. "These two go at it all the time. Two totally different types of cops, you know? You ought to try working with them every day. I'm stuck here until this gets better."

He tapped his bum leg with his cane.

"Some old lady backed her car up on me when I stopped to help her with a flat. I should have known better than to let her sit behind the wheel and wait. Apparently, she thought I was done. I wasn't."

"Sorry to hear that," Lisa said. In a more polite mood, she would have asked a few questions, like how much longer before he could get back on the road. She felt bad for the guy, and he was kind of cute in his own way, but she was anxious to get going before the lieutenant, or the sheriff changed his mind.

Deputy Donlin seemed to take the hint. He found the report within minutes and tried to waive the copying fee, but Lisa didn't want any favors. She didn't want to owe anybody in this place anything, not even a few cents. She couldn't bear to look at the paperwork right there, in front of the deputy. So she took it outside, got in her car, and drove through the light drizzle that followed the storm. Lisa kept going until she reached the McDonald's near the highway on-ramp. She pulled into a parking spot, turned off the engine, took a deep breath, and picked up the papers. There were two reports: the incident report and the arrest report. She started with the incident report.

The arrest took place at one minute past seven on a Sunday evening. Marty was driving erratically, the deputy wrote, and had a busted taillight, so he pulled him over. The deputy, a guy named Larsen, immediately noticed Marty was slow to react and fumbled with his wallet when asked for his license. He told Marty to get out of the car, and he performed a sobriety test on him—walk a straight line, touch the nose, the works. Marty passed the test and the portable breathalyzer. He said he was just tired and had worked fourteen hours straight. Then this Larsen guy glanced into the car and saw a large bag of weed sticking out from underneath the back seat on the passenger side. Closer observation of "the suspect" revealed the possible smell of marijuana on his clothing and blood-shot eyes. So Larsen cuffed Marty, gathered the evidence, and brought Marty in.

Lisa looked up from the report and stared out her fogged-up window. So Marty had smoked pot. He smoked and drove, and then he left the bag in plain sight. Stupid. Really stupid and definitely dangerous, but that was it. Nothing dramatic. No cocaine. No heroin. Nothing that indicated he had connections to any drug dealers and would make a good informant. No pending punishment big enough to scare him into working for the cops. Or was there? The report said "a large bag." How much was in that bag? What happened to it? Did they book Marty? She didn't remember reading anything about possession on the rap sheet.

Lisa picked up the report again, read it through one more time, and flipped it over. She did the same with the arrest report. Nothing. Nothing that showed how much pot they found in the car. No follow-up report. No back-up called in. No one involved who might file a related report. In fact, it seemed no one else was involved at all. Just Deputy Larsen. Marty was charged with driving while under the influence of drugs, but not with possession. Maybe the deputy wanted to leave that up to the prosecutor? But this wouldn't be a grand jury case. It was too obvious and objective. The charge would be based on the amount of marijuana the deputy found. It's

34

cut and dry. And Deputy Larsen shouldn't have needed lab tests to verify that the stuff in the bag was pot, at least not to charge him. All he needed was a scale or a good eye.

But then this was Mohawk County. Maybe this Larsen guy wasn't the brightest. Marty had no convictions on his record, so this case obviously didn't make it to court. She had assumed that he pleaded—cut a deal with the prosecutor like most first-time offenders—but now she wondered whether the deputy just screwed up so badly that the prosecutor didn't have enough to go on. It shouldn't matter. She got what she was looking for, but something about this arrest bothered her. Something wasn't right. If the deputy could screw up this badly, then how could this department be sophisticated enough to take on drug informants? How would Deputy Larsen even know where to start? He must have left something out of the report on purpose. They had more on Marty. They must have had more.

It would be easy enough to find out.

She turned the key in the ignition, peeled out of the parking lot and headed back to the Mohawk County Sheriff's Department.

Chapter Six

I
t had to be a coincidence, the fact that Sheriff Weidenfeld was available with an open door, a clear desk, and a welcoming smile when Lisa returned. He ushered her into his office and offered her coffee, which she declined.

"How can I help you, Ms. Jamison?" the sheriff said, shutting the door and motioning Lisa toward a straight-backed, wooden chair positioned opposite his worn, metal desk. He sat on the edge of the desk with one foot on the floor, closer than Lisa would have liked. The air was dry in his box-of-an-office, dry and too hot. She wished he would have left the door open.

She cleared her throat, suddenly more nervous than she should be.

"I have a few questions I'm hoping you can answer about this case. From what I understand, Martin Delano was never prosecuted despite the fact that a bag of marijuana was found in his car. He wasn't even charged in connection with it. And this report," she said, looking through the papers on her lap, "it doesn't say how much marijuana Deputy Larsen found or what he did with it. That would be awfully important to note, wouldn't it?"

Sheriff Weidenfeld laughed.

He took a sip from his coffee and set the mug down on a sandstone coaster bearing a Native American design. The decorative coaster seemed out of place in such a barren room. The walls were empty except for a small, outdated poster of the ten most wanted criminals in Central New York. No sweater or jacket hung over the sheriff's chair. His desk top held a computer monitor, a black phone, a large desk calendar, and a pad of yellow Post-It

36

notes. Even the garbage can beside the desk held only a few crumpled sheets of white paper. The room had an irrelevance about it, a transient feeling like the sheriff was either just moving in or had just packed up to leave.

"Yes, it would be," the sheriff said, folding his arms across his chest. "Sometimes, our deputies get a little excited when they come across drugs and forget procedures. We're just a small county, you know. Not much besides drunks breaking into barns for cans of gasoline to fuel their ATVs. Larsen got better over time, but they all have their learning curves."

"That's funny," Lisa said. "I thought you guys handled drugs a lot in this county, what with the lake and the Canadian border and all. It would make sense that dealers would run their stuff across Lake Ontario or down the St. Lawrence Seaway. Just three weeks ago, one of our reporters in a bureau north of here covered a bust where the DEA seized a whole yacht full of cocaine."

"That was the DEA," the sheriff said. "We cooperate with them and with the Coast Guard whenever we can, but they're the pros in this kind of thing, not us. Certainly not Deputy Larsen. He's not even with us anymore. Moved on to private security. Sears, I believe. Not much tax money in this county either. We just don't have the equipment or the force to monitor the comings and goings of yachts on Lake Ontario."

"But what about the bag of marijuana? Shouldn't Deputy Larsen have weighed it?" Lisa asked. "Shouldn't someone have put it in an evidence locker? It seems that even the most inexperienced deputy would know not to leave a bag of pot lying around. If it was as large and as obvious as it sounded in the report, it could have been a felony. I would think an inexperienced deputy would get pretty excited about the potential for a felony drug bust."

Lisa paused and thought a moment, tapping her pen on her notebook.

"You know what? Maybe I'm wasting your time. Maybe it's the DEA I should be talking to. Maybe Martin Delano was informing for the feds when he got shot, and somehow they got this whole thing with the pot swept under the table. Maybe there were even other drugs in the car you're not telling me about and you passed the case on to the DEA," she said. "That would make more sense, wouldn't it? That would explain why the case was never prosecuted."

Lisa thanked the sheriff for his time, and gathered up her reports, her notepad, and her pen. If she hurried, she would have enough time to get back to the city and over to the federal building before her shift started. The DEA was tough to crack, though. They loved to show off when they made a bust, but they didn't like to talk until it was over and done, and their investigations sometimes took years. Lisa started to get up, but the sheriff stood first and gently, but firmly, pushed down on her shoulder before she could move any further. His other hand was on the gun in his holster. Lisa was too surprised to resist. So she sat.

"Now it's my turn to waste your time," the sheriff said.

When Sheriff Weidenfeld appeared satisfied that Lisa was settled, he returned to the chair behind his desk, picked up a pen, and fiddled with it, flipping it like a baton with the fingers of one hand. Finally, he set the pen down on his desk, leaned back in his chair, and fixed his eyes on the blank wall, like his mind was in some other room, some other place or time.

"It's hard to be professional when things get personal, isn't it?" he said. "Sometimes, we need to just let things go. We all make mistakes. We all want to believe the people in our lives are perfect, but, if we dig too deep, we find out that isn't so. And that revelation isn't very pleasant, especially when that person is dead and when dredging up the past, the negative, will do no one any good."

He said nothing for a moment, letting the silence hang between them. Then he leaned forward, fixing his eyes on Lisa.

"What child wants to hear her father was a drug dealer? Especially a teenager, someone so easily influenced, so full of hormones and energy. Martin Delano ran a couple of convenience stores and helped his mamma pay her bills. He sold a little meth on the side to help make ends meet. Then he got shot. You can put a good spin on that, can't you? Make him out to be a hero for your little girl?"

Lisa's throat immediately went dry. How could he know? Only a handful of people knew about Lisa and Marty, and she hadn't had any contact with those people since social services sent her to live on the farm. And why should the sheriff care? Why should he know? Why should he know anything at all about Lisa and her daughter?

"Now, I think you'd best be getting along," the sheriff said, standing to open the door for her. He offered no smile this time. "I'm sure you have deadlines to meet and much more important stories than this one. Wouldn't want to lose your job over a story that isn't really there, would you?"

For just a moment, Lisa couldn't move. She'd interviewed killers, stumbled over dead bodies at accident scenes, been lunged at in prison walkways, walked brazenly through the worst neighborhoods in the city in the dead of night, but she'd never been this frightened before. Had she misheard him? Misinterpreted him? Was he really threatening her and her daughter?

It didn't matter, she told herself. She would have to deal with it later. She could not afford to be vulnerable. Not now. Not in front of him. So she closed her eyes and did what she'd been doing since she was a child, drew on the one valuable technique her parents had taught her. She pretended she didn't care. She was good at it. Within seconds, the wall was up, her fear sealed behind it.

Lisa stood. Slowly. Gracefully. She turned to the sheriff and offered her hand, which he took.

"Once again, thank you for your time, Sheriff Weidenfeld," she said. "It's been enlightening. I'll let myself out."

And she left.

Chapter Seven

Lisa woke up the next morning with no recollection of slipping under the covers and with very little memory of the rest of her previous day and night at work. Somehow, she'd gotten through it. Her daughter had left for school hours ago, and Dorothy had left a note saying she was teaching a workshop at the library. Lisa hadn't gotten a chance to talk with Bridget about skipping. It seemed less important after her interview with the sheriff. Her anger was gone, displaced by a different kind of concern. Lisa longed to hold her daughter and tap into Dorothy's endless reservoir of comfort and advice, but part of her was relieved they were both gone. She could never seem to hide her emotions from her daughter, not when they were running deep, and Bridget didn't need any more burdens right now. They'd had enough trouble lately. As hard as she had worked, as close as she had tried to keep her, Lisa felt like she was losing Bridget.

She knew no mother-daughter relationship was perfect, but it seemed Bridget had started younger than most. By eleven years old, she had mastered the art of eye rolls accompanied by huffs and sarcastic comments under her breath. Every other day Lisa "didn't understand her," was "so mean" and "couldn't possibly know what it was like." Bridget would storm out the front door and sit on her old metal swing set with her head down and her feet dragging, kicking the dirt and grass every now and then. In foul weather, she would take her frustration and anger into her bedroom, slamming the door, blaring her stereo and sketching, always sketching, in a diary Lisa was not allowed to see. Lisa knew from experience she would only make things worse if she tried to comfort her. And that hurt. That hurt more than anything.

But that was every other day. On the better days, Bridget was still Lisa's little girl. She still hugged her mother and snuggled into her. She still cried when other girls were mean or unfair and then washed away the tears with new coats of nail polish for both of them or an ice-cream cone or a couple of seats at Chandler Field, where the minor league team played. Lisa still read to her in bed on the nights when she was home, introducing Bridget to books she never would have considered and initially rejected only to find her immersed in them for a few days afterward, unable to put them down until she was done. These were the days that cleansed Lisa of her doubts and reassured her Bridget would not make the same mistakes she did, that Lisa was not like her own mother, that their relationship was a strong one.

As Bridget grew older, her reactions became less volatile. The angry days were fewer and less overt. For that, Lisa was grateful. But, as the strength of her anger diminished, so did the strength of every other emotion. Bridget became more complicated and secretive, more protective of herself, and Lisa became more confused. Instead of lashing out at her mother, Bridget grew distant. Instead of talking about problems with her friends, she only hinted here and there, leaving Lisa to play detective and surmise the rest. Dorothy assured Lisa that everything was okay, that Bridget's behaviors were normal for a teenage girl, and Lisa tried, so hard, to accept that.

But then came the big blow six weeks ago.

Lisa felt dizzy just thinking about it. She rarely conversed with the parents of other kids from Bridget's class. She didn't have time. But on that day, she got stuck behind a familiar man in the grocery store while the cashier tried to flag down a supervisor to help her with a void. The man had looked familiar, it turned out, because he was the father of Bridget's best friend. Lisa hadn't seen him for a few years. She had seen only the mother. His hairline had receded, and he'd lost weight. The beer belly was gone. He smiled weakly when he saw Lisa.

He was sorry, he said, that their daughters weren't speaking anymore, but that's the way girls operate. As soon as Bridget started dating his daughter's ex-boyfriend, they were done even though his own daughter had already broken up with the boy. Don't worry, though, he assured Lisa. They'll be friends again the instant Bridget and the boy, whose name was Benjamin, broke up. Because they will, he said. That's what they do at sixteen, and they'd been together now for two months.

"That's got to be a record at their age," he laughed.

Lisa laughed with him, but her laugh was insincere. She was angry. Very angry. That anger blocked out all other emotions and ruled her the rest of the afternoon. Bridget had gone to the beach with some friends that morning to enjoy the final days of summer. Most likely, those friends included Benjamin. Lisa called in sick to work, something she rarely did, and waited on the front steps for Bridget to come home.

It wasn't good.

There were so many images playing in Lisa's head. His hand on Bridget's breasts, breasts that had been nothing more than nipples on her rib cage only a few years before, skin that still had that childlike softness. His lips on her throat. His body pressing against hers. And more. So much more. Lisa had to make it stop and screaming, yelling, anger—that was all she could do to force those images down, deep down, where she wanted them to stay.

Bridget apologized and offered to bring him by so Lisa could meet him, but Lisa wasn't ready for apologies or meetings. It wasn't the fact that Bridget had hidden the relationship that bothered her so much, and it didn't matter what kind of guy he was. It was the fact that teenagers are ignorant, rebellious, and hormonal. They easily mistake that hormonal attraction for love because they haven't known love. Lisa had no reason to believe that Bridget was above that, that she had some sort of secret lease on maturity. Love leads to crazy things, to physical expression, and a desire to be closer in every way. At that age, a week seems like forever. But two months? Lisa was probably already too late.

She barely slept that night because, by midnight, she had made a decision, and she felt an urgent need to act on it. That need left her too anxious for sleep, too restless. She had decided she was too late, that they'd probably already had sex, and that nothing she could do or say would stop them. So instead, she would call a truce with Bridget and offer to take her to a gynecologist for birth control. She'd sell her on it with promises of lighter periods with fewer cramps and start times that were predictable almost to the hour. She'd pay for it, too.

The next morning, Lisa waited in the kitchen for Bridget to wake up. Bridget was a late sleeper, but she remained in bed even later than usual that day. It was past eleven, and she hadn't even gotten up to use the bathroom. Lisa figured that, like her, Bridget had probably been up thinking for much of the night and hadn't fallen asleep until the wee hours of the morning. So she didn't bother to check on her.

Just before noon, the front door opened. In walked Bridget with a grease-stained bag from Dunkin' Donuts, a cup of chocolate milk with a lid and a straw, and a soft smile. She was dressed for the day and full of energy. Lisa watched her silently, unable to speak as Bridget told her that she had thought about what she had said—about not knowing what love was—and that she had decided Lisa was right. So she'd slipped out of the house at six in the morning and walked to Benjamin's house. His bedroom was on the first floor, so she tapped on his window until he woke up. And she told him. It was over.

She had expected to feel down, depressed, to feel something. But she didn't. She didn't feel much of anything at all. She didn't even feel empty. That proved, she supposed, that Lisa really was right because if she'd been in love, she would have felt something, wouldn't she? As she spoke, Bridget cocked her head, letting her curls fall lightly across her face, and looked at Lisa through slightly squinted eyes. It was a familiar look, the same look that Bridget had given Lisa so many times as a child whenever she had questions that she knew only Lisa could answer. It came from a time when her daughter never doubted her, rarely disobeyed her, and loved her unconditionally. It was a look that Lisa greedily accepted because it filled her up, lifted her, made her feel needed, loved, trusted. Complete.

And that was when Lisa realized what she had done. She had just screwed up. Badly. But she had no idea how to fix it. Mandy got back with Benjamin after that, and the girls were best friends again. But it wasn't the same. Lisa could feel it. She could see Bridget was playing a role with Mandy, acting a part. She was doing the same with Lisa, except that she was avoiding her too. Nothing had prepared Lisa for this. Nothing at all.

Lisa found herself drawn into Bridget's bedroom. She fixed the comforter, fluffed the pillows, and looked around. The walls were still covered with little girl things—butterflies, stars, the mural of fairies on a pond that filled the wall beside her bed and was worn in spots where she had caressed the paint until she'd fallen asleep. Nothing in this room indicated that a teenager lived here, nothing besides, maybe, the make-up bag on the dresser.

The coffee that remained from the morning was cold, and she didn't want to make a full pot, so she grabbed a tea bag and microwaved some water in a mug. Too many things were happening at once. Bridget, Marty, the sheriff. Her mind was jumbled. She needed to sit and think.

Yesterday still seemed so unreal. Had the sheriff actually threatened her? Maybe she was reading too much into it. When he put his hand on his gun, was that a threat or just a subconscious gesture, something he did out of habit? But then how did he know about Marty and Bridget, that Bridget was Marty's daughter? It was all so impossible. Yes. It was a threat. It had to be. There was no other way to read it. He was telling Lisa to back off or something would happen to Bridget. Marty and his death were somehow connected to the sheriff, but how? Why?

She didn't even have any photos of Marty to show Bridget. She had nothing. The people she hung out with back then didn't take pictures. Most of her friends couldn't afford cameras, and they certainly couldn't afford to develop the film. They had fun, though, and looking back, Lisa thought they were good people. Yes, some of them smoked pot, and they chugged beers or whatever they could get a hold of, but who didn't? It's not like they were hurting anybody. They usually just hung out, listened to loud music and played pool or cards, or talked about who was hiring—McDonald's or Burger King. It didn't matter who their parents were. Some parents were cool, and some weren't. It wasn't about the parents.

Sometimes, she actually missed those days.

As Lisa moved toward the dishwasher to put her mug away, an official-looking slip of paper caught her eye. It was just sitting there, waiting to be found, but not wanting to be found, and it was written on school letterhead. The official note from the dean of students. Lisa was supposed to sign it and return it to school with Bridget. She kicked the dishwasher, leaving a small dent near the base and regretting it instantly. She did not want to deal with this, too. Guilt washed over her for the nostalgic thoughts of her runaway days. Was it rubbing off on Bridget? Had she not filled her in enough on the bad parts? Perhaps she should tell her about the nights she slept in abandoned cars hiding on the hard, dirty floors so the cops wouldn't spot her, or the days when the only thing she got to eat was ketchup from packets she stole from a diner or maybe she should describe the blood that permanently stained her shirt after the shooting, how she had to wear it again anyway because it was all she had. What was she doing wrong? What was happening to Bridget?

She sighed and took a good look at the dent. She might be able to pop it out with a plunger. The paint was scratched, though. That would be harder to repair. She signed the note and left it where she found it. Maybe it was time to bring in a third party, possibly a school psychologist. Maybe Lisa just wasn't any good at this thing. Maybe poor parenting was hereditary.

Lisa was still tired when she stumbled into the newsroom ninety minutes later, emotionally drained and exhausted. She hadn't thought to bring clothes that would be appropriate for the calling hours that evening, and she still planned to go, now more than ever. So she called Dorothy, quietly telling her that Bridget's father had died and that she would be stopping by the house to change. She could only hope no one was eavesdropping on her conversation. That was a habit of reporters and editors, and she wasn't any more innocent than the rest.

"I'll only have a few minutes," she said, trying to keep the emotion out of her voice. "I just found out the other night, and my brain is kind of fried. I've got to finish this feature if I want to take the time off, and even then, I still have to keep my cell phone on me just in case something big breaks."

"No worries," Dorothy said. "You've got those black wool pants. I'm on my way back to the house now. How about I steam the wrinkles out for you and find a blouse to match? You can wear your black boots, the simple ones

45

with no designs on them. Someday, I'm going to make you wear something other than boots, boots, and running shoes."

Not a single question. That was Dorothy. She knew when to ask and when to act. Lisa would have to fill in the details for her later, maybe in the morning when Bridget was gone for the day. That would be nice, she thought, allowing her eyes to close for a moment. First, she would take Bridget to school. Then she would have coffee and a bagel with Dorothy, who would spread cream cheese with hands already stained with splashes of paint from her latest project. She wouldn't get much sleep, but she could make up for it the next day. It was worth the lack of sleep to drive Bridget to school once or twice a week. Sometimes, those were Bridget's most talkative moments, when she was nervous or excited about something on the way to school. Of course, she'd have to bring up the school-skipping thing at some point. That was something she could not let slide. The sooner Lisa could get that out of the way, the better.

"You're awesome, Dorothy. Give Bridget an extra huge hug for me, would you? I'll call this afternoon, and I'll try to wake her tonight when I get home. I've really got to get some better hours."

"You know I will," she said. "Just take care of yourself. These things have a way of hitting you when you least expect it."

When Dorothy hung up, Lisa found herself wishing she was already home, sitting on the sofa with Bridget's bare feet on her lap and Dorothy in the recliner sipping on Merlot. She wished she and Bridget could just call a truce for a night, and things could go back to the way they used to be, just for that one night. Instead, she turned to find Jacob hovering over her desk, riffling through a pile of press releases. He was all business. He couldn't have heard.

"I need something quick," he said. "Ten inches worth. Do you mind?"

"Go for it," Lisa said, handing him another stack from the other side of her desk. "Some cop won a national award for physical fitness. The release is in there, along with a photo. He works days, so you can probably reach him at the station if you try now. Should be the end of his shift. I've got an email from the PR flack I can forward you, too."

"Thanks." Jacob scooped both piles in his arms. "I'll get these back to you in a bit."

That was the strange thing about this business. No matter how much she disliked Jacob, she still had this unshakable sense of obligation and loyalty toward him, simply because he was part of this whole weird world of hers. And he seemed to reciprocate, despite his constant jibes. Maybe his way was healthier. Maybe it would be better to distance herself from the people she interviewed and wrote about, to numb herself more often, and to see her job as just that—a job. But she wasn't sure she would ever be able to do that. She couldn't understand how anyone could do anything for so many hours a week without being truly passionate about it. But, she supposed, there were passions she didn't understand. From what she could see, Jacob was motivated by a sense of importance, the minor celebrity status that came with the job. But maybe there was something else. Maybe there was more to him than she knew. She hoped, for his sake, that there was something else.

For the next couple of hours, Lisa alternated between deadline work and searches for information on the sheriff. She didn't find much. He had risen through the ranks in one of the local village police departments to chief. After a few years with that title, he ran for county sheriff and won. It was an easy race. He was endorsed by both parties, which wasn't uncommon in Mohawk County. He was married, and his children were grown. He'd had a few big cases over the years, but nothing that would cast suspicion on him. He was generally uncooperative with the media unless the story involved praise for the department or one of his deputies. He refused to endorse candidates for other offices for either party, though he was a registered Democrat.

Nothing stood out.

At six p.m., Lisa climbed into her black Ford Taurus, stopped home just long enough to change her clothes, and left for Nottingham Funeral Home on the west side of the city. She had told her editor only that an old friend had died, and that she needed to attend the calling hours. Her editor was good about that stuff and told her to take whatever time she needed. An intern would monitor the scanner. She was fortunate. There were other editors who had no lives beyond the newsroom and no empathy either. Children, friends, relatives—they were irrelevant. Those editors—and some reporters too—came in when they were sick and infected everyone else. They only took vacation days when they were forced to, and their social lives consisted of the once-a-year company picnic. Lisa worked hard, and she worked long hours, but her time off was for Bridget, and Bridget always came first.

She was trying not to be nervous. What were the chances that Marty was still in touch with any of the guys they had hung out with so many years ago and that they would remember her? She was only fifteen at the time, with long stringy hair that fell into her eyes, baggy jeans, and old T-shirts. She was older now and much better dressed. But still, someone might recognize her. Not that it should matter. It shouldn't matter. It shouldn't make her heart beat so fast, and her chest hurt.

Lisa swallowed hard. She couldn't let herself think this way, or it would show. She had to think like a reporter, think of this like any other assignment. Go. Feel it out. Talk to a few people quietly here and there. Listen to conversations. Shake hands with his mother and offer condolences. Tell her she was an old friend who just happened to see the obituary and wanted to pay her respects. Leave it at that, gather what information she could, and make a quick exit.

She parked, turned her phone on vibrate, and stepped out of the car. The lot was packed. Lisa hurried up the front steps, but stopped abruptly when she saw the small, compact woman who blocked the door. It was her. Marty's mother, standing alone, her deep brown, almost-black eyes staring at Lisa like she'd been waiting for her all along. She wore no coat over her tailored black dress despite the autumn chill that had come with sunset, but she didn't look cold. She looked angry. Deeply, deeply angry in a way that seemed oddly sane.

"Um. Hello." Lisa held out her hand. "I'm an old friend of Marty's. I—I just want to say that I'm so very sorry for your loss."

Lisa stood strong and still, but she quivered inside. She had seen Marty's mother from afar several times as a teenager, watching from across the street, pressed alongside a building, waiting for her to leave for work so she could slip into his house and take a quick, hot shower. But she'd never met her. Marty couldn't really introduce Lisa to his mother. What would he say? "Hi, Mom. This is my girlfriend, Lisa. Where does she live? Oh, anywhere with a spare bed. Her parents didn't care whether she lived or died, and they were too busy partying to notice anyway, so she left. By the way, she's carrying my baby."

Marty's mother did not offer a hand in return.

"I know who you are," she said, through tight, pale lips. Her eyes narrowed, focusing intently on Lisa. Despite her nervousness, Lisa couldn't help but notice the dark and swollen skin under her eyes. It wasn't just for lack of sleep. It was the darkness of mascara smudged by tears and covered with foundation, and the swelling that came with rubbing the tears away. Rubbing hard and often.

"I am going to appear angry with you," Marty's mother said, "like I hate you, and you should appear equally put off by me. Trust me and do as I say. Stay clear of me while you are inside. Avoid me. Wait for me to go into the ladies' room and follow a few minutes later. We're being watched. I'm sure we are. They watched him; they're watching us and, maybe listening, too. If they think I like you, they might think I'm telling you something."

With that, she whirled on the heels of her pumps and turned inside.

For a moment, Lisa could not move. Her eyes remained fixed on the door that had slammed shut behind Marty's mother, and her hand remained slightly outstretched. This was not the encounter she had imagined. So she knew about her relationship with Marty. That much was clear. Did she know about Bridget? Did she know about Marty's letter? Was she angry that Lisa had not introduced them before he died? No. She said "appear" to be angry. Something else was going on here, and Marty's mother was afraid. She had to be, or why would she take so much care to meet her privately? Why would anyone be watching them or listening? Maybe she has just gone mad. Maybe Marty's murder pushed her beyond her limits. Lisa had seen that kind of thing happen before. She shivered though she was warm enough between her nerves, her wool pants, and her dress coat.

49

Why was she even here? Part of Lisa wanted to turn and run. Get the hell out of there and leave Marty behind for good. She could do that, and everything could remain as it was. Or could it? If he hadn't sent the email... God, she wished he hadn't sent that email. And then the sheriff—if she hadn't pushed it even further, going to see him the first time and then the second time. If she had just let Marty die and be dead, her life would be the same. Lisa turned to survey the parking lot. As far as she could tell, no one had witnessed their exchange. She took one last deep breath, placed her hand on the brass doorknob, and slipped inside.

Chapter Eight

T he orange and yellow tabby was so skinny Bridget could easily count her rib bones with her fingers. She was barely more than a kitten, maybe eight months old, and she was unconscious, unaware that soon they would be taking from her the ability to carry a litter of her own. The operation was for her own sake, for the good of her unborn kittens, and for the health and convenience of society. Bridget knew all this, and she knew the surgery was the right thing to do, but she still couldn't help wondering whether this was what the tabby would have wanted had she been able to speak.

This was Bridget's first stray day, the day the shelter brought stray animals in to the vet for neutering or spaying. Today, they'd had two dogs and five cats. The tabby was the last one for the day. But there was another special addition in one of the crates where Dr. Robbins kept the animals that spent the night. This was a pregnant dog, due any day now, that someone had found under a porch. She was a mutt, but an adorable one with medium-length chocolate fur, a pinkish nose and lips, and a body the size of a Beagle. Her belly was so full that she could barely drag herself to her feet for a few sips of water. Dr. Robbins said it would happen any day now. He promised to call if she gave birth while Bridget was off work.

"Got to be a good seven or eight in there, I suspect," Dr. Robbins said as he bent down to offer her a small treat. Bridget stopped petting the tabby and watched closely as the dog's belly changed shape several times with what looked like an occasional paw, head or butt taking turns sticking right out through the skin. "I just hope we can find homes for them all. That's what people don't get. Puppies are cute, but good luck finding them families. The cuteness wears off when you're stuck with half a dozen of them."

Dr. Robbins sighed as he left the room, and Bridget squatted to caress the mother's head. The dog closed her eyes and seemed to fall into a deep sleep as the babies settled down inside her. Bridget tried not to think about what might happen to the mother and the puppies once they were born. The shelter would try to adopt them out, but who would want the mother with her sagging teats and her worn-out body? Would the babies cry when they were taken from their family and given human parents and siblings in their place? Would the mother be sad or relieved when they left her? It couldn't be easy to care for an entire litter on her own without even a dad dog to share the load. Bridget had something in common with these babies. Apparently, they didn't know who their father was either, and he wasn't barking at the door demanding to be a part of it all.

Bridget saw that her mother's bedroom door was open this morning, a sign she wanted her to say goodbye before she left for school, but she ignored it and slipped out of the house quietly. She had wanted to talk to her yesterday, to tell her about the man in the woods, but her mother replied to her texts with "We'll talk later." Later never came, and it wasn't a conversation Bridget wanted to have before school. After she'd had a day to think about it, she decided the guy wasn't worth worrying about, anyway. She just happened to be in the woods the same time he was. Even if he was some kind of pervert, he probably spent his days there, lurking and leering at any girls who went back there for a smoke. She could avoid him by staying away from the woods and the creek.

But then, after Grandma Dorothy dropped her off at school, she swore she saw him across the street, wearing the same shirt untucked, sort of like a jacket. He was staring at her from behind a thick maple, and he ducked fully out of sight when she looked his way. He was creepy, and she was scared. She didn't want him to know where she lived or worked, so she called Dorothy after school and asked for a ride to the vet's office, saying she'd pulled a muscle in her leg. She had planned to tell Dorothy the truth in the car, but she couldn't. She'd brought this on herself by skipping school.

It was her own fault.

She'd felt numb in the car, too numb to speak. She felt that way a lot lately. It was like she was watching her life on TV. Bridget belonged somewhere else or, at least, she needed to go there for a while. That was what had attracted her to this job at the vet's office. She wanted to be part of something different, something unfamiliar, where she didn't have any preconceived notions about anyone, and they didn't know her either.

The ad was in the weekly paper, and she noticed it when she was gathering newspapers together for recycling day. It said they were looking for help just two days a week for three hours at a time with the dogs and cats that were coming in for surgery. They wanted a teenager, she later learned, because it didn't require much training, and they knew few adults would accept a six-hour work week. The office was nearby, so she stopped on her way home from school one day and filled out an application. She was surprised when she got the call last week and relieved that Grandma Dorothy hadn't asked who it was.

The woman on the phone asked her to come in for an interview the next day. It took almost an hour, and that made Bridget late coming home from school, far later than usual. Grandma Dorothy was annoyed, but only annoyed. Not mad. Bridget made up an excuse about staying late for help in science and changed the subject, asking her about the color combination on the canvas in the living room and, soon, her lateness was forgotten. She wasn't sure what had kept her from telling Grandma Dorothy or her mother that she had been at the vet's office, interviewing for the job. It just wasn't something she felt like sharing. If she didn't get the job, she wanted to be the only one who knew.

Dr. Robbins, an older man with bushy, tangled hair and a belly that jutted out from his short frame, was welcoming and encouraging. He told Bridget she was more mature than the other candidates and that he had a feeling she would work out. His assistant, a woman just a bit younger than her mother with no need for make-up and an obvious love for cats, agreed. Bridget immediately felt comfortable there, warm, connected again. So she was thrilled when Dr. Robbins called later that same evening and offered her the job. He wanted her to start right away. Grandma Dorothy scolded Bridget for going on the interview without permission and tried to call her mother, but her cell phone was off, and she wasn't in the office. Finally, Grandma Dorothy agreed to let her work, but only after talking with Dr. Robbins herself and making Bridget promise that she would tell her mother the first chance she got.

She meant to. She really did. But Bridget was off with her friends most of the weekend and, with her early morning school schedule and her mother's late-night work schedule, they'd barely seen each other since. The timing had seemed wrong last night when her mother stopped by the house for a quick dinner. She'd seemed so upset in a lost kind of way, like a kid, really. And the way she looked at Bridget—like she was so scared, like Armageddon was coming or something—it just freaked her out. Bridget couldn't seem to bring herself to say much of anything, especially after skipping class the other day. She'd have to get through that lecture first before she could tell her about the job, and she just didn't feel like hearing it.

Everything seemed strange lately. Bridget's mother had never mentioned any old friends, and now she seemed obsessed about some guy from her past who had died. She couldn't imagine her mother just hanging out with a bunch of other kids, goofing off. She wanted to know more about them and more about her father. At the very least, she wanted to meet her grandparents. It wasn't fair that her mother had kept her from them just because she didn't get along with her own parents. As soon as she got her driver's license, she was going out there to Mohawk County to introduce herself. They couldn't be as bad as her mother said, and maybe her mother was the one with the problem. Maybe she was the one who didn't care enough to make it work.

Bridget bent over and soothed the pregnant dog one last time before leaving for home, breathing in her dander. She'd never asked her mother about getting a dog. She never thought about whether she might want one before. But maybe, if she promised to take care of it herself, maybe she would let her have this one. Maybe if her mother met her, she would fall in love with her, too. Who could say no to this?

Chapter Nine

It took a moment, but Lisa finally spotted Marty's mother standing near the open casket, receiving hug after hug with an awkward smile. The restrooms were located on the far wall near the center of the room, slightly to the right. This particular funeral home had a comfortable feel with soft, beige carpeting and plush sofas and armchairs scattered about in various corners. As she scouted out the potential obstacles to her views of both the ladies' room and Marty's mother, Lisa couldn't help thinking that this was all too surreal, too much like an episode of *Murder She Wrote*.

The line to view the body was several people long. Every time a few people moved out of it, more moved in, so it grew neither longer nor shorter as the minutes passed. Lisa had no desire to see Marty's embalmed and made-up body. Her first viewing was enough.

She had intended to find out more about him. People talk more freely among those experiencing grief, even when the grief is not their own, and strangers are the perfect earpieces. They would tell her with ease who was beating on who, who was dealing what, who killed who even if they knew, in less emotional times, that those revelations could put them at serious risk. She'd always been careful about that as a reporter, never wanting to abuse that vulnerability by assuming that their words were intended for publication or pushing them too far. But right now, she needed it. She hoped for it. She was willing to abuse it relentlessly.

But she couldn't keep her eyes off that bathroom door long enough to strike up a conversation with anyone.

Lisa weaved slowly in and out of the crowd, suddenly, and for the first time in years, feeling nervous and socially inept. People generally came to calling hours with others or to meet others, to share their grief in small clusters. She had come alone, and she didn't want to share, so that left her standing by herself, obvious in her estrangement. Finally, she spotted an elderly man to the right of the main doors who seemed to be talking to no one in particular. He was the cover she needed, someone who was eager to converse but couldn't care less whether she was listening. Lisa approached him, smiled, and said, "Hello" with the enthusiasm of an old friend. Then she positioned herself across from him so she could see the bathroom door with a slight sideways glance, and she pretended to hear him. She nodded. She shook her head. She didn't worry that her timing was inappropriate. Only that it appeared to anyone who might be watching that she was deeply involved.

Then she saw her.

She checked her watch, pushing her sleeve off it ever so slightly as if she simply had an itch. Seven thirty-six. She would wait three minutes, she decided. Lisa kept her hands low in front of her, holding one wrist with her opposite arm so she could gracefully glance down at her watch. The next minutes were endless. Finally, at seven thirty-eight and thirty seconds, she grasped the old man's hand in her own, interrupted him, and said, "It has been such a pleasure seeing you, even under these circumstances. I really hope we get a chance to speak again in better times."

She smiled and pulled away and, as she did, she saw him tap on another shoulder. A thick, silver-haired man with a chesty laugh turned. He wrapped an arm around the older man's shoulder and gently pulled him into his own conversation. The old man didn't miss a beat. He seemed content to continue his mutterings even as the others talked over him.

Lisa pushed through the mourners. In place of sobs, she caught appropriately muffled snippets of conversation about such things as insurance and kids and upcoming BBQs. Most people, Lisa had learned during her years of crime reporting, are capable of holding it together during calling hours. It's the funeral that does it. The ceremony of it all. The eulogy. If the show is convincing enough, tears will explode even for those who don't deserve them.

The path to the door bearing the word "Ladies" in raised antique cursive had seemed long, too long to reach within thirty seconds. But once she arrived there, Lisa worried that she had been too fast. Still, she knew better than to look around. She pushed the door open with one hand and charged right in as if it were the most natural and comfortable thing to do. But her heart was not comfortable. Her chest ached. Her hands shook. It didn't help that Marty's mother was standing immediately before her, staring into the mirror and washing her hands at the sink.

As the door swung shut, Marty's mother (*Celeste. That was her name*, Lisa remembered. *Celeste Delano*.) turned to face Lisa, whose vision had not yet adjusted to the bright, fluorescent bathroom lights. Lisa struggled to see her, noticing that her olive skin was pale in the same way that Bridget's skin paled whenever she was tired or sick or sad.

"Quickly," Celeste said sharply, shaking the excess water from her hands and reaching into her oversized pocketbook. She pulled out a small, bulky manila envelope and shoved it at Lisa. "Take this and slip it under your coat. Now, Lisa. Do it now."

Lisa did as she was told, opening her jacket and tucking the envelope under her armpit in such a way that she could still move her forearm and shake a hand if she had to. She glanced into the mirror. The jacket was large enough. It didn't show. Thank God she had decided to wear it.

"The envelope contains a DVD and a microcassette tape. Marty hid a copy of the DVD in his apartment wall, knowing that if they killed him, they would not stop searching until they found what they were looking for. They knew he wasn't stupid. They knew he'd keep some evidence against them. The sheetrock was in pieces. They think they have it. They don't know he gave me a copy, too."

Marty's mother grabbed some brown paper towel from the dispenser and rubbed her hands dry over and over, no longer looking at Lisa. Instead, her eyes shifted to the door with a nervousness that Lisa had not seen during their earlier meeting.

"They don't know about the cassette tape. He didn't leave them a copy of that," Celeste said, her voice cracking slightly. "Now flush a toilet and wash your hands. Come out immediately after you're done. Your timing has to be right."

With that, Marty's mother tossed the paper towel in the garbage can and pushed through the bathroom door, adopting a look on her face seconds before she left that said that the last place she wanted to be was in a bathroom with her dead son's ex-girlfriend. A look that Lisa found herself hoping was part of the act.

Lisa quickly opened a stall and flushed a toilet with her foot. She turned on the faucet and let cold water rush over her hands, forgetting about the soap. While she dried her hands, she took in a breath, counting four seconds as she did. Then she released it with a count of eight, just as she'd done when she'd labored with Bridget. If you can control your breathing, you cannot panic, she told herself. You cannot panic. You cannot panic.

One last round of deep breathing, and she left the bathroom behind, trying her best to appear slightly agitated, the way she might look if she'd been rebuffed by her daughter's grandmother. She understood that it was best to acknowledge that they'd had an exchange of some kind, even if they simply did so with their expressions. It would be impossible for the dead man's mother and the mother of the dead man's child not to exchange some words even if they had never spoken before.

Pausing only for one last glance toward the smooth, polished coffin, Lisa headed for the door, always conscious of the package under her arm. She had made it more than halfway when she felt a gentle hand on her shoulder and heard a familiar, though older and deeper, voice speak her name.

"Lisa? My God, it is you." It was Kevin Donnelly, part of the old gang during her runaway days. He was taller—much taller and more filled out—but so much else about him had remained unchanged. He had the same unruly brown hair. The same grayish-blue eyes set against lightly freckled skin. The same habit of cocking his head slightly to the left when he spoke.

"Wow. I really didn't think I'd see you here, but I guess...," He stopped short and rolled his eyes in apology. "Man. I don't know what I'm saying. I'm just surprised, that's all. It's been a long time."

"She's sixteen, Kevin. It's been sixteen years."

For a moment, just a moment, she forgot. Forgot about the package, forgot about Marty's mother, forgot that Marty was dead. This was the first time she'd seen anybody from back then, from that night. And that panic she'd felt in the morgue, that feeling that she'd been caught, that she'd been living a lie, returned. But she hadn't lied, she reminded herself. She had never lied, and she had never intentionally deceived anyone. There was nothing to expose and nothing to fear. She had to remember that. There was nothing wrong with simply leaving the past in the past.

"So it was a girl then," Kevin said. She wondered whether he still drank Jim Beam, his drink of choice whenever they raided his father's liquor cabinet. Lisa was sure that she and Marty were the only sober ones on the last night they all hung out together. She didn't drink back then, not even a few sips of beer, and drugs were out of the question. Even now, she couldn't stand the smell of beer. It reminded her of too many mornings of picking empty cans out of the kitchen sink so she would have enough room to get a glass under the faucet. Though she liked wine, dry red wine. Her parents never drank wine.

"And you...and you kept her? I don't mean to be rude," he said quickly. "It's just that you were so young, and so was Marty, and you were on your own. And then there were the cops and the shooting, and everything was such a mess. It would have made sense, to give her up. God, I'm doing it again."

"Kevin, it's okay. Her name is Bridget, and she's beautiful. She's smart, and she's beautiful."

The package shifted. It was starting to feel awkward now, and she was breathing too fast. A part of her, a strong part of her, wanted to stay. She wanted to know more about Marty. She needed to know more, and she had to admit that, on a certain level, it was a relief to talk with Kevin about the old days. She never thought it would feel that way. But she had to get out of there. Fast.

"Look," she said, gently grasping Kevin's arm. "I sneaked out of work to be here, and I have to get back, but I really want to talk with you. About Marty.

About you. About everything. I work at the paper. I'm a reporter. Could you call me there? My name is the same. Just dial the main number and ask the operator to connect you."

"Um, yeah. I could do that. Just a second." He reached into his pocket and pulled out a business card. "If I can't reach you, just call me. My cell and work numbers are on the card. I wondered if that might be you in the paper. But then I thought about how hard that would be, to go through what you did and end up becoming this awesome reporter."

He shook his head and smiled.

"I should have known, though. I should have known you'd do it, anyway."

"Thanks, Kevin. You look great, by the way."

She wanted to hug him, but she couldn't. Not with that package under her arm. So she simply returned his smile and walked away, leaving Kevin and Marty's body and Marty's mother behind, along with all those people who knew Marty and understood him and could have helped her. She didn't care. She just had to get out that door and into her car. She tried not to race down the funeral home stairs for fear that she might trip, and she couldn't help wondering whether someone might be in one of those darkened cars in the parking lot, watching her. Who? The sheriff? Who else? Why?

Lisa tried to open the car door, but it wouldn't budge. It was locked. That was strange. She'd been good about locking up since her notebook and the letter had disappeared, but she couldn't remember pressing the button on her key chain before she went into the funeral home. She'd been distracted by the sight of Marty's mother. Maybe she did it without thinking. She fished her keys out of her jacket pocket, unlocked the door, and pulled it open. The interior light came on, and she immediately noticed the print-out of the obituary was not where she had left it. She was certain, absolutely certain, that she had folded it in two and stuffed it between her seat and the console. But there it was, open with the print facing upward on the passenger seat. Other things seemed a little out of place as well. The pack of gum on the console was turned the wrong way. She always had a pack of gum there, and it was always in the same position, with the open end turned slightly toward her so she could grab a piece while driving.

CHAPTER NINE

Carefully and slowly, she peered into the back seat. Nothing. She didn't dare pop the trunk. She would be too vulnerable standing out there, looking into it. Lisa suddenly felt unsafe. She jumped into the driver's seat and slammed the door, locking it deliberately this time. She shoved the keys into the ignition, revved the engine a little too much, put the car in reverse, and hit the gas. She didn't bother taking the envelope out of her jacket or even buckling her seat belt until she was well underway. She didn't stop driving until she reached the newspaper, and she didn't open the envelope until she was safely inside, past the door that could only be opened with the swipe of a cleared employee's pass card.

She left the DVD inside the envelope, but she shook out the cassette tape and put it in her pants pocket, fearing she might crush it or lose it in the larger envelope. Lisa started toward the newsroom, but then stopped when she realized it would be too busy in there. Some editor would see her and pull her into the deadline frenzy. Better that they think she was still at the funeral home. So she turned down a darkened hallway and headed for the conference room adjacent to the publisher's office, the only place she could think of where she could watch the DVD unseen and uninterrupted. No one would be in that wing of the building now, not even the janitors. They were gone for the night. The door was open, so she turned on the lights, turned on the television and the DVD player, and slid the disc in. Then she settled into a chair to watch.

Chapter Ten

This was the Marty she wanted to remember, this man who sat before her on a dining room chair in his cramped, disheveled kitchen talking into a video camera. She wanted to close her eyes, to keep him there in her mind—alive, strong, healthy, and even more handsome in adulthood than she could have imagined, forcing out the image of the lifeless shell in the morgue. She wanted to bask in the inflections of that voice, that same deep voice that had soothed her when she was scared, laughed with her when she told stupid jokes, seduced her when she didn't really need seducing. That voice that had gotten excited, not angry, when she told him she was pregnant.

But Lisa's eyes remained open, afraid of missing even a moment, and as he continued speaking, his voice started to frighten her. She began to see, feel and hear something in this older Marty that she had never experienced before, not even on that last night together when they watched as their friend put a bullet through his head. What Lisa was witnessing on that video was terror, absolute terror. First, he simply identified himself—name, birth date, address, and social security number. He rambled for a moment about his mother and his job. And then he said it. He just came right out with it: "If you are watching this video, you know I am dead. I just hope you're the right person, the person who can make it right."

Marty gave the words a moment to sink in. Then he leaned forward and stared directly into the camera as if he were searching, as if he knew she was there and he was desperate to reach her on the other side. She could see the tension in his muscles, see the sleeplessness in his face and skin. She wanted to reach in after him, to pull him out and bring him back. His eyes seemed wider than ever, permanently on guard. Every few seconds, his eyes darted about the room, scanning every space before they came back to the camera.

"I am not a good man," he said. "Don't mistake me for that. I could have gone to the FBI. I could have done something, anything. But I didn't always know that I had choices, and by the time I figured it out, it was easier just to keep on doing what they asked. It felt safe, and I always believed it would end. I just wanted it to end, and I wanted everyone to be okay. I don't think it's going to happen that way. Not for me. But I hope this video helps. I don't have enough evidence just yet, but I'm trying. This is a start anyway. During this video, I am going to tell you how it happened and what they demanded of me."

Marty started right in, sometimes stopping mid-sentence, breathing deeply for a bit, and forcing himself to move on. He described climbing into the driver's seats of refrigerated vans that waited for him at pickup points, inserting the keys he had picked up elsewhere earlier on those evenings and driving nearly five hours to a New York City warehouse, where he delivered bodies and sometimes, body parts, through darkened back doors. He took the cash they gave him and brought it back to predetermined spots in Mohawk County, where someone, he didn't know exactly who, watched from a distance, presumably waiting until it was safe to retrieve it. They told him ahead of time how much to keep. Marty took the money they paid him, dumped the vans and keys where they told him and stashed his own money in a safe deposit box, intending to give it to his daughter, Bridget, someday.

Lisa swallowed hard when she heard their daughter's name pass through his lips. She'd never had the chance to hear him say it before. She had to force the distraction from her mind and listen, listen hard to what he was saying. He did it, he said, because he knew what would happen if he failed to follow through.

"I really thought I had no choice and, in the beginning, I did not," he told the camera. "I don't know who I've been working for, but I know it's someone in the Mohawk County Sheriff's Department, maybe more than one person. That much I'm sure of, that it was a cop, a sheriff's deputy, maybe."

63

The first trouble he'd had with anyone there was during a speed trap, he said. He was going about sixty-five in a fifty-five-mile-per-hour zone, and a couple of deputies were there with all their red lights flashing. They were just finishing up with another driver. Someone took his wallet, which he thought was odd. Usually, they just wanted license and registration during a traffic stop. About twenty minutes later, the sheriff himself brought it back to him and apologized. He said they had a new guy who didn't know any better. He wrote him a ticket and Marty left.

"I knew the sheriff," Marty said. "Not well, but I knew him from the store. All those deputies, the sheriff, too, would stop by when they were on patrol to load up on cigarettes and coffee. Free coffee. I always gave it to them free. None of them ever hung out at the store, though, until after that day, after the traffic stop. I don't know why, but the sheriff suddenly started drinking his coffee right there in one of those two booths by the rest rooms."

Sometimes, the sheriff would bring a file with him or finish up some paperwork from a citation or a traffic stop, Marty said. He never really said anything. But most of the time, Marty noticed, his eyes focused on the door like he was waiting for something to happen. Occasionally his eyes rested on Marty. They rarely spoke more than a few words. Sheriff Weidenfeld made Marty uncomfortable, very uncomfortable, he said. Marty tried to spend as little time as possible there after that and started focusing more on his other store.

About two months later, Marty got pulled over again. This time, it was a guy named Deputy Larsen who told him his taillight was busted. Sure enough, the red glass was cracked, and the bulb was shattered. It wasn't like that when he drove to work. Marty was sure of it. He would have noticed. While he was inspecting the light, he heard another patrol car pull to the side of the road, but he barely even glanced at it. Deputy Larsen went back to his patrol car to call in Marty's license and registration, and Marty was too focused on the taillight and the glass to notice anything else.

"Too damned focused," he said, leaning back in his chair for the first time since he'd started taping and staring off to the side. "If I had just turned around, even for a second, I might have seen him. Things might have been different."

Marty said he was down on one knee, pulling shards out of the casing when something hard crashed against the side of his head. Then he vaguely remembered coming to in the back of a patrol car. He was lying there with his hands cuffed behind his back. His head was pounding, and he couldn't see straight. But when he struggled to sit up, the driver reached back and covered his mouth with something. Something that smelled terrible. And he was out again. When he finally regained consciousness, he was cuffed to a tree with a blindfold on, and someone was talking to him through what sounded like a voice changer. Whoever it was said he had a photo in his hands, a picture Marty had taken of Bridget from afar when she was ten and had performed Christmas carols with her class in the city square. Bridget's full name, the date of the concert, and the name of her school were written on the back. It would be too bad, the voice said, if anything happened to her. That photo had been in Marty's wallet. It went missing the night of the traffic stop.

"Whoever this was, he was desperate," Marty said, nervously scanning the room for at least the tenth time and then focusing on the camera again. "He knew who I was. He said he'd been watching me and researching me since the speed trap and that he knew all he needed to know about me. He knew he could get to me. That was four years ago. It was the year that woman Annette Baker disappeared from her own house, the lady who left her baby behind. He told me if I didn't behave, I might disappear, too, or that maybe Bridget would because Annette Baker didn't run away like it said in the paper. She was his courier, and she tried to quit, so he killed her, and now he had a vacancy. His only regret was that he couldn't sell her body, too. It was too risky to sell a murder victim. The bodies they sold were mostly cremations of people no one cared much about. They gave the families animal ashes, and no one was any wiser. He said he panicked and buried Annette Baker, but that he wouldn't do that this time. He wouldn't worry about the risk involved in making a transport himself either. He said he already had a vacant truck ready for me."

He chuckled. A nervous, unsteady chuckle. "Of course my mother is super religious, and she doesn't believe in cremation. If I died and there was no body, there would be hell to pay. I told him that. He didn't appreciate it."

Marty took a moment to compose himself, drawing in a deep breath and blowing it out. "Anyway, the witnesses who saw Annette Baker in Texas partying at some bar, they weren't real. This guy, he either investigated the case or tampered with the investigation. Somehow, he convinced the DA that she just took off, didn't want to be a mom anymore. But she didn't take off. He killed her. She wanted to quit, and he didn't believe her when she said she wouldn't tell anybody. That's what he told me. He was proud of himself."

The guy laughed and kept laughing for a few minutes after he told Marty about the killing, sometimes so hard that he coughed and spit, Marty said. Then he told Marty that he had set him up, tossed a bag of pot in the car when Deputy Larsen wasn't looking, and then made it look like Marty had resisted arrest. Like the two of them had scuffled. He knocked Marty out and told Deputy Larsen to finish the paperwork while he took Marty to the hospital. Larsen was an idiot, he said. He'd believe anything, and he'd screw up the report, anyway. Marty could go to jail for a long time, he said, probably prison because there was a lot of pot in that bag, and then there was the resisting charge. All this guy had to do was hold Larsen's hand while he filled out the report, just to make sure he got it right, he said.

Marty was sweating right through his dark curls. Bridget's curls. His voice was growing weaker, cracking. "He offered me a deal. One time, he said. That was all I had to do. Just make one run for these perverts and he'd leave me alone, make sure the charges never went anywhere. He said I owed him and that if I thought back real hard, I'd remember why. I don't remember why. I don't remember owing anybody. I've tried, but I don't."

Marty looked down at his lap and then back up. "But he didn't leave me alone. There was a surveillance camera at the pickup point. There were photos of me making the delivery, photos of me dropping off the money. There was a wiretap of the phone call he ordered me to make when the drop was complete. If he went down, I would go down, he told me, and if I stopped making deliveries, Bridget…"

Sweat flowed so freely down Marty's face by now that it was impossible to tell whether he was crying. His lips quivered. He rolled his reddened eyes up toward the ceiling and then dropped his face into his hands, rubbing hard. Marty took several more deep breaths and pulled himself together. He lifted his head and stared directly into the camera.

"He would kill Bridget. That's what he said."

Marty reached toward the camera, like he was going to shut it off. Then he stopped and slumped in the chair with his head in his hands once more. Finally, he looked right into the camera with a tight jaw and thin lips. He clenched his hands together in his lap, squeezing them tight. He looked like a man who might just explode.

"I could have stopped it, you know. I could have asked the FBI for protection. I could have tried to get more evidence sooner. I could have let them wire me, but this is the thing about me. I'm a coward. They only called me for a delivery once every couple months and…and every time, every single time, it seemed easier to do it just once more. Easier than thinking they might kill me if I got caught wearing a wire, or kill Bridget, or that the FBI might not believe cops were involved, and I might end up in prison for a couple of decades. I told myself it was okay to keep going because at least those people were dead already and the money, the money would go to Bridget—for college. It would be something, just one thing I could do for my daughter. I've been a lousy father. No, I haven't been a father at all. I have never contacted my daughter. Not once. I've stood so close to her, I could have reached out and hugged her, but I didn't tell her who I was. I didn't even try. I was a coward about that too. I was too afraid that she wouldn't like me. So, don't feel sorry for me. Don't think I'm some kind of hero. I pushed Annette Baker out of my head. I made myself forget these guys killed someone. I'm not much better than them, so whatever happens to me, happens."

He reached for the camera again, and this time, the recording ended.

Chapter Eleven

At first, she just wanted to vomit. But as Lisa sat there hugging her knees to her chest and staring at the blank screen, her nausea subsided and numbness took its place. The words, his voice, the reality needed time to sink in. She wasn't sure how long she'd stared at the screen, but she knew it had been a while and that she had to get back into the newsroom or the night editor would be looking for her. She couldn't tell him about this. She couldn't tell anyone. Marty's DVD was upsetting and intriguing, but it wasn't evidence. Not by itself. Marty couldn't even identify the guy who was behind all this. It would be a dead man's word against whose? She needed something harder, something real. She needed to find out more about Annette Baker, and who handled the investigation, and how involved the sheriff was in all of it. This was no longer just about Marty. The sheriff had threatened her daughter, and he knew Lisa was poking around. Bridget's life might still be in danger. Lisa's too. And all over corpses. What were they doing with those bodies? Who would want a corpse?

She took the DVD out of the machine and slid it back into the envelope. She had to hide it, and she could think of only one person who was trustworthy enough and who would be available in the middle of the night. Alex deserved to know anyway. His office worked under contract with all the smaller counties in the surrounding area, including Mohawk County. Someone in his office might be involved, pilfering bodies and shipping them to New York. Most likely someone who had access to unclaimed bodies. Maybe someone who worked in the crematorium. She didn't want to see him get in trouble. She owed him. She'd owed him since they first met eight years ago and had never really had the chance to pay him back.

It was a double murder, her first fatality of any kind, and the investigators had wanted someone from the ME's office on the scene while they collected evidence. Alex was just an assistant then. Unbeknownst to Lisa, he was watching when a cop insisted that they talk near the fire truck just as the firefighters were bringing one of the bodies past on a stretcher, preparing to take him to the morgue. He saw that they had intentionally brought the body, with its arm almost fully separated from its shoulder by some kind of blade, past her. He saw how the cop kept her attention diverted until they were close enough that she could almost smell the blood and then stepped away in just the right moment so Lisa would be forced to see, to look at the dead man. He watched as they passed her too closely, pinning her against the fire truck so she couldn't possibly turn and hide from the body or hide her reaction as the procession moved slowly, nearly allowing the fingers to brush against her jeans.

Alex also saw, he later told Lisa, how she paled, but refused to cover her mouth in horror, refused to look away, refused to let them see the effect the ordeal had on her. She waited until she thought she was alone in her car, which was parked a block away, to throw her head back, close her eyes, and then clutch her stomach and double over with her forehead resting on the steering wheel, believing no one could see her. But Alex saw everything. He felt sorry for her. He didn't like reporters much, but he liked something about Lisa, he later said. She was clearly intelligent in more ways than one. Alex knew what they were doing. There were certain cops and firefighters who like to haze reporters, especially the new, young and female reporters. They were trying to see whether they could break her, make her go running back to her editor begging for another beat, any other beat. More than likely, they had already placed their bets.

So when Lisa called the morgue for more information on the cause of death the next day, Alex made an offer. He'd like to see her stay on the beat, he said, and not be driven away by a couple of idiots who didn't realize that it was to their benefit to have someone with brains writing about their profession. He'd also like to see all of them lose their bets, every single one, even those who gave her a year or more. He invited her to spend a day at the morgue, off the record, for educational purposes, to see how things work and to learn how to view dead bodies differently, as nothing to fear or be sickened by. Her editor agreed, excited that a reporter would finally have an "in" at the ME's office, and so she went.

That was when she first met Anita. Anita, who was Alex's equal at the time, was appalled when she walked in and saw Lisa in the morgue, standing alongside Alex and peering into a chest cavity as he prodded a man's heart. She was so appalled and so angry that she didn't bother to ask why Lisa was there or ask anything at all. Instead, she simply hollered at Alex to get Lisa out and marched away, right into their boss's office. Had she waited, had she asked questions or calmed down for even a minute, she would have learned that Alex had permission from the chief medical examiner and that Lisa had signed confidentiality forms. She would have known that their boss had agreed that it was a good idea to educate a reporter, especially one who might be around for a while. Anita might even have improved her chances of being selected to replace the medical examiner when he retired three years later. Unfortunately, she was known for her tendency to make assumptions and to jump down people's throats before they could speak, something Lisa later realized was a control issue. Anita wanted to have the upper hand, always, and feared that without it, she would be perceived as weak, as a typical female. And this incident only made her control issues more obvious, and it was a factor in the decision that, although Anita was highly skilled and knowledgeable, she wasn't ready for a higher-level supervisory position. So Alex was chosen instead.

Anita had to make peace with Alex, eventually. He was her boss. But Lisa could still feel the weight of her anger whenever Anita looked at her, especially when she was anywhere near Alex. She clearly still hated them both.

Lisa's legs were unsteady when she stood, so she grasped the back of the chair for support. She had just tucked the envelope back under her jacket when the conference room door flung open.

"There you are. I've looked everywhere. The security guard said you came in almost an hour ago, and you're not answering your phone." It was Gil, the night editor. If the phone had gone off, Lisa didn't even notice. She pulled the phone out of her back pocket. She had switched it to vibrate mode before entering the funeral home, but she had forgotten to turn it back on. It showed three unanswered calls and one voice mail message.

"We've got a rollover on Clough Parkway I need you to check on. Sounds nasty. They called for a chopper." He held the door open with his small, beefy hands while she passed through and then caught up with her for the walk through the empty halls to the newsroom.

"Hey, you all right? What were you doing in there anyway?" he asked, between breaths. Gil was Lisa's constant reminder that she needed a life beyond the newsroom. He was round and greasy, and his skin had a grayish cast to it. He worked until two a.m., drank until five a.m., and slept until it was time to eat and come back in to lay out pages once again. Even with all that was on her mind, Lisa found it ironic that he would ask whether she was well.

"You look a little pale," Gil said. "I hate calling hours myself. Funerals aren't so bad, but calling hours stink. Everybody making small talk. You want me to call someone in from regional? Ask them to pick it up for you?"

"No. I'm fine. I need a good distraction," Lisa said, struggling to come up with words that would satisfy him. "Thanks anyway. It's just kind of strange when old friends die, you know? Makes you realize you're not so young anymore. I just needed a few minutes alone."

That seemed to satisfy Gil. He peeled off toward his desk when they entered the newsroom, grabbing a few proofs off another editor's desk along the way. "Okay then. Just let me know when you've got something. I'm going to need at least a brief by twelve-fifteen. Two inches for the paper and whatever you've got for online."

It was too late to go to the accident scene and too early to get any real information. So Lisa picked up the phone, called the dispatcher and got the basics—time of call, location, number of vehicles involved, number of people transported to local hospitals. She would check with the hospitals just before deadline, and hope the officer in charge of the accident would call her back. They usually did. They were good about that.

Then she called Alex.

"Hey, I need to stop by after work. Will you be there?"

"Lisa, if it's about this ex-boyfriend of yours, I've told you all that I know. You're going to get me in some trouble here," Alex said. "You really need to step back and breathe a little." He sounded tired and annoyed. Lisa knew she was pushing it with him. He took risks every time he talked with her and asking him to let her into his office in the middle of the night twice in a week was taking advantage of their friendship. But she had to see him.

"Please, Alex." Lisa lowered her voice. "I have something. Evidence. And I can't keep it on me. I can't explain now, but I can't go to the police. Not just yet. I know you must think I'm insane, but I need you. I need you as a friend, not as a source." She paused. The words that followed seemed surreal, like she was listening to someone else's voice, someone far away. "I think whoever killed Marty might come after my daughter. I really, really need you."

Lisa heard nothing for a few seconds, not even his breath. He was taking too long to answer. Alex thought she was crazy; she knew it. Contacting him was a mistake. She could feel that quiver in her throat again. The nausea that had overwhelmed her in the conference room had returned. Her mouth was dry. She needed water badly. She was about to apologize and hang up when he spoke. Alex's voice was calm and level. Lisa could feel her muscles relaxing already.

"Okay, but be sure no one sees you, and don't tell anyone where you are going," he said. "I don't know what you've got, but for now, I'm going to believe that you and your daughter are in danger. If that is the case, you need to take every precaution to make sure no one knows you have evidence. Evidence in the hands of a civilian when murderers are involved can be seriously fatal."

Lisa spent the rest of her shift working on the accident brief and, as far as Gil knew, finishing up a feature for the weekly neighborhood section. Most of the articles about Annette Baker had been written by Jacob back when he first started at the newspaper in the Mohawk County bureau. Baker's fiancé had filed a missing person report when he stopped by her apartment after working all night and found the baby alone, hungry and unchanged. At first, the whole community searched for her. But when that turned up no leads and investigators could find no evidence of foul play, rumors started to surface. The rumors led to the Texas bar and statements from witnesses who said she was drunk and drugged up. Those statements led to a warrant for her arrest on child endangerment charges. The theory was that she had been partying and had only meant to leave the baby for a few hours, but then she got doing drugs and took a road trip. When she realized what she'd done, that she'd face charges if she returned, she decided to keep running. Her family didn't believe it, especially her fiancé, Dan Hadley. He insisted that she didn't do drugs and never had, that she would never intentionally leave their baby alone.

Lisa took advantage of Gil's sympathy and left the newsroom early. Her car was parked in the newspaper's secured lot, which was monitored by video cameras and a guard who sat in a booth at the entrance. But that was no comfort on this night. Lisa still found herself turning quickly to look behind her back every now and then, and she checked her car thoroughly through the windows before she got in. She locked the doors immediately. She'd feel much better, she knew, when that DVD was out of her hands. As he had promised, Alex was waiting just inside the morgue entrance at twelve forty-five a.m. when Lisa arrived. Through the glass doors, she could see him studying the parking lot. He almost seemed more nervous than she was. Finally, she saw his hand move and heard the lock turn.

"Come on in." He held the door open and made sure it locked behind her. "Are you okay?"

"I can't explain right now, Alex. I have to get home. I need…I need to see my daughter. But it's all on this disc." Her hands shook as she pulled the envelope from under her jacket and gave it to him. She didn't tell him about the microcassette tape in her pocket. If she had, he probably would insist on taking that, too, and she wanted to be the first to hear it. For now, she could throw the recording in her desk drawer at home with the rest of her old interviews, and no one would know any better. It would be safe there.

She could pull out some earbuds and listen to it in private.

"You need to see this," she said. "I think someone from your office might be involved, or maybe it's a funeral director you know. You're the only person I trust with this, and I hope and pray that no one followed me here or saw me give it to you. I don't want to put you in danger, too."

"Hey." Alex tried to laugh. "If anybody asks, we're having a passionate affair right here amid the corpses." He opened the envelope and started to pull out the disc. Then he stopped as the hum of a floor polishing machine drifted down the hall from another room. He quickly pushed the DVD back in and tucked the envelope under his arm. "You never know. That might even make me more popular with the county board."

Lisa was too tired to spar with him. Too wired. Too scared. She stared down at the dirt-stained tiles of the morgue floor. She just wanted to go home and hold Bridget close and tight. She wanted to hold her and never let go. Alex put a hand on her shoulder and then lifted her chin so he was looking in her eyes. Once again, his voice was calm. Reassuring. "I'll take care of this, Lisa. Don't you worry. But you need to let me get it to the right people. I could get in some big legal trouble if this does turn out to be evidence, and I withhold it. And I certainly don't want anything to happen to you. Hopefully, you're all worked up over nothing, but you have to understand that I'm going to do the right thing here, and then you have to leave it alone."

"I know," Lisa said. "I know, but just give me one more day. This DVD isn't enough. It's just Marty's word against some unknown cop, most likely the sheriff, and, right now, it could easily look like some desperate drug dealer's lame attempt to ensure his own freedom if he ever got caught. But I know what I saw on that DVD, Alex. That was the Marty I knew. He wasn't making this up."

Alex sighed. "Okay. One day, Lisa, but that's all. And you call me if you find anything at all. Don't go confronting killers on your own, and especially don't go around accusing cops. That's not usually a good idea. I'll just say that I didn't watch the video right away, that I thought you were off your rocker."

"Thanks, Alex." Lisa leaned over and kissed him lightly on the cheek. Then she pulled her coat tightly around her and pushed open the door. The cool night air felt good on her face. It would snow soon, in another month or so, and then everything would look different. It was funny how quickly things could change. "I seem to be thanking you a lot lately," she called back as she headed for her car. She felt better just knowing that the DVD was in his hands.

Chapter Twelve

The clock read five-twenty a.m. Lisa had slept all of three hours. She hadn't meant to fall asleep right away when she got home, but her body had defied her. Now it was defying her again. Her muscles ached, especially in her shoulders and lower back. Her head ached, too, and her body felt like lead. But her mind was racing, and she knew that further sleep was beyond her reach. She sat up, forcing her feet to the floor, and rubbed her face hard. She knew she couldn't put it off any longer. She had to tell Bridget. This whole thing was a mess.

By the time Lisa had showered and dressed, Dorothy was already in the kitchen brewing coffee. Folgers. Good and strong. The way Lisa liked it. Coldplay blared from Bridget's alarm clock. *Viva La Vida*. Any moment, she would stumble through her doorway and into the bathroom, locking herself inside for a good thirty minutes before emerging, looking like something from a Maybelline ad, but with a bit of an early morning, cranky edge. That was thirty minutes alone with Dorothy. Thirty minutes to figure out how to do this.

Lisa slid onto a stool at the breakfast counter, exchanging "good mornings" with Dorothy. She couldn't look up at her. Instead, her eyes rested on Dorothy's hands, following them as they pulled out two mugs from the dishwasher, two spoons from the silverware drawer, and a container of sugar from the cupboard. Dorothy's hands, Lisa noticed, had aged. They were no longer smooth and glossy, the result of endless applications of Curel. Creams and lotion were not enough anymore. Rather, her friend's hands were rutted with blue veins, and the skin appeared taut and thin. But they were far from fragile.

Despite her age, Dorothy still had the upper body of a weight lifter, sculpted with acutely defined muscles earned by hour after hour, day after day, of holding brushes up high while she translated the moods and thoughts and ideas in her head into colors and shapes on canvases and walls. Her hair was gray, flecked with white, but it fell in a long, thick youthful braid down the center of her back. The skin on her face was creased, but its tone remained healthy and vibrant.

It would be easy to believe that Dorothy had lived a life with no worries. But Lisa knew better. Dorothy talked about herself rarely, but Lisa was a journalist. It didn't take her long to fill in the gaps. Lisa didn't know Dorothy when she'd lost her family, but she found the story easily in the newspaper's library. It had made the front page. It was the first day of hunting season in the first hour of sunlight. A group of five men had been hunting together. They spread out through the woods in the same area that they had christened every year on opening day. Dorothy's husband took the first shot. He shot without thinking, too excited to notice the movement beyond the deer. Then, when he saw what he had hit, he turned the gun on himself. It was their only son. He was nineteen years old. Their son died instantly, but her husband lived three more months—three long months—and Dorothy spent every possible minute at his side.

There was more pain behind those eyes. Lisa was sure of it. She could tell by the way Dorothy reacted to certain things when she thought no one was looking, the way her smile would suddenly fade, or she would cringe just slightly or lose her expression entirely. Lisa had learned to read her that way by paying close attention to the minutia. Yet, despite all of it, Dorothy had this glow that seemed to come from a certain kind of reconciliation, a peace she'd made within herself long before Lisa had even met her. Dorothy never dwelled on her past, at least not openly, and she never let it suffocate her. Worries had their place, and the room she allotted them in her soul was appropriately small. Before her husband and son died, she had been a stay-at-home wife and mother. It was a few months later that she discovered her talent for painting. She had taken just one art class and, within six weeks, she was commissioned to create the print that would be sold at the city's bicentennial celebration. Since then, she had easily earned her living selling her canvas works and painting murals in people's homes, on city buildings, and in schools. Still, sometimes Lisa wondered whether Dorothy's way was healthy. Sometimes it seemed like she was overcompensating, like that peace of hers came with a price.

"I figured you'd be up early," Dorothy said, pulling up another stool and settling at the end of the counter. She was already dressed in her usual work clothes—faded, paint-stained jeans and a loose, white, cotton T-shirt—and ready to start her day. "That kind of stuff eats you up inside, you know. No way you can sleep with that level of mental destruction going on."

"Yeah. It's been a tough couple of days." Lisa shoveled a few extra teaspoons of sugar in her coffee in hopes of getting a quick jolt before the caffeine kicked in. "Sleep is not a priority right now."

"Is it Bridget? You have to just tell her," Dorothy said. "Tell her all of it. She'll be mad at you, but she'll be more angry if she thinks you're holding anything back. And don't make up excuses. Apologize, explain, but no excuses."

"You're right. You're always right, but there's more to it, Dorothy, and I'm—God, I don't even know how to say this." Her own hands trembled as she lowered her mug to the counter. She swallowed hard and lifted her eyes to look squarely at Dorothy, hoping to draw from her some of that strength. "I'm scared, Dorothy. I'm scared for Bridget, and I'm scared for you. They killed Marty, and I think they might come after her too, maybe even you."

For a moment, they were silent, and Lisa wasn't sure what to do or say next. She wished she could just take her words back. Maybe if she didn't say it, didn't tell Dorothy anything, it wouldn't be so. Everything would just be the way it was before. No Marty. No Sheriff. No DVD and tape. Nothing to hide and nothing to fear. Or maybe, now that she knew, Dorothy would leave her, save her own life and leave Lisa to protect Bridget on her own. Her chances would be better that way. Dorothy would have to worry only about herself. Who could blame her?

"Oh no," Dorothy said, the firmness in her voice startling Lisa. "You can't throw something like that out there and just freeze up on me. Out with it. If somebody's going to put a bullet to my head, I at least want to know who to haunt when I come back for revenge."

Dorothy smiled and calmly took another sip of her coffee.

That was all Lisa needed.

Lisa gave Dorothy a condensed version. She wanted to give her a chance to digest it before Bridget came flying through the kitchen for her usual orange juice and peanut butter toast. She decided to skip the part about the recordings, for now, telling Dorothy that she didn't have time to explain how she knew all this. Marty's mother had said they were listening. Listening and watching. Lisa understood that paranoia now. Though the sheriff had no reason to believe that Lisa was a threat any longer, she couldn't shake that feeling that someone might be bugging her house. She could give Dorothy more details later at a busy café, in the grocery store, or while they took a walk.

When Lisa finished, Dorothy stood up, poured Bridget's orange juice into a small, thin glass, and put two slices of wheat bread into the toaster. She pulled out a plate and the peanut butter, removed the lid, and grabbed a knife. Then she turned to Lisa.

"Tell her only what she needs to know. Tell her that her father's killer is still out there and that you have reason to believe that they know she is Marty's daughter, but don't tell her she's been threatened. Tell her that we need to take precautions until the killer is caught, but it won't help to scare the pants entirely off her. And don't tell her just yet. Wait until after school. Come home and tell her. Teenagers don't take anything well first thing in the morning."

The toast popped up, and Dorothy began smoothing the peanut butter across its surface, slowly, evenly, and perfectly, allowing it to melt just enough that it didn't pour off the sides. Then she set the glass and the plate on the small, round table in the nook beside the counter. It all looked so normal, peanut butter toast and orange juice on the kitchen table. Just like an ordinary day.

"We want her to be aware, to know why we are being so strict with her and why she shouldn't trust anybody. But we want her to keep her wits about her. I'll pick her up after school and stay with her. She can come with me to load up on art supplies, and then we'll meet you back here whenever you can get out of work. I won't even let her sit in another room by herself. I'm pretty sure I can protect her."

Lisa was about to speak when Dorothy lifted a finger to her lips and turned back to the cabinets. She opened the spice cupboard and reached inside, pulling out an oversized, brown container marked "oregano." To open the lid, Dorothy had to squeeze the sides and turn, like the child safety caps on medicine bottles. When her hand emerged from the container, it held a small, black automatic handgun.

With a wink at Lisa, Dorothy placed the gun on the counter and pulled an ankle holster from the back of the pots and pans cupboard. She strapped it on, tucked her gun into it and pulled her pants leg over it. Nothing showed. She was just an artsy older lady with baggy jeans.

"See what I mean?" Dorothy said. "We'll be just fine."

Chapter Thirteen

The air in the kitchen was uncomfortable when Bridget came in for breakfast. Both of them—her mother and Grandma Dorothy—stared at her while she ate, taking sips of their coffee at regular intervals like they weren't even paying attention. Bridget glared at them, not thrilled to be under a microscope while she chewed and swallowed, but they didn't even acknowledge her. She wished they'd just come out with it, say what they needed to say. Finally, Grandma Dorothy broke the silence, announcing she would be picking Bridget up after school.

"You're not working today, are you?" she asked.

"Working? What are you talking about?" Her mother suddenly came to life, putting down her mug and sitting up a little straighter. Her gaze shifted from Grandma Dorothy to Bridget and back to Grandma again. Now she was really in trouble. "What's going on?"

"Bridget, you didn't tell her?" Grandma Dorothy patted her mother's hand and smiled. "She got a job at Dr. Robbins's office two days a week for a few hours after school last week. She had to give him an answer right away, but you weren't around, so I checked it out and told her to go ahead. I didn't think you'd mind. I guess you two haven't been around each other this past week, or I'm sure Bridget would have told you. They say she's a natural with the animals."

"I'm sorry, Mom," Bridget said, intentionally stuffing another bite in her mouth. She didn't want to deal with this right now. Bridget looked up at the clock, grabbed her orange juice, and washed down the rest of her toast. She would have skipped breakfast altogether, but that was something neither

her mother nor Grandma Dorothy allowed. "Oh God, I've got to go. No, I don't work today, but I have to be there tomorrow. I'll meet you in the parking lot near the gym."

Before her mother or Grandma Dorothy could speak, Bridget grabbed her backpack and bolted out the front door. Something was going on in that kitchen, something heavy, and she was sure it was about her. Probably something else she'd done wrong—stared at a boy for too long, worn her jeans too tight, put on too much lipstick. She didn't care and didn't want to know. Usually, one of them drove her to school, but she wasn't in the mood for a stuck-in-the-car-forced-to-listen lecture. Maybe they knew about the pictures. Maybe they knew she'd intercepted them. Bridget checked her backpack one more time to be sure they were still there. She'd found them in the mailbox last night when Dorothy asked her to get the mail. Her mother's name was scribbled across the front of the manila envelope in large, bulky letters. They were photos of Bridget—in the creek, at school, and leaving the vet's office.

That man in blue knew where she lived. He knew the things she'd done wrong—skipping class, working at the vet's without telling her mother. The note inside was in the same handwriting. It said, "I'm watching her. She is my purpose." Her mother had hired him. She didn't trust Bridget. That was the only explanation. The next time she saw him, he'd get some close-ups, close-ups of her breaking his camera because that's what she planned to do.

Bridget shoved the envelope back into her pack. She had barely reached the sidewalk in front of the house when she heard a low moan, a horrible, low moan coming from the driveway. Part of her wanted to keep on walking, terrified of what she might find. The sound was painful to hear. Someone or something was hurt. Badly. She could go back into the house. She could get her mother or Grandma Dorothy, but she didn't want to deal with that either. That would just give them another opportunity to drive her, especially if this made her late.

Slowly, she made her way around her mother's car, where the sounds seemed to be coming from. With each step, the moans grew both louder and weaker at the same time. Then she heard something like a squeak. Oh, just get it over with, she thought, forcing herself to move faster. Then she saw it, and she screamed. She screamed and screamed and screamed. She screamed so much that she didn't see her mother come and wrap her arms around her. She didn't see Grandma Dorothy run inside and grab blankets or the neighbor who came outside and used her bare hands to push the mother's innards back inside and hold her body together. She watched from some other universe as Grandma Dorothy and the neighbor ripped a sheet and tied it around the mother's belly, wrapping her puppies in the rest—the dead one and the ones that were still alive.

But then something happened. She stopped screaming, and something inside her clicked. A practical side that remembered Dr. Robbins was always in by seven a.m. to feed the animals who spent the night.

"He's there," she yelled. "Dr. Robbins is there now. Get them in the car. I'll ride with them in the back seat."

The neighbor and Grandma Dorothy looked at each other. Grandma looked at Bridget's mother, who nodded. Bridget just wanted them to hurry. Please, hurry. They lifted the mother dog and her puppies into the back of Grandma Dorothy's car since it was a bit larger while Bridget eased in beside them.

"Are you going to be alright back here?" her mother asked. "There's only room for one of us. Wouldn't you rather ride up front?"

"I'll be fine. Just get in," Bridget said firmly. She turned the dog and caressed her fur just as she had done the day before. "Oh you, poor, poor dog. Who could have done this to you? Why would anyone do this to you?"

The puppies were so tiny, but only a day or so from their due date. One wasn't moving. Not at all. If they could get the rest to the vet, get them warm and fed, maybe he could save them. But the mother—she was bleeding everywhere. She'd been sliced right down the middle like someone had tried to do a c-section with a steak knife. As Bridget held her, she felt it. She felt the life go out of the dog's body and felt the body go limp. There was something about her that told Bridget that she hadn't just passed out. A feeling. A connection between them that was instantly lost. And that's when Bridget did it when she let herself cry.

"God, Mom. Why?" she asked, for once wishing she was little again. Wishing her mother could just make up a story, a lie of sorts, a slight distortion of the truth to make the bad things seem not so bad, or at least not so scary. But her mother just looked nervously at Grandma Dorothy, who was driving, and then looked down at her lap.

"We've got some things to talk about, Bridget, but let's take care of these animals first."

Dr. Robbins rushed to the door when Bridget pounded and opened it wide. A police officer stood inside by the reception desk with his notebook open. The officer looked shocked to see the animals, like he might throw up, and Dr. Robbins put his hand over his mouth. He went right to work, telling them to put the mother down right there on the floor and to take the puppies into the exam room. He checked the mother first and confirmed what Bridget already knew. She was dead.

"Officer, whoever took her out of my office slit her open," he said. "This is a sick, sick person we're dealing with."

While Dr. Robbins worked on the puppies, the police officer sat down with all three of them. Someone had broken into the office overnight and had touched nothing but the mother's crate. The intruder left no fingerprints and so signs of how he or she got in. The place had been locked with the security alarm set.

"This has got to be the strangest case I've had yet," the officer said.

No one spoke, and Bridget couldn't take it anymore. She didn't care anymore why her mother had done it. She wasn't even mad. The man in the blue plaid shirt could help them find the person who did this. Nothing else mattered. Whoever killed that poor dog would pay. She took a deep breath.

"What about the man, the man you hired to follow me?" she asked her mother. "Maybe he saw it happen. He might have photos."

But her mother didn't answer. Instead, everything went quiet, and everyone stared at Bridget, including the police officer. Her mother's face paled, and her eyes grew wide. She put her hand over her mouth and looked like she was about to either cry or scream. Dorothy put a hand on her mother's arm.

"You didn't hire anyone, did you?"

Bridget's mother shook her head with her hand still over her mouth.

"Bridget, who has been following you?" Dorothy asked with a firmness that scared Bridget. "What are you talking about? You need to tell us everything."

A chill surged through Bridget, and her limbs started to quiver. She was cold. So cold. She pulled her jacket more tightly around her body. Her mother hadn't hired the man. Bridget had planned to approach him today, to tell him off. What would have happened? If he was capable of this, then what would he have done to her? He must be the one who killed the dog, but why? What had Bridget ever done to him?

She told them everything, about the creek, about seeing him at school, about the photos. The photos. She ran out to the car and got them, showing the officer the note and the writing on the envelope. The officer listened carefully and encouraged her to tell him everything she remembered about the man. She'd been so focused on the shirt that she couldn't remember much more. Average height cropped brown hair. That was about it. The officer read the description over his radio. Then he turned to her mother, asking her about anyone who might want to get to her through Bridget. The officer didn't see it, but Bridget did. Her mother and Dorothy locked eyes, and Dorothy gave her a look that said she should keep quiet. Her mother looked uncomfortable, but then she straightened up in her chair, looked right at the officer and told him she had no idea. She was lying. Bridget could see that. But why? Maybe she really had hired someone to follow Bridget, and maybe it went badly. Maybe he was crazy and decided to punish Bridget for skipping school.

The officer started to ask another question, but Dr. Robbins interrupted.

"If you like, you can come see the puppies. We lost one to the knife wound, but the other six are doing just fine. I'll need your help with the bottle feedings, Bridget, if you feel up to it after all this. But I understand if you don't want to come back until we know who is responsible."

Bridget looked down at her hands.

"Do you want me back? Whoever did this must have done it because of me. They stole a pregnant dog from the place where I worked, cut it open, tore the babies out, and left them all in my driveway."

She couldn't help it. The tears came again, and they wouldn't stop.

Dr. Robbins came over and took a seat beside her.

"Bridget, there are a lot of sick people out there, and that's not your fault. Whoever did this would have done something to someone, eventually. He or she is ill. I do think it might be best if you give the police some time to make sure you are safe, but maybe Dorothy or your mother could bring you down here just to help with the puppies in the meantime. You still have a job here. You do fabulous work. You're a natural. And keep in mind, this might not have been about you. It could have been someone who was angry that I gave you the job, someone who would have gone after anyone who took it."

Bridget wiped the tears off her face and tried to catch her breath. She looked at the mother dog lying lifeless in a corner, got up, and knelt down beside her. Her own mother followed, kneeling down next to her. Bridget ran her fingers through the dog's fur once more and then covered her face with part of the sheet. She sat back on her heels and just stared, unable to take her eyes off the creature that had been so full of life just the day before.

"It is absolutely not your fault, Bridget," her mother whispered, stroking her hair with her fingers. "Absolutely not."

Then her mother took her by the shoulders and hugged her tight. Bridget wanted to push her away. If she hired that man, this was her fault. But her arms felt good in a way Bridget hadn't experienced in a long time. Her mother's embrace felt secure, like she would never let her go, never let anything or anyone hurt her. It felt good to be loved so completely and to just give in. And that wasn't all. Bridget finally felt something at this moment, despite the horror that she'd been through. She felt a part of something, a part of her mother again, even just for a few seconds, and that was good. That was real. One little good thing, and she couldn't bring herself to reject it.

"You have my cell phone number and our address," her mother said, turning to look at the police officer. "You'll keep us informed, right? And maybe increase the patrols near the school and in our neighborhood? This guy sounds like a predator, like he was waiting for a victim to show up at the creek. Maybe he's done it before. Kids smoke out there and hang out in those woods when they don't want to go to class. I'm calling the school as soon as we get home."

"I'll request that," he said. "I'll get my supervisor to station an unmarked car at the high school, too. What this person did to the dog is bad enough, but breaking into this office to steal her is also a felony. Nobody is going to just let this go."

Bridget's mother stood up and offered her a hand. As she took it, she couldn't help noticing how much more their hands looked alike. Bridget didn't have little kid hands anymore. Her fingers were long and lean like her mother's. Her nails grew long and strong, like her mother's. Only their skin was different. She wanted to know more about that skin, and now, more than ever, she was determined to find out. She was tired of arguing, and she was tired of evasive answers. She needed more than her mother. She needed her father, her grandparents, and all those other people who were out there somewhere and had a biological link to her.

As they walked to the car, Bridget felt her mother's arms fall over her shoulders once again. She leaned over and whispered into Bridget's ear. "You're not going to school today. We have to talk. Some things have happened, and you have to know."

Chapter Fourteen

The talk with Bridget had definitely not gone well. Lisa tried to ignore the pain ripping through her upper chest as she eased her car into a parking space in the gravel lot. Every turn of the wheel was like a fresh injury. She had expected anger from Bridget when she told her the truth about her father, and lots of it. She had expected yelling and tears, accusations and pleas. But she had not expected fists. Another fifteen minutes or so and the Tylenol would kick in, she hoped.

What Lisa had done was unforgivable. She knew that now. God, did she ever. It had never occurred to her—never in all of her daughter's sixteen years of life—that Marty was not the only person Lisa had denied Bridget. Lisa had chosen to leave her parents. She left them because they didn't want her. They wanted to party all night and sleep all day, but they didn't want her, didn't care whether she ate, slept, drank, smoked, went to school, showered, dressed, whether she existed at all. But at least Lisa knew who they were and where she had come from. She had a sense of belonging, even if she didn't really belong there. It had never once crossed her mind that Bridget might need that too. That she might need more than just Dorothy and herself and the support that they provided her.

She did have Leo and Winnie, who had given up their working dairy farm not long after Lisa left in favor of a few acres just outside the city. They were growing older, and most of the pregnant girls they had taken in were less bright and less motivated than Lisa. It all got to be too much in their older age. For the first few years after Lisa moved out, she visited Leo and Winnie often with Bridget in tow. But over time, their relationship had been reduced to cards, photos, and long notes at Christmas and on birthdays. And they weren't real family. Maybe to Lisa, but not to Bridget. Again, that was Lisa's fault. She'd gotten busy with her job, and then Dorothy came along. Lisa was the one who didn't make enough time. Bridget remembered Leo and Winnie well, and she adored them, but she was seven when she last saw them, even though they lived only about fifteen minutes away.

Lisa had always made it clear to Bridget that her maternal grandparents were off-limits in all ways. She had never met them, and she never would. They would have rejected her—or worse yet, dismissed her—the same way they had dismissed Lisa. Lisa thought she was protecting her daughter by keeping her away from them, but what she did not know was that finding that window locked and darkened, Bridget had flung open another. She had spent her short lifetime leaning out that open window, dreaming, imagining, and planning, just waiting for the day when she would finally meet her father and his family and, hopefully, figure out where out there, outside of this life with Dorothy and her mother, she belonged.

And then, with the news of Marty and his death, Lisa slammed it shut.

Not only did she shut it, but in doing so, she took all the color out of the landscape, all the freshness out of the air, all the promise and hope out of Bridget's heart, and Bridget responded like anyone would: physically. She pounded on her mother's chest over and over and over, and Lisa simply let her. It was Dorothy who finally decided that both mother and daughter had had enough.

"Time's up," Dorothy said, wrapping her strong arms around Bridget from behind and peeling her off Lisa. Bridget struggled for just a moment before her body started shaking, and the sobs came. She collapsed into Dorothy's arms, first yelling and then mumbling, "I hate you," in Lisa's direction until, finally, the tears took over, and she said nothing at all.

"Me, too," Lisa said to herself. "Me, too."

By the time Lisa left, two hours after she had started talking, Bridget was sleeping. She was sleeping that emotionally drained kind of slumber that can last for hours. When she awoke, Lisa knew Bridget would feel achy, depleted, swollen, and numb all at the same time. It was a familiar feeling for Lisa, one she had hoped her daughter would never experience. It made Lisa's own pain—the sharp, physical nature of it—seem welcome.

The man in the woods and the dog incident had escalated everything. Lisa hadn't dared tell the officer about Marty and his allegations, not if the neighboring sheriff might be involved. The officer might not believe her, and she didn't have any real evidence. If the cops thought Lisa was crazy, they might back off the investigation. She needed them out there looking for this guy. And Bridget. How could she believe Lisa would hire someone to follow her? Had they really grown so far apart? Damn her hours. If Lisa had been home at a more reasonable hour, Bridget might have told her sooner. How could Bridget tell her something so difficult when she's always rolling in at two or three in the morning?

But that poor dog. It was clearly a warning, a horrible threat from someone who had lost his humanity. She hated to leave Bridget today, but she had to put an end to this, and she couldn't do it sitting around at home. Besides, Dorothy had her gun and had promised not to leave Bridget's side, and the police officer had said they would add extra patrols. That was of little comfort, but it was some.

Lisa winced as she stepped out of her car and stuffed her long, narrow reporter's notebook into the back pocket of her jeans. The parking lot at The Spoke & Wheel was full, even though it was just barely eleven-thirty in the morning. Most of the patrons had probably been there since the night shift ended at the nuke plant, around seven a.m. It was the only place in Mohawk County that served shots with breakfast.

She had planned to visit Dan Hadley, the boyfriend of Annette Baker, father to Annette's baby, at his home. According to the articles, he was the one who had protested most loudly when the sheriff declared her a runaway and the DA closed the case, insisting that she would not take off like that, that they had planned to marry, that she had never touched drugs, not even alcohol. After Annette disappeared, he took custody of the baby and moved in with his mother. But when Lisa knocked on the door, his mother said he was rarely home. He spent most of his time, when he wasn't working, hanging out at The Spoke & Wheel.

"He ain't done so well since she left," his mother said, pausing for a moment to turn her head and blow smoke out the door. She was thin and fragile with that tight, tanned, translucent skin that comes from a lifetime of sucking down cigarettes in the sun at backyard BBQs and keg parties in open fields. "Can't seem to believe she would take off like that. But I tell you, like I always tell him, you don't really know people. You never do."

Lisa left her phone number with the mother just in case she missed Dan Hadley at the bar. She paused on her way to the car to survey the house and its yard. No one had tended the exterior in a long time. The white paint was peeled and chipped all over, and a gutter hung from the porch roof. The bushes that separated the driveway from the yard were overgrown, and an old tractor lawnmower with no hood over its engine filled the ditch near the roadway. But Lisa noticed a small, metal swing set to the left under a large maple tree. Boards were nailed into the tree's thick trunk horizontally at intervals, making a ladder that led into its branches. It had been more than four years since Annette Baker's death. Her daughter would be in preschool or in kindergarten by now. Lisa wondered how different it must be for a little girl to be raised by her father instead of her mother or instead of both parents. How were Bridget and this little girl different? Did it change the way they interacted with the world?

Dan Hadley's mother pushed the door open again and stuck her head out. "Forget something?" she asked through another drag from her cigarette.

"No," Lisa answered, resuming the trek to her car. "I was just admiring your tree there."

The smells of eggs, bacon, stale beer and cheap cigarettes overwhelmed Lisa when she opened the door to The Spoke & Wheel. Smoking bans clearly didn't apply here. It was dark inside, almost windowless. She stood there for a moment allowing her eyes and lungs to adjust to the haze, looking for something, anything, to get her through this whole thing. Bridget was lost to her in one way right now, but she couldn't stand the thought of losing her in all ways forever. She couldn't even imagine what that felt like, what Annette Baker's family and her boyfriend must feel. She would not imagine it.

"Can I help you, young lady?"

The din quieted as the bartender leaned across the smooth wood and shouted in her direction. Lisa still couldn't see well, but she could feel them all watching her, curious. A few stood at the bar, but most sat at small, square tables with red and white checked, waterproof tablecloths, and cheap napkins in plastic holders. She didn't like beer, and she couldn't stomach the thought of wine so early in the morning, though it might take the sting out of her muscles. She felt nauseous just breathing it all in.

"Just coffee, please," she said as she moved closer.

That was enough for most patrons, who simply chuckled and then turned back to their pool games, flirtations, drinks, and conversations. Just a few refused to break their stares, and Lisa recognized them. They were the regular types. This was their home, even more so than their houses or apartments, and they wanted to know who this stranger was who had just stepped over their threshold. She did her best to ignore them, to shake off their stares.

"I'm looking for Dan Hadley," Lisa said as the bartender poured her coffee from a glass carafe and offered her packets of cream. The coffee smelled bitter, old. She declined the cream and sugar, figuring there was no way she'd really drink this, anyway. "Is he here? I just stopped by his house, and his mother said I'd probably find him at The Spoke & Wheel."

"His mother, eh?" The bartender said with a grin. "Yup, Dan's our momma's boy alright. He's right over there at the other end of the bar. The tall, skinny guy with the black T-shirt. He eats plenty and drinks plenty more. Just never looks like it."

Lisa pretended to take a sip of her coffee and tossed a five bill onto the bar.

"Thanks," she said. "Keep the change."

She could hear bits of their conversation as she approached. Dan Hadley was talking with two other guys about a recent warning from the state Department of Environmental Conservation concerning the fish in Lake Ontario. The warning had been in the newspaper the day before. It recommended eating only one fish from the lake per month because of high levels of chemicals in the water. The city desk and the bureau had already gotten lots of angry calls on that one.

"Those people are idiots," the husky guy on his right said, taking a swig from his bottle of Budweiser. "I grew up eating that fish at least a couple times a week, and I ain't dead yet."

"Yeah, but you ain't too smart, either," Dan said, and all three of the men, barely more than boys really, laughed. They stopped when they saw Lisa standing behind them. She cleared her throat and apologized for bothering them.

"Are you Dan Hadley, by chance?" she asked.

The smile faded from his face.

"Why?"

"I was hoping I could talk to you for a few minutes…about Annette. You see, I work for the *Sun Times* and I have some new information—"

"Get out."

The words came out in a low growl.

"But I think I can help. I know you don't believe she ran off, and neither do I. I think I know what happened to her, but I need—"

"You need some help?" He slammed his beer down onto the bar. "I'll give you some help if you don't get out of my face right now. You reporters are all a bunch of assholes. Dragging her through the mud like she was some kind of whore screwing around."

"No, no. You don't understand."

But Lisa knew it was too late. Once they'd been burned by some jerk, they lumped all reporters into the same category. She wasn't going to get anywhere with him, and he made that even more clear when he lunged toward her. She stepped to the side just as his buddies grabbed him by the T-shirt. The bar grew quiet again, and this time, Lisa sensed something far more dangerous than curiosity. Loyalty to one of their own. At that same moment, she felt a hand on her arm, and she turned to see a worn-out, old man with stained teeth, pearly eyes, and clothes that barely clung to his thin frame. He smiled, and when he spoke, his voice was surprisingly level and smooth.

"I think you'd best go, dear," he said. "Let me show you to the door."

93

The two men still held their friend and were trying to turn his attention back to his beer, satisfied that the old man would take care of things. Slowly, people started talking again, but it was cautious talk. Lisa was more than just a stranger now. She was a reporter, and these were clearly people who treasured their privacy. Lisa went willingly, but not without a new, even heavier feeling in her chest. She was stuck. Unsure who to turn to next. She would need time to think this through, yet she felt like time was something she was running low on. There were other leads—Deputy Larsen, for instance—but the local Sears store said he had transferred to Nashville. She had left a message for him at the other store, but he had not yet called back. For all she knew, he could be on vacation, or, like Dan Hadley, he might be anti-reporter. Maybe he'd been burned too.

"I think it would be best if you just got into your car and drove away," the old man said, pushing open the door for Lisa and stepping outside with her. He removed his guiding hand from her arm, turned to face her, and extended his other hand to shake hers.

"I do hope you come again sometime, perhaps when our wild boy there is off at work somewhere," the man said with a slight bow.

Lisa found his behavior odd, kind of eccentric, but she reached out to accept his hand, anyway. When she did, his other hand clamped on top of their joined hands, and she felt a small piece of paper make its way through her fingers. She took advantage of his attempts to shield their exchange and grasped it, curling up her fingers as they broke their hold on each other.

The old man winked and turned away.

"Drive safely now," he hollered without looking back.

She drove until she was well out of sight of The Spoke & Wheel before she pulled over next to a cornfield and smoothed out the note. What she found was a phone number with these words: *Call at eight p.m. from a payphone.*

Chapter Fifteen

A payphone? Where would she find a payphone these days? A payphone that worked? Her mind was so full of the note and its possibilities that Lisa didn't even notice where she was going. Instinctively, she had taken a right when she should have taken a left, and then she continued for several more minutes even after she realized she was headed the wrong way.

The houses and landmarks were all too familiar: the gas station and deli at the corner, with the caged-in selection of propane tanks out front and the sign offering a special on pepperoni pizza; the rod and gun club up on the hill; the small Methodist Church that stood all by itself on land that a farmer had donated more than a hundred years earlier with a parking lot carved out of cornfields.

She used to do this all the time, drive up and down the slight hills, through the rural neighborhood of fields and trees, past the house where she grew up, not knowing why or what she expected to see. But it had been years since she'd felt the need or the desire. She thought that she had put this urge behind her. It was ridiculous. What did she expect to accomplish?

Yet she couldn't help it this time. She felt drawn, compelled.

She slowed as she neared it, pulling onto the wide dirt shoulder of the road as soon as she was within sight. It was a simple house, a split-level ranch with two bedrooms and a spare room, and no master bath. Her parents owned nearly two acres, but the portion of the yard closest to the woods was swampy and attracted swarms of mosquitoes, making it nearly impossible to enjoy the back deck in the summertime. The nearest neighbors were two or three suburban-sized lots away. The two houses to the left and one across the street were similar split-level ranches sold around the same time and constructed by the same developer. The house to the right was the original farmhouse in the area, and it was still owned by descendants of the original farmers.

Lisa had always admired that house. The people who lived there were not farmers. The husband was a retired mechanic, and the wife had been a school secretary. Their kids were already grown when Lisa was a child. They had sold off all but five acres decades ago to the developer who built her parents' house and put the profits into restoring their home, which was large and lumbering with a comfortable wrap-around porch on the front and a tree-lined drive that squirmed and squiggled. Other houses along the rural road were a mix of old and new, two-story and one-story. Some had several acres, and some had only one, but none had less than one. Everyone here depended on leach fields, septic tanks, and wells. Building codes required a certain amount of land. Just about every house had a dog or two and cats that roamed freely back and forth across the road and through the fields.

Most of the homes were well kept. The lawns were trimmed, and the paint was fresh, or at least not cracked and peeling. Lisa's childhood home stood out even though it was several yards back from the road. The cedar siding was dull and dry. It had probably not been sealed since she tackled it herself at twelve years old, inspired by the promise of a twenty-dollar bill that she never received. The front yard was barren of the flowers that had trimmed its borders and filled its corners when she was very young, and the bushes along the sidewalk leading from the driveway to the front door were so overgrown that a path had been worn in the grass where people were forced off the concrete.

If not for the cars—a rusted Toyota pickup truck with a cap and a tiny Saturn—in the driveway, it might have appeared empty, abandoned. The grass was mown, though not perfectly, but it was mowed. It was good to see that her parents still cared enough to at least do that.

Lisa didn't talk to people at work about her past, about this house or neighborhood, and she'd been with the newspaper so long that no one bothered to ask her those things, anyway. She got the feeling that most people who knew about Bridget and bothered to make the mathematical calculations assumed her family had helped her through high school and college. She could feel it in the way that some of her colleagues talked to her, especially those who considered themselves experts either through upbringing or journalistic experience, like they had to explain poverty or neglect because she might not understand.

Every now and then, a cause would pop up—a support group for pregnant teens, a program for children of drug addicts, the opening of a shelter for runaway kids—and she would think, this is the time to tell my story, to make something good come out of it. But she couldn't do it. She had severed herself from this life completely, and she couldn't publically restore that connection.

She was fascinated by others, by the stories of obstacles they had overcome and the achievements that came after. Those were stories she most enjoyed researching and writing. But she shuddered to think of anyone associating her with this place, this family, this past. As Lisa sat there in the car that she owned, that was fully paid off, wearing clothes that she'd ordered from upscale catalogs and shoes she'd bought at a specialty store, she started, for the first time, to understand why.

She was afraid. She didn't want to be a "loser," as Jacob would put it. She could have told someone what her parents were up to back then, how there was never any food in the house, how the kitchen counter would often be coated in cocaine dust and how she would sometimes sneak to school early to shower because she'd found some passed-out stranger in the bathtub. But then she would have been pitied and labeled and placed in a foster home, and everyone would have known about it. They would have known that she had become trash, that her parents had sunk so low since they had been part of any real social circles that they had discarded any right to respect. Any sympathy they might have earned even a few years before was spent. In Lisa's experience, that label was almost impossible to overcome. She would always be considered trash if she had stayed home or sought help. The only way to escape it was to hide it and before that, to disappear, run away.

She got lucky. When she was found and taken into the system, no one from home knew about it. They didn't know that she was just thirty miles away at Leo and Winnie's farm and, when she attended college, she kept her head down and her mind focused. She worked on the college newspaper, and she interned at the city paper, but she didn't let any of her classmates get to know her. She steered clear of anyone who looked even remotely familiar. It wasn't hard. Her name had been Melissa, but she had started using Lisa when she ran away from home, and it had stuck. Most of her former high school classmates had wanted to get away from Mohawk County, anyway. Few attended college locally, and if they did, they went to the community college in the city.

With each success—her degree, her job, the front-page stories, the car, the house, the clothes from the upscale catalogs—Lisa put a little more distance between her old self and her new self. Or at least she thought she had. The problem was that it kept creeping back, this person that she used to be. And at times like this, the two merged and confused her. It shouldn't matter that they had never come after her. She didn't love them anyway, and she shouldn't care. But she couldn't help wondering. Did they really not want her, or had she imagined it, distorted it? She could not imagine not loving her own child. How could they not love her?

As she sat staring at the house, the front door flew open, and a middle-aged woman emerged wearing baggy sweatpants, a bright pink T-shirt, and about thirty extra pounds on her small frame. Her hair was short and spiky. It was not her mother. The woman held a cigarette in one hand and a letter in the other. She walked around the bushes and toward the mailbox, close to where Lisa was parked.

Then Lisa saw him, hollering something to the woman from the doorway, just as thin as ever in his old, white T-shirt and jeans, but older. A little older. Suddenly, she realized how exposed she was, parked on the shoulder of a rural road less than fifty yards from the old house, practically in front of the neighbor's house. Nobody parked on these roads. Not unless their cars broke down. She panicked, hit the gas, and yanked at the steering wheel, pulling out into the road without looking. A pickup truck swerved around her, the driver laying on his horn and cursing her through his open window. As Lisa struggled to regain control, she saw her father peering in her direction. He'd seen her. She knew that he'd seen her. But did he know who she was? She floored the gas pedal again and focused on the road, driving away from there as fast as she could.

Chapter Sixteen

After the incident at the old house, Lisa was nervous. People might still know her here even though it had been sixteen years, seventeen really, because she had left before Bridget was born. It wasn't much of a community, though. Most of the people out this way moved here because property values had plummeted, thanks to the nearby nuke plant, and because doublewides and ranch houses were cheap to erect. Their extended families were in surrounding towns, in other communities. Lisa's own parents had met in Utica, just over an hour to the east, and had moved here shortly after they married. Her mother was a hairdresser and had a good job in a shop a mile or so outside the city. Her father worked in a factory that made packaging for ice-cream and other frozen foods. He was a foreman on the night shift when he started calling in sick too often and lost his job. He tried to fight it when they fired him, but too many people had seen him in too many places. They knew what kind of sickness he had.

Lisa's tank was still three-quarters full, but she pulled into the One-Stop anyway and topped it off with gas. Then she pulled away from the pump and into a parking space near the door. An interview here had not been in her plans today, but she figured she might as well get it over with since she was in the area. There would never be a good time. The store was busy. People seemed to file in and out constantly, buying coffee and gas and cigarettes and lottery tickets. The clerk behind the counter was a young woman, maybe in her mid-twenties, with silky black hair and dark skin. French, Lisa guessed. She would have been beautiful if not for the gum she constantly snapped and the curse words that flowed from her mouth. She looked Lisa up and down when she approached the counter and then demanded her pump number.

"Number five," Lisa said, pulling out her wallet. "I am with the *Sun Times* and I'm doing a profile on Martin Delano, the manager who was murdered. Is there anyone here who was close to him that I might be able to talk to?"

The clerk rolled her eyes.

"He was weird, I know that much," she said. "I know the guy is dead and everything and I shouldn't say anything bad about him, but he was seriously fucked up. He was always either moping around or looking at everybody real suspicious-like. He didn't trust anybody. He just seemed mad all the time. Sucked to work for him. Bull Dog knew him better than me, though. He's in the office back there. Bull!"

A broad, thick man with a crew cut emerged from a door behind the counter. He was younger than Lisa, not much older than the clerk. Despite his linebacker build, he had a soft face, pudgy in the cheeks and neck, and dimpled. He wore a Looney Tunes t-shirt featuring Marvin the Martian.

"What now?" he said.

"Lady from the newspaper wants to talk about Marty," she said, giving Lisa her change. Lisa dumped the change into her purse and pulled out her notebook and pen. She smiled and tried to give him her least intimidating look.

"I just need a minute, if you don't mind," she said. "The name is Lisa. Lisa Jamison."

Bulldog motioned toward the office with a nod, and Lisa followed. Papers, manila envelopes, files, and register receipts were scattered all over the desk, covering the computer keyboard. She stepped over a few that were on the floor. He cleared a few binders from a folding chair and offered Lisa a seat. Then he fell into the swivel chair behind the desk, nearly tumbling over backward. He looked so out of place with his large frame, so bewildered.

"Corporate asked me to take over for a while until they find someone else. Heck, I play football. I'm studying to teach Phys. ed.," he said, throwing his hands up in the air. "There's a reason I'm not a math major. Find me Marty's killer, and I'll do him in myself just for this. I still can't believe he's dead. The worst thing Marty ever did was fire an idiot or two. But maybe he fired the wrong idiot. You never know."

"How well did you know Marty?" Lisa asked. "The cops are thinking that he might have sold drugs and turned informant. Does that sound possible to you?"

Bull Dog laughed.

"Marty? Drugs? No. Not Marty. The guy was totally straightlaced. By the book. His only crime was drinking too much Mountain Dew. He drank a lot of Mountain Dew. Something was going on, though. He kept talking about taking a transfer to Florida, but he wouldn't let me tell anyone else, and he wouldn't say which store. He said it was better if I didn't know where he was for a while, but then he'd clam up. I figured it had to do with corporate. Maybe they were going to fire a manager down there, and that guy didn't know yet, so I didn't push it."

"What about the sheriff or the deputies? Did they come here often? Did he ever act strange when they'd come in?" Lisa scribbled in her notebook, pretending to jot down every word Bull Dog said and flipping the page every once in a while. She didn't need to take notes. She knew she wouldn't forget one bit of this conversation.

"Not that I noticed. Most of them just paid and left, anyway. The sheriff hung out sometimes, but I haven't seen him in the last few days. Heard his daughter is having a baby soon, so I'm guessing he's busy with that. I don't think he and Marty liked each other much. He was kind of strange himself. We wouldn't see him for months at a time, and then he'd be back again, sitting at a booth every day for half an hour or so doing paperwork. A different time each day. We never knew when he'd come in. It made the clerks kind of nervous because they weren't always good about checking IDs. Marty never talked to him. Not once that I saw. He'd always make someone else take the register."

"Was Marty ever sick? Did he ever take time off?"

At that, Bull Dog grunted.

"Not scheduled time off. Never. No, he'd just call me at midnight or at one in the morning and ask me to come in right then and there and take over because he had a family emergency or he was suddenly feeling really sick.

Then he'd be out for two days or so, and he'd turn into a real jerk when he came back. It didn't happen much. Maybe once every couple of months. We all figured he had mental health issues and went for treatment or something. He never talked about it."

"Is there anything else you can tell me? Do you have any guesses about who might have killed him, or do you know anyone else I can talk to? Did he leave anything behind?" Lisa said, looking around at the mess of paperwork, "that might have any meaning? Anything personal?"

"Not that I know of, but I want you to know that this isn't my mess." Bull Dog leaned forward on the desk and lowered his voice. "We're only closed for four hours each night, from two to six a.m., and someone broke in here the morning Marty died. They tore everything apart, but they didn't take anything as far as we know. We called the sheriff's department, and they investigated, but they couldn't find any fingerprints and, whoever it was, managed to disable the cameras first. That's kind of why I thought it might have been someone he fired. Whoever broke in knew what to look for and how to avoid getting caught. The thing is, though, it's like I said: Marty only fired idiots, and an idiot couldn't have done this."

"Who was here from the sheriff's department?" Lisa asked. "Did the sheriff himself come?"

"Oh yeah. It was him and a couple of deputies. They scoured the place for prints. Then a couple investigators from the city came, but they didn't find anything either. I'm not supposed to say anything, though. The official word is that we were closed for the day because of a water leak. But corporate's not fooling anybody. There were patrol cars in the parking lot for hours, and Marty was dead. Duh. People figured it out."

Lisa pulled out a business card and wrote her cell phone number and home phone number on the back. Then she stood up and handed it to him. "Thanks for taking the time, and I am so very sorry for your loss. If you think of anything else or if there is anyone else who might want to talk to me, just call. Anytime."

"No problem," Bull Dog said. "I just want to graduate and get out of here."

Lisa bought a Diet Coke on her way out and walked to her car. When she approached, she noticed something pinned underneath her windshield wiper. She assumed it was an advertising flyer and yanked it out, but then she took a closer look. It was another photo, blown up and somewhat grainy. A copy of the photo Marty described from his wallet, and whoever left it had circled Bridget's face in red ink.

Chapter Seventeen

I t was impossible not to panic as she drove. Lisa blew a stop sign, passed a car that was already going sixty on a two-lane road, and flew down the highway. She was relieved to find Dorothy's car in the driveway when she reached the house. No red lights or sirens. No broken-in doors or shattered glass. No more dead dogs. And she could see the glow of the television through the living room curtains. She could finally loosen her grip on the steering wheel and breathe.

He was trying to scare her. Lisa had to remember that and stay cool. Dorothy had a gun. Bridget was safe, or at least safe for now. He must have been following all along—when she stopped at Dan Hadley's house and then at The Spoke & Wheel, even when she had pulled to the side of the road by her parents' house. He must have known Lisa would investigate and targeted Bridget right away. He was doing the same thing to Lisa that he did to Marty, using Bridget to keep her quiet. Was he trying to recruit her as his replacement? Was that what this was all about? The sheriff couldn't possibly have been in all those places—on the road following her today, at the creek photographing her daughter. He had a day job, after all. Someone else had to be helping him. She was too angry to be embarrassed or frightened. Whoever did this—left the photos and killed the dog—he was probably following her now, knowing she would immediately go to check on her daughter. He was telling her not to do anything stupid. She would have to be careful, even more careful than before.

She hadn't bothered calling Dorothy first. Lisa didn't want to make Dorothy panic or have an emotional break-down on her cell phone in her car. She needed to see that everything was okay and allow herself to calm down first. She also didn't want to know what kind of fury Bridget had in store for her. She would have to face it, regardless. Sometimes, she knew, it was better to be unprepared. What she found was Bridget curled up on the sofa with her hair gathered in a loose ponytail and her body swaddled in a blanket, watching Cupcake Wars on the Food Network. Dorothy sat on the other end of the sofa, reading a paperback.

Only Dorothy looked up when Lisa walked in.

"Hey there," Dorothy said, peering over her reading glasses. "I haven't thought about dinner yet. Will you be staying?"

"No, unfortunately. Got to get back to work," Lisa said, dropping her purse into the recliner. "Besides, that old friend I met at the funeral home called my cell phone. He wants to meet for dinner at The Pasta House tonight. I'm hoping he can fill in some blanks for me…and for Bridget. It's been a strange afternoon, and, after this morning, I'd prefer it didn't get any worse. Is everything okay here? Any word from the police?"

"Not a word. Strange that man would wear such a bright shirt, though, and wear it both times she saw him. Not very stealthy of him. Hopefully, he'll keep wearing it. He'll be easier to catch."

Lisa decided against telling Dorothy about the other photo in front of Bridget. That could wait. Instead, she nodded toward her daughter, and Dorothy shrugged her shoulders. Then Dorothy slipped a bookmark into her novel and got up, making room for Lisa on the sofa. "I think I'm just going to stretch my legs a bit," she said, heading for the kitchen. "Been sitting on that sofa far too long."

For a moment, Lisa just stood there watching her daughter. She wanted to wrap her arms around her and hold her tight, but she knew better. Bridget wasn't in the mood. Her eyes were locked on the TV, but nothing in her face changed as the host announced the winner of the cupcake competition. Nothing at all. It was that numbness. Bridget wasn't taking it in. She was trying not to think, and Lisa couldn't blame her.

Lisa climbed onto the sofa beside her and carefully reached out with one hand, brushing a few strands of hair from her daughter's face. Bridget's cheeks were blotched from hours of tears, and the last thing Lisa wanted was to trigger that flow again. Finally, Bridget sighed and spoke in a flat voice without looking her way.

"I don't hate you, Mom. I didn't mean that."

"Oh sweetie, I know you don't deep inside, but I wouldn't blame you for hating me for a little while. I was just a kid when I had you, just a year younger than you are now. I didn't have my parents to help me sort through anything, and the longer I was away from Marty, the harder it was to bring myself back to him again. Do you know what I mean?"

Bridget said nothing. She just pulled the blanket more tightly around herself and continued staring at the screen. Lisa sank back into the soft cushions and let her head rest against the fabric. She focused on the ceiling tiles, noticing for the first time how ordinary and drab they were. They were old and worn, almost industrial looking. Not at all comforting or cozy.

"I can't really ask you to understand. How could you? It was selfish of me. I know that. But I didn't know this was going to happen. I just wanted a couple months, a little time to tell you about him, and to get up the guts to let him back into my life. His mother didn't even know about me. I was terrified."

Bridget broke from her gaze, sat up, and turned to face her mother.

"Look, Mom." This time her voice was hard and strong. "I just found out that the dad I never knew is dead, murdered even, and that he lived so close all along, I might have bumped into him a thousand times. But I would never have known that it was him. And now I can't know whether I ever might have seen him before, whether he knew who I was, because he's dead. I don't even have a photo to look at. I have nothing."

Bridget paused and stared at her mother. It took all of Lisa's energy not to crumble, not to pull her daughter close, cradle her, rock her and beg her to never, ever run away or leave her forever or cut her out of her life. Lisa had been so determined to be different from her parents that she hadn't realized that there were other ways to betray a child, many other ways.

"I said I don't hate you, and I meant it," Bridget said. "But I could use a minute or two, you know? You can't expect me to work on making you feel better right now because that's what you really want. Isn't it? This isn't about you. I just need to feel lousy for a while, and you need to let me. Just... just let me be."

Lisa released a long breath she didn't even know she'd been holding. Bridget was right, very right. Lisa was making this about her. She desperately wanted Bridget to feel better, as much for her own sake as for her daughter's. The important thing was that she and Bridget were on the sofa, talking. Bridget was okay, or as okay as she could be, and they were still mother and daughter. That should be enough for now.

"There is one last thing I really need to tell you, though, Bridget, and it is a bit selfish, I know. But I need you to understand this." Lisa couldn't look at Bridget. She stared ahead at the darkened living room wall, focusing on the closed drapes and the silhouette of Dorothy's easel in the corner. "I want to tell you about the last night your father and I saw each other. I want you to understand why it was so hard for us to see each other again, for any of us who were there that night. I didn't even realize until your father died that I had been blocking out that part of my life, not thinking about it or anyone who was part of it. I was in shock. I was horrified, and I think I still am."

And she told her. She told her sixteen-year-old daughter everything, every gruesome, awful detail that she had never in her life told anyone before. She told her how none of them had taken the game seriously, how none of them had even considered that there was a bullet in the gun. They were used to being invincible, all of them. They were sure that they were until that shot blasted through the room, and Brian's head blew into pieces. He was gone. Just like that and, until now, she hadn't realized just how much that had scared her, just how afraid she was that Bridget would be ruled by that kind of invincibility. But she was wrong. Bridget was a different person, very different, and Lisa had no right to assume any differently.

"I'm just sorry. I am so, so very sorry."

Bridget was listening. She knew she was. Lisa didn't look at her as she told the story. She couldn't even bring herself to look in Bridget's direction. It was too hard, but she could feel her daughter's eyes on her. She could hear her breathing, hear it quicken ever so slightly. And she heard her words, which came out as barely more than a whisper. "I know you are, Mom."

Telling Bridget about Brian had taken everything out of her, but she knew she couldn't stop there. She had to tell her everything about what was going on, or she would lose her nerve and her energy. This probably wasn't the right time, but there might never be a right time. It was true. She had been thinking only of her own emotions and of her relationship with Bridget. She had to tell Bridget the rest despite what Dorothy had said about keeping her in the dark, not scaring her. There was no time to dole it out piece by piece and wait for Bridget to forgive her over and over again. So, she reached over just as Bridget was about to fall back into her catatonic respite, shifted her own body to face her, and put a hand on her arm.

"There is one more thing, Bridget, and this is important." Lisa's stomach tightened, and she could feel her heart race. She drew her hand back and fought the temptation to simply curl up in a ball, staring blankly at nothing for hours like Bridget. "God, I don't want to tell you this, but you have to know. For your own safety."

Bridget sat up a bit straighter.

"I told you I didn't hire the man who followed you, but I didn't tell you everything. Whoever killed your father, I have reason to believe...no, that's not true. I know that he knows who you are and that your father had wanted to get in touch with you sooner, but that this man threatened to harm you in order to make your father do things that were illegal. That's why he was killed, because he stopped, and I'm guessing that's what this dog thing was about. But Marty, your dad, collected evidence to blackmail him, to make sure you would be safe, and I'm pretty sure that you are safe, too. The evidence is in the right hands now, and I'm trying to find out more to make sure this guy goes to prison for a long time."

Bridget's eyes were wide open. She looked like a five-year-old again, like she had that first time she truly witnessed the darker side of human nature when she some teenagers dump soda on a homeless man who had been curled up on a city bench. She looked scared, really scared. And, if the house really was bugged, Lisa had probably said too much, but at least she stressed that someone else had the evidence, someone in authority. Maybe that was the right thing to do. Maybe that would scare Sheriff Weidenfeld off. He'd be stupid to harm Lisa or her daughter if he knew that someone in another agency knew she suspected him.

"You're safe. I believe that. But just in case, I want you to be extra careful. Don't talk to any strangers whatsoever. None at all. Not until this guy is arrested. And don't go skipping class. That man in the woods…just don't skip class. And Dorothy will be with you at all times. If I'm not in the room, she'll be in the room. I'll drop you off at school and pick you up in the afternoon. And I'm going to embarrass you. I'm going to walk you to the door and pick you up at the door. Okay?"

There was silence between them again, and Lisa began to second-guess herself once more. Maybe she shouldn't have told her. Maybe she should have listened to Dorothy and not burdened her with all of it. No. She had to stop thinking that way. She had to stop leaning on Dorothy for all the big decisions. She was Bridget's mother, and she had to tell her. It was the right thing. Bridget was almost an adult, and this was her life at stake. Still, Lisa couldn't imagine how frightening that kind of information might be to a sixteen-year-old girl.

"So, he sold drugs because someone made him? Because of me?" Bridget said in a voice that shook. "How did this guy know he was my father if even I didn't know? Who was it? Who is the asshole who killed my father?"

Lisa moved closer to her daughter, draped her arms around her shoulders, and gently pulled her head into her chest. Her entire body was shaking. She held her there against her breasts, stroking her smooth hair. And Bridget let her.

"He didn't sell drugs, but I can't tell you anymore, honey. The guy who shot him or had him killed doesn't know that I know or that anyone suspects him. I can't take the risk that you might do or say something that will make him want to hurt you. In a couple of days, it'll be over, and I'll tell you everything."

If he was listening—the sheriff or his buddy—Lisa wanted him to know that Bridget was ignorant and, therefore, harmless. Lisa kissed the top of Bridget's head and felt the wetness of her daughter's quiet tears soak through her shirt. It seemed she had no energy left for sobbing or hitting or anything.

She was spent.

"I love you, Bridget, more than anything. And I am so, so sorry."

Chapter Eighteen

The black market for corpses was rich.

Lisa sat at a small table in the university library with copies of a dozen of articles that had cost a small fortune in printing fees. It was worth it to get them in their entirety from the journals that were referenced online. She could have asked the newspaper librarian to print them out for her, but she would have asked questions Lisa didn't want to answer. The first one she found was about a gang in South America that had slain obese people, targeting those who weighed at least three hundred and fifty pounds. They hung their decapitated bodies from a specially made wrack in a warehouse to drain, harvested the body fat, and then melted it into gallon-sized containers for sale to cosmetic companies. They took in sixty thousand dollars per gallon.

Dermatologists quoted in the article said there was no scientific basis for adding human fat to cosmetic formulas. Human body fat has no role in preventing wrinkles or smoothing skin, they said, but they added that some people will believe anything if they are desperate and that desperation comes in many forms. The creams and lotions were also sold on the black market, mostly to wealthy women who feared losing their wealthy husbands, and to owners of exotic spas. Investigators insisted it was an isolated case and highly unusual, that no other similar gangs existed and that there was no longer a market for human fat.

But Lisa knew better. With news of the arrests, more potential customers most certainly had read about the creams and started demanding to give it a try. Someone else out there, someone cold and unfeeling with a fiscal need, had most certainly started slaughtering people again, filling the vacancy. A crooked chemical engineer or scientist or someone else with just enough education to be dangerous had formulated his or her own lotions and creams, selling them for a bundle. The market was still there. It had to be. The publicity surrounding the investigation and the dark, vain side of human nature ensured that.

Next came the stories about medical research and transplants.

Three funeral directors were arrested in California for removing leg and arm bones from corpses and replacing them with PVC piping. They made their cuts on the backs of the limbs so that they would be undetected by family and friends even during open-casket funerals. The trio had been doing it for years, selling the limbs for about five thousand dollars apiece to companies that provided bone tissues to doctors for transplants and to medical researchers who didn't want to go the legal route. They had harvested hundreds and hundreds of parts, pulling in three hundred thousand bucks in just one year. But they made too many mistakes. They simply deposited the money in their checking accounts, drawing suspicion from bank clerks and the IRS. They bought high-end sports cars and took expensive vacations. One of them repeatedly slept with an expensive escort to whom he told everything. She tried to blackmail him. When that didn't work, she went to the police, who gave her immunity and dug up several clients of all three funeral homes. The PVC piping was still in good shape.

Lisa had not considered funeral directors as possible suspects, but now that seemed obvious. Funeral directors probably handled more bodies per year than medical examiners, and most of them had crematoriums. They were the last people to see the bodies, and there was very little legal oversight. It wouldn't be all that hard to pretend to cremate a body and to then fill the urn with bits of animal bone and ash. What relative is going to pick apart the contents and analyze them? And they could remove bones from corpses just as easily as these guys did. They'd just have to be more discreet, more careful with their money. The sheriff would know how to do that. He could advise them on their finances.

She tried to think of the funeral directors she knew. Most, she had only talked to over the phone. There was the guy on the east side who did primarily black funerals, often for next to nothing if the family couldn't afford it. He was considered an activist and was as respected in the community as any pastor or priest. When the Pullman girl was killed, and the cops arrested the guy next door and found body parts stashed in various parts of his house, he was the one who led the fundraising effort to pay off their mortgage and help the parents move far away from the source of their nightmares. She knew him, and she knew it couldn't be him. That would be too much of a stretch.

There were plenty of funeral directors who were a bit too chatty, always willing to drop an address or a phone number or two for a reporter. They were possibilities. Some of them might have the necessary lack of ethics. Then there were the funeral directors who simply emailed obituaries and never checked back or took follow-up calls. Those were the ones who were most protective of their clients and their families. Reporters never got anything more out of them than what ran in the newspaper in the obit column.

Lisa didn't know many of the funeral directors in Mohawk County or in any of the other surrounding counties. The parlor that handled Marty's funeral in the city wasn't all that familiar to her either. Could Marty have become a victim himself? Could some of his bones be missing? For a moment, Lisa panicked. Then she remembered that they had lost their runner. Marty's body would remain intact because it was unlikely that they had found a replacement for him yet. Still, Celeste's paranoia might have been even more appropriate than Lisa had thought. The funeral director himself might have been watching them.

Lisa pulled more articles from the stack. Several stories reflected on the growing need for cadavers in medical schools and in medical research. In some Far East countries, journalists were investigating reports left and right about the sale of executed prisoners or dead indigents. In some of the poorest areas, people claimed to be related to the unidentified dead so they could claim bodies, sell them and collect the money. Still others signed contracts allowing surgeons to harvest kidneys, bone tissue, and skin tissue while they were still living for what we in the United States would consider ridiculously small amounts of money. One reporter interviewed a man who had sold three fingers for transplants for a grand total of a hundred and fifty bucks.

How desperate would you have to be, Lisa thought, to sell three fingers? She stared at her own hand, which was holding a pencil, using her thumb, index, and middle fingers. How would you decide which to give up, or would the buyers do that? Would it be better to lose two from one hand and one from another, or to take all three off one hand? The thought of it all made Lisa too nauseous to ponder further. She shuddered and picked up the next article.

This one was the strangest by far because so little money was involved. It had happened two years ago. A medical examiner was fired and then arrested after several strange incidents involving corpses and missing body parts. He had boiled limbs down to their bones, bleached the bones, and taken them home, where he had a collection he'd built up over the years. He had a fetish for limbs with deformities and had converted an entire room in his basement into a museum of sorts dedicated to their display.

Apparently, he appreciated other people's fetishes as well. He had a deal with a guy who liked to snuggle with corpses and then take pictures of himself with them. The guy paid the medical examiner fifty dollars per visit and was supposed to keep the pictures to himself. Unfortunately for the medical examiner, he showed them to a thirteen-year-old boy he had lured into his home. During that investigation, he told the cops that while he was with the bodies, the medical examiner was in the parking lot stirring his bubbling pots. That led to searches of the morgue and his home and to headlines in both the legitimate papers and in all the tabloids.

Lisa pushed her chair back from the table and stretched her legs. She'd been at it for only about an hour, but already she'd found an astounding amount of material. Corpses were easy prey. They didn't fight back, and they didn't tattle. No one cared much about them except for the ceremony of burying or cremating them. She had checked the box on her own driver's license that made known her desire to donate her body to science when she dies. When Lisa made that decision, she was full of doubts. She knew what they did with cadavers in medical school, joking about the dead, goofing around sometimes with the preserved hands or feet, calling them by silly nicknames. But now, she was sure she'd made the right decision. She'd rather her body was already claimed that some legitimate agency was waiting for it and would protect it from serious misuse than take a chance on something like this.

The last article Lisa read was about the porn industry, the darkest side of it. There were the sadists who recruited young runaways and then killed them on-screen during the commission of sickeningly deviant sexual acts. Lisa skipped over those paragraphs. She couldn't stomach them. But then there were the filmmakers who catered to a different market, those who preferred sex with the already dead. These guys would pay top money for good corpses, corpses that were fairly fresh and fully intact. Sometimes they got them off the streets immediately after death or on the verge of it. Homeless drug addicts were the easiest prey. They could be wrapped in blankets and stashed in trunks with barely a glance from a passerby or fellow inhabitants of the alleyways. Apparently, fans didn't care much whether they were young or old, beautiful or not. But they generally had to be female. The viewership was mostly male.

When Lisa looked up again, it was three p.m., and she was supposed to be at an interview for a feature story in thirty minutes. She suddenly felt dirty, disgusting, like everyone around her knew what she had been reading and was judging her. She knew it was irrational. Still, she scooped up the articles, folded them in two, and shoved them into her purse.

Which of these stories described Sheriff Weidenfeld and the people he worked with? Who was he selling to and was it whole corpses or just body parts? How could Marty have done this for so many years, even with the threats he faced? Did he ever see the people he transported? No wonder he was so difficult to work for and to get to know. He probably didn't want to know anyone. Lisa knew that she would be ashamed even if participation was forced upon her, and she figured Marty probably felt the same way. He had planned to move to Florida, according to Bull Dog. Lisa doubted the sheriff and his partners would simply let him go. They had killed Annette

Baker when she wanted out. Maybe he had wanted to warn Lisa when he asked to meet Bridget, to tell them to flee because he was getting out of the business and just couldn't bear it anymore, not even for Bridget. Could she blame him?

As she walked out of the library and into the campus quad, she had a greater appreciation for the clear sky and the sun that burned in it. It was the kind of fall day that made her feel good to be alive. Still, she couldn't help herself. Every person who passed by Lisa envisioned as a corpse in one of the scenarios she'd read about. Would that woman be more marketable as a dead co-star in a porn flick or as a tool for research? Did the guy with the crutches have a broken leg or an abnormality that would have pleased the medical examiner? What about that huge professor who had to shuffle from one foot to the other to move and stop every few steps for a breath? How much fat could they get from him? It was sick, and Lisa needed something to take her mind off it.

She pulled out her cell phone and dialed the Sears store in Nashville again. She had to reach Deputy Larsen. He knew who killed Annette Baker. He just wasn't aware of it. The woman who answered said he was not in and that he was off for the next two days. She offered to leave him a message but refused to call him at home no matter how much Lisa pleaded, even when Lisa explained that he had information about a murder. He was a security guard, and he'd busted plenty of crackpots, the woman said. How did she know Lisa wasn't one of them? If there had been a murder, then the cops should be calling him, not some reporter, she said. Then she hung up on Lisa.

Lisa paid for an online search of his phone number but couldn't even find a P. Larsen in the area. She couldn't go back to the sheriff's department for help in tracking him down. She didn't know who else was working with the sheriff. When she had time, she decided, she would have to find out where he had lived and try enlisting the help of friends or former neighbors. Time was the problem, though. She knew she'd never get that far before Alex insisted on turning in that DVD. At least, if she gathered enough other evidence, the state troopers or FBI would be able to find him. That gave Lisa the assurance she needed. All she had to do was put together the rest, and who knew what the old guy had to say, the guy from The Spoke & Wheel? Anything would help because already there were so many pieces that the picture was starting to take shape. Anything at all.

As Lisa was about to pocket her phone, she saw that she had a message. It was Anita Ulman and, as always, she sounded angry. "You did it again. I have you on video at the morgue well past midnight. This is unacceptable. This behavior must end, or I will report both you and Alex to the county. You don't know what you're getting into, Lisa. I mean it. Stay away from the morgue and stay away from Alex. I will not warn you again."

Good luck with that, Lisa thought. There was no evidence that either she or Alex had done anything wrong, and if anyone looked closely at that video, they would probably see her come with an envelope and leave without it. When all this was done, her visit to Alex would make sense. The threat itself didn't bother Lisa, but she was intrigued by the fact that Anita Ulman had become so upset. Why? What did Anita Ulman have to lose or gain? Someone was providing those body parts, and maybe that someone was Anita Ulman. The sheriff and the assistant medical examiner—they could make a bundle together. It made sense. This wouldn't look good for Alex, the fact that she was stealing body parts under his watch. The county would be looking for a scapegoat. They would blame him, and he would likely lose his job. It was too much to think about.

Lisa needed to distance herself for a bit, to mentally regroup. So, she got in her car and drove off to interview a boy who had defied death to recover nearly fully against all odds. Miracles did happen. Good things did happen. Human nature was generally good. Those were the things Lisa needed to remember.

Chapter Nineteen

She was the cause of all this, Bridget thought. She was the reason her father was dead and the reason the rest of the family was in danger. She'd already ruined her mother's life by being born when she was only fifteen. Her mother had never said so, but Bridget knew it. When her mother chose to keep her, to give birth to her and raise her, she also chose to give up the rest of her childhood—sports, proms, hanging out at the mall, the senior trip—all of it.

Bridget sank into her bed, grabbed her iPhone and her earbuds, and flipped through her music. Times like this called for a loud dose of some old Ellie Goulding, music she could get lost in. She turned up the volume and tried to drift with the lyrics—the lights, the voice, the dark that's too hard to beat, the queen, overthrown.

But it wasn't working. Not this time. Her mind raced anyway.

Bridget knew her mother wouldn't go back and change things even if she could, but the whole thing still made her angry sometimes. Why did she keep her? If her mother had just given her up for adoption, Bridget wouldn't have to carry this guilt. Adoptive parents are desperate for babies. They know what they are getting into when they sign all those papers, go through all those interviews and then wait and wait and wait for a baby to become available. They know what they want, and Bridget would have been sure that she was it. She would have understood, when she was ready to hear it, that her mother gave birth to her at fifteen and couldn't care for her, wouldn't she?

Or, if her mother had aborted her, she would never have felt any guilt

119

or anger at all. She just wouldn't exist. If anyone felt guilty after that, it would be her mother. Better yet, her mother could have skipped the whole sex thing altogether or maybe made a little detour to Planned Parenthood. Now there was a thought. She lectured Bridget constantly about abstaining and using protection, yet she obviously had no self-control at fifteen and no common sense. Sometimes it was unbelievably hard to sit through that lecture with a straight face. Bridget was not stupid. She was not careless. She did not want to get pregnant. Not now. Maybe not ever.

She should just leave. Just pack up and go, and then nobody would be able to use her like that again. Nobody else would have to die or do horrible things for her sake. Bridget knew she could make herself lost. She could find a waitressing job somewhere in California or Arizona and lie—say she was eighteen. She had two thousand dollars in her savings account. That would get her a bus ticket and at least the first month's rent on a decent apartment or a room in some boarding house. At sixteen, she could even get legally emancipated, make herself independent of her mother or any other guardian. She could stay in school that way and enroll wherever she landed. A girl in her class had done that after her father took off and her mother drank herself into rehab for the fourth time. She didn't want to move away with relatives, so she rented an apartment from a friend's mother, got a full-time job at a Mobil station, and enrolled in the alternative education program so she could take classes at night. But in order to do that, Bridget would have to file papers, and the courts would probably contact her mother. That wouldn't work. No. She would just have to go. What difference would the papers make, anyway? She'd just wait until she was eighteen and get her GED.

Who was she kidding? How could she do anything like that right now, with her mother and Dorothy watching her like hawks? And she had to admit that after seeing that dog, she was scared. Her father had been shot from across the street. The killer probably never saw his face, never saw the blood, never heard him moan or groan. It would be easy for the shooter to convince himself that he was just playing some harmless video game.

But the dog. Whoever killed the dog was less than human. He must have held the dog and braced her with one arm while he sliced her open with the other. He had to have seen those puppies and been completely unmoved. He had to be dangerously cold and unfeeling to have left her like that, with the puppies spilling from inside her, and to have killed her in hopes of terrifying a sixteen-year-old girl and her mother. He was worse than evil. She was sure of that. He was something out of a horror movie.

Would the killer follow her if she left? Would he find her somehow? Would she always have to be afraid of the dark, of alleys, of empty houses, knowing that he might be waiting for her with a knife or a gun or a rope to strangle her with? And what if he came after her mother? What if he killed her and Bridget never knew? What if she was never there to say goodbye, to kiss her and hold her tight and tell her she loves her? What if she died because Bridget wasn't there to save her? Suddenly, Bridget felt unbearably nauseous. She tore off the earbuds and ran into the bathroom, dry heaving over the toilet bowl. She clutched her stomach and wretched some more. Then a moist washcloth appeared in front of her, and she felt a warm, familiar hand rest on her back. It was Dorothy. What about Dorothy? What if he did to her what he did to that dog?

She heaved again.

Chapter Twenty

The kid was amazing, and Lisa was grateful.

He was amazing because of his attitude.

He was lucky because the earth was wet at the time—when he fell five floors—drenched from a week straight of steady rain. His doctors believed that's what saved him. The softness of the earth absorbed some of the impact.

Lisa was grateful because he was the distraction she needed to get through the day. She had seen him that day. She had watched as the paramedics peeled him off the ground and slipped a board underneath him, strapped him on tight, and lifted him into an ambulance. The cops were shaking their heads. He was unconscious—maybe comatose—barely a pulse, and he had several broken bones. No way would he survive.

But when Lisa interviewed him this afternoon, one year after the accident, he was sitting at his parents' kitchen table, talking about computers and books and whether his parents would get him a skateboard for his eleventh birthday. They were protective of him, and Lisa couldn't blame them. The retina in his left eye had nearly detached when he fell, and they feared another hard crash, even just a tackle in a football game, would leave that eye blind.

This was the kind of story she needed to write now and then, especially now. The good stuff. The happy endings. This, she knew, would make the front page because regardless of what some readers believed, good news made the papers too. And it was easy to write. She could lose herself in it despite all that she'd been through in the past few days, despite all her worries, and be done with a first draft before her dinner meeting and before she made the phone call.

Kevin Donnelly had called her cell phone when she was driving back from Marty's store in Mohawk County. She was too focused on getting home and making sure Bridget was alright to think. Dinner could have waited for another night, another week. But now, she was glad she had agreed to go. She was anxious to hear more about Marty, but she was curious about Kevin, too. It was interesting, even with everything else that was going on, to step into that old life and to see that it wasn't necessarily the backward step that she had feared. She was different, but so was Kevin. He wasn't going to invite her to some keg party in the basement of a vacant house. From the sounds of it, he was more likely to invite her to a cocktail party at his own house, where she would meet his wife, his kids, his newer friends and maybe some of his business associates or clients.

It was good that they were meeting during Lisa's shift, though. It gave her an excuse to end the evening just before it was time to call the old man. She chose the Pasta House because she remembered they still had a payphone there in the corner near the bathrooms. She just hoped it worked. She'd tell Kevin her cell battery was dead and decline if he offered his, saying it might be a long conversation, and she didn't want to hold him up. The restaurant was within walking distance of the newspaper, so she would say her goodbyes before the call and tell Kevin she'd get back on her own. The old man was right to be cautious. Scanners could pick up cell phone conversations. You never knew who might be listening. He must have heard her talking with Dan Hadley. He must have something. Why else would he want her to call? He certainly wouldn't insist on all the precautions if he was just some pervert looking for a date. What could some old guy in a bar possibly have to tell her?

Lisa wrote furiously, weaving previous interviews with the boy's doctor, the investigators, his teacher, his mother and his friends through the boy's own words and his own memories. She loved this part, crafting the story, putting it all together. Just as she typed the last word of the final paragraph, the phone rang.

"Hey, it's Alex."

"One more day. Just until tomorrow, Alex," Lisa said. "That's all I'm asking."

"It's okay," Alex said. His voice was calm, easy. "I'm just checking on you. I watched the video. Those are serious allegations. Any chance he was making it up? I mean, there were witnesses who saw that woman in Texas."

"Yes, but who were the witnesses? I talked to the reporter who covered that story. He tried to track them down, but he couldn't find them. The bartender didn't remember her, and he wasn't familiar with those people who claimed to have seen her. Sounds a little fishy to me," Lisa said, keeping her voice low.

That reporter was Jacob, who had worked in the Mohawk County bureau at the time. And she didn't really talk to him in great detail, but Alex didn't have to know that. Lisa already had a pretty good idea about what had happened. Jacob was so anxious to be one of the guys, to be the reporter that the cops took inside the lines, cracked jokes with and swapped stories over beers with, that he hadn't really questioned the sheriff's findings or the decision of the DA, who did double duty as coroner.

He had talked to Lisa about the case once, after making a half-hearted attempt to track down witnesses, who seemed not to exist, and Lisa had suggested that he confront the sheriff. Next thing she knew, Jacob's byline was on the front page. He'd gotten an in-depth interview with Sheriff Weidenfeld, something no other reporter had ever achieved. The fact that Jacob had gained his trust impressed the city desk editors. A few weeks later, he was offered the daytime city crime beat opposite Lisa.

Jacob's story was full of accolades for the sheriff and the deputies. No mention at all of the missing witnesses in the Annette Baker case, or of her fiancée's doubts. When Lisa asked him what the sheriff had to say about the investigation, Jacob shrugged his shoulders. "She was a loser," he said. "Why do you care?"

That's when Lisa stopped trusting Jacob.

"Lisa...," Alex said. "I wish you would drop this. I really do. I know the people who work here. I know everyone. I hired most of them. I can't think of a single one who would be desperate or stupid enough to steal bodies or anyone who needs the money that badly. I really can't."

She debated telling him about Anita Ulman, about the message and her threats, but it didn't seem right to broach it over the phone. Like he said, these were serious allegations, and she was his second in charge.

"One more day, Alex."

She didn't tell Alex about the photos or the dog or the man in the woods either. He would just become more insistent that she turn this over to the police. She wasn't ready. How could she prove anything? How could she prove that Sheriff Weidenfeld put those photos on her windshield? Or that Anita Ulman was stealing corpses and body parts? She just needed a connection. Anything to connect them with Marty or Annette Baker.

"One more day, and that's it," Alex said, hanging up.

Even with the cubicles, Lisa could hear the muffled clicking of computer keys throughout the newsroom. It was deadline for most of the daytime reporters, especially those who had families to go home to. The place would empty quickly. Suddenly. By seven p.m., the newsroom would be empty of most everyone but the night editors and a few reporters who had projects to work on or breaking stories to finish up. That was Lisa's favorite time to work.

"Gil!" Lisa yelled over the top of her cubicle wall to the city desk where the editors sat in a sort of rectangle with low dividers. The assistant city desk editor, who was Lisa's direct editor, was already gone for the day. "I'm meeting a source for dinner, and I'll stop at the police station on the way back."

"You got your cell?" Gil hollered back.

"Yup."

"Is it charged?"

"It's charged," Lisa said, gathering her things.

"Is it on?"

Lisa scurried out, pretending not to hear him. Of course, it wasn't on.

In the stairwell, Lisa stopped, leaned against a wall, and turned the cell phone on. She dialed the Nashville number again and asked for Phil Larsen. This time, a man answered. He said he'd been warned that someone might call for Larsen and that he was supposed to hang up. What, he wondered, did she want with him, anyway? The guy sounded nice enough, and he didn't disconnect her, so Lisa decided to take a chance. She told him. She told him that Larsen had been involved in a traffic stop with another member of the sheriff's department and that she believed the other person recently killed the man they had pulled over, a man named Martin Delano. The trouble was that this other deputy, or lieutenant, or the sheriff or whoever, was not named in the report, and she needed his identity.

"Then why do you think some other deputy killed the guy? Why don't you ask the sheriff? Why isn't the sheriff doing the calling, anyway? Man, I should have just hung up like I was told. You are crazy, lady."

And the line went dead.

Lisa turned the phone off again and stood there for a moment, just staring at the beige concrete-brick wall. She'd blown it. Now she really did seem like a crazy lady. She wouldn't even call herself back if she were Phil Larsen.

Kevin was already waiting by the time she got outside. She probably should have driven herself to ensure he didn't wait for her to finish her call, but she hated to park at the police station, and she had to check the blotter entries on her way back. The lot for the public safety building was closed at night, and the spaces out front were usually taken. Besides, it wasn't worth the trouble to drive. The restaurant was only about a mile away, but it was atop a steep hill overlooking the city. Walking back was no big deal, but the one time she walked up, her calves ached for days afterward.

"Hey there," Kevin said, reaching across the passenger seat to open the door of his Jeep Grand Cherokee. She couldn't help noticing the infant car seat and the booster in the back. A Ziplock bag of Goldfish crackers lay between the two seats, along with a green sippy cup covered with little cartoon frogs. It was so hard to picture Kevin as a dad, to picture anyone from back then as a parent.

"A toddler and a baby, huh?" Lisa said, climbing in. "Boys? Girls? One of each?"

"Both boys," Kevin said with a smile as she buckled up and he pulled away from the curb, "and a stepdaughter who is turning seven on Friday. I'll force the photos on you when we get to the restaurant. How about you? Did you ever get married? Any other kids?"

"Nope. No time," Lisa laughed. "Besides, I can't imagine worrying constantly about more than one. Bridget is enough. Hey, is your wife okay with us having dinner? I mean, she knows we're just old friends, right?"

"Yes and no," Kevin said. "It's not that you're another woman. It's how we know each other that bothers her. She was that way with Marty, too. I can't blame her. I'd be a little freaked out if she started hanging out with some guy she last saw when another friend shot himself in the head. But she'll be all right once she gets to know you. She got used to Marty."

They drove only a few minutes before they were at the restaurant, and already Lisa was feeling that comfort that comes from old friendships, from being in the presence of someone who already knows your history, your core likes and dislikes, and your innate quirks. They found a booth far away from the din of the kitchen and the bar where they could talk quietly. But Lisa couldn't quite get entirely comfortable. Celeste's warning was still with her, her insistence that they were always being watched.

Marty and Kevin had gone their separate ways after the shooting, too. Kevin's parents enrolled him in private school, and then he went off to college. They bumped into each other at Marty's store a few years ago and fell back into their old friendship. Marty was different, though, Kevin said. He had a cautious way about him, and he didn't smile much. That was one reason Kevin had such a hard time believing what the cops said about him dealing drugs.

"He just wasn't the drug-dealing type," Kevin said. "Not that I really know what that type is, but you know what I mean. He was serious and responsible, and he was definitely no salesman. He didn't even drink anymore. Not even a beer. I couldn't imagine anybody wanting to buy drugs from him, somebody who was looking to get high. He was kind of a downer. Besides, this whole thing—the problems he had with Tyler and Abe—that was all about drugs. He almost got killed over it. You saw Tyler. He was going to shoot Marty himself, and he would have if Brian hadn't jumped in."

"What?" Lisa nearly choked on her water, and she struggled to put her glass down without spilling it. "What are you talking about? What happened with Tyler and Abe, and why would Tyler want to kill Marty?"

"You didn't know, Lisa? You honestly didn't know?"

Kevin ran both hands through his hair and released a long, deep sigh. Then he leaned forward and spoke in a near-whisper.

"Man, Lisa. I don't even know how to tell you. I just assumed he told you everything. Tyler and Abe had hooked up with some gang. They were selling coke, heroin oil, 'shrooms, you name it. We grew up with these guys. We all went to kindergarten together—played under the fire hydrants in the summers, went sledding on the ball field hill in the winter, stole gum from the big barrels at Sam's Market. You know. Harmless stuff like that. But this was big, and this could ruin them. Marty tried to talk them out of it. We both did, but Marty wouldn't let up. He threatened to turn them in. For their own good, you know? I told him to back off, but he wouldn't listen."

"I don't understand. That whole Russian roulette thing—that was just a set-up? They knew the fourth shot would be the last. Oh my God, he could have died right then, right next to me, before Bridget was even born." Lisa suddenly had trouble getting air in her lungs. The sights and sounds of the restaurant seemed far away, unreachable and dim. Then she felt Kevin's hand clamp fast to her arm.

"Lisa. Lisa. Take another drink of water. This was long ago. It's over. Tyler's dead. He was killed in juvie. After the shooting, they impounded his car and found a whole bunch of stuff in there. He ratted on Abe, who was arrested too. Word is that the gang wanted to make an example of him. A couple of guys knifed him for ratting on Abe. And Abe is long gone, too. He's serving time in prison for robbery. His third conviction. He'll be locked up for most of his life."

He released Lisa's arm and patted it lightly.

"It's okay. It was long ago."

"How could I not know, Kevin? I was his girlfriend. I was carrying his baby."

"Kindergarten, Lisa. That's how long we were all together. I'm sure he loved you and all, but how long were you dating? A year? It was complicated, and he probably wanted to protect you. To him, these guys were the same old guys, the kids he grew up with. He couldn't see what I saw, that they weren't the same at all. They were dangerous, and he pushed them too far. Brian is dead. We can't change that. But they didn't kill him. He took that gun, knowing the chance he was taking. He wanted to take that risk. He wanted to die, and he did. That's how the night ended. It was screwed up, totally screwed up, but it's over."

Lisa felt nothing but numbness inside. Kevin changed the subject, and Lisa tried to listen, tried to respond politely. Kevin said he asked Marty about her and about the baby a couple of times, but that Marty made it clear the subject was off-limits. In fact, most anything, even remotely personal, was off-limits. They mostly did what other guys did when they hung out, Kevin said. They watched football or baseball or basketball or whatever was in season. They didn't talk much.

"I was just surprised that you two didn't get back together," he said. "You seemed so tight. I still remember when you first started dating, when you came to that party in the city just before you left home. Do you think you would have left home if it weren't for us? I've always wondered that because we kind of took care of you, all of us. I mean, you stayed in my clubhouse for about three weeks, remember? That old shack? Then Shannon's mom let you stay with them for a while until you got pregnant. She said you were a 'bad influence.' How could anyone be a worse influence than her own mom? Are you still in touch with Shannon? She's still the same. Still smoking and drinking her life away, just like her mother did."

Sometimes Lisa wondered that herself, whether she would have left home if she hadn't fallen for Marty. Marty had given her something to look forward to for the first time in her life. He made her happy. He made her laugh. He paid attention to her. There was something about the way she had to sneak around to see him, too. Not that her parents cared, but the school did. It seemed the only times her parents ever really noticed her back then were when the truancy officer called. That was probably because he usually called at about eleven a.m. and woke them up.

Marty lived in the city, and he was too young to drive, so she hitched rides there. Sometimes it was easier to just stay overnight than it was to go home, go to school the next day and then come back. So, she started coming back home less often, and then, one day, after she found out she was pregnant, she decided not to go home again at all. That's when she started to become a fixture in the homes of her new friends, sleeping on their sofas or on their living room floors. She never stayed at his house, though. His mother, from what she knew, was the opposite of her parents. She was a widow, and she was tough. She would not have approved of Marty dating at fifteen, especially not someone like Lisa.

She was sure now that she was never really in love with Marty, not the way that other people love their spouses. Maybe that was one reason she didn't contact him after Bridget was born. But she had liked him a lot, and she had needed him. Still, Lisa had no regrets. No regrets about leaving home, being with Marty, or getting pregnant with Bridget. All those things combined were what had lifted her out of her circumstances. Without Marty, Bridget and Winnie, and Leo, Lisa might never have gone to college. She might never have become a reporter. She might never have understood what it meant to completely and wholly love another human being. It would have been easy to keep living as she had been, with no sense of self, no feeling of self-worth. So many people she knew droned on about their past and blamed the stresses of their childhood struggles for all their faults in adulthood. They looked for pity, excuses. But, Lisa knew, those were things to be grateful for. Without them, without Bridget, who would she be?

Lisa tried to keep the conversation balanced, asking Kevin questions about his family and his job, but it was hard not to focus entirely on Marty, especially after what Kevin had told her. The only thing that Kevin found unusual was that every now and then, Marty would have to cancel their plans at the last minute, like it was an emergency. He wouldn't talk about it and, the few times Kevin had stopped by the store to check on him the next day, he was exhausted and irritable. It'd be weeks before he would contact Kevin again.

"I suppose that could have been it," Kevin said. "Maybe that's when he was selling drugs, and the emergencies were calls from users who really needed it bad, but it just didn't feel that way. Whatever it was that was taking him away, it made him angry. I can't explain it, but he was definitely angry."

Dinner ended with Lisa demanding the check and Kevin conceding, only if Lisa, Dorothy, and Bridget would come over for dinner sometime. He'd like his wife to meet her, he said, and he'd love to find out how Bridget and his kids clicked. They could always use a good babysitter, he said. As she expected, Kevin offered to wait while she made her phone call and drive her back to the paper, but Lisa insisted he go ahead. She had no idea how long she'd be on the phone, and it was a nice night for walking. She needed time to absorb what he'd said, and the walk would be a good opportunity, she said. It was good to reconnect with him, and she found herself craving more of that, more of the person she once was.

Lisa lingered a minute or two, sipping water and flipping through her notebook after Kevin left. It wasn't quite time yet, and she didn't want to call too early. She had already located the payphone and checked for a dial tone. It was an old phone, but it had been upgraded to take credit cards. The booth was open to the restaurant, but it was tucked in a corner opposite the bathroom doors, so she had at least some privacy. It didn't seem to get much use, and she could easily tell if anyone was near enough to listen. The sheriff couldn't possibly know what she was about to do, and he'd have to have a whole network of cop-criminals at his disposal to tap that payphone fast enough. At one minute before eight p.m., she walked to the phone. No one was using it. No one was around. She picked it up and dialed. He answered on the first ring.

"That you?" he asked.

"This is Lisa Jamison," she said.

"I'm going to talk fast in case anybody tries to trace this. I heard you asking about that Baker girl, saying you don't believe she ran away. She didn't. I was there when she was buried, and somebody's got to know about it. I've got to tell somebody. I keep having these dreams, you know? Can't sleep. I've seen what you do, how you write. I like you. People think I ain't smart, like I don't read the papers. I do. I read them every day. I just don't go bragging about it."

The old man's voice was breathless, like a kid who just couldn't get the words out fast enough. He'd been out drinking that night, he said. Drinking a lot—beer, whiskey, maybe some vodka, too. He'd driven to the bar, but he was so drunk, he couldn't find his pickup truck or the keys when he left, so he gave up and hitched a ride with two younger guys, some guys he'd never seen before, who were leaving at the same time. They were too nice, he said. He should have known better.

"It was a pickup truck, too. A Ford, or maybe a Chevy. I don't know. The one guy got in the middle and offered me the window seat in case I had to throw up. I was stupid. I saw those looks between them. I should have known they were up to something, but I was too wasted to do anything about it. A few miles down the road, the jerk reached over, opened my door, and shoved me out. Right in the middle of nowhere on Route 49. That's why I was walking," he said. "Scraped my leg up pretty good, too. Didn't even slow down. Not a bit."

The old man stopped to cough, a sickening, wet cough that seemed to last forever. For a moment, Lisa was afraid he wouldn't be able to continue. But he picked up right where he had left off. He said he woke up a few hours later in the woods by the Essex River. His watch said four a.m. He must have come down the path from the dirt pull-over just before Cheese Factory Road, he figured, and passed out right there. Headlights woke him, and when he saw it was a patrol car, he figured he'd better keep low. He'd been in trouble a few times before—little stuff like peeing in public or walking in the middle of the street, stopping traffic. Nothing he was proud of.

"I couldn't see too well because it was dark, but I saw someone, someone in uniform, open that trunk and drag her out of there. She was wrapped in something. Soon as he got her out, he moved her to the side of the path, into the woods a bit, and then just drove off. I waited until he was gone, and then I took a peek. It was her alright. Shot in the chest a couple times, it looked like. I didn't know who she was then, but I saw her picture in the paper a few days later. Then I heard him coming back. He was walking through the woods from the other direction, and he had a shovel over his shoulder. Must have hidden his car somewhere else. I flipped the tarp back over her and crawled behind a tree. Wasn't more than a foot or two away when he passed me by. Thought I was dead right there and then. But he didn't see me. Didn't hear me, neither. He dragged her down by the riverbank and dug a hole. Took him a good hour. It wasn't at the end of the path. Kids still hang out and drink there now and then. Wouldn't have been safe. He took her a couple yards up river, but still close to the bank."

The old man barely stopped to take a breath. His words rolled into each other, and Lisa had to ask him to repeat himself several times. He said he was too scared to move long after the killer was gone, but just when the sun was starting to come up, he crept over there and started digging with his hands. It wasn't hard because the soil was still loose. He just wanted to make sure that he hadn't been dreaming or that he wasn't still drunk. He started at a boulder near the riverbank and counted his paces diagonally away from the water: fifteen steps. He counted because he wanted to remember.

"I saw her again. She was still fresh. I keep seeing her. Every night. Every day. I covered her again, and I picked my way home through the woods the long way. Took me all day. I didn't want nobody seeing me coming out of there. They'd pin it on me. I know it, especially if cops were involved. They can lift fingerprints from anything, you know, and say they found them somewhere. Two state troopers were just busted for that."

He paused.

"So, you got that?"

Lisa was stunned and nervous, but excited. Very excited.

"Got it. Have you told anybody else about this?"

"No way."

"What's your name? How can I contact you?"

"Who? You never talked to me. And don't go looking for me at the bar. I'm taking off for a while. I don't want be around until this thing is good and over and I know that guy is dead in the electric chair."

And with that, the old man hung up.

Chapter Twenty-One

L isa replaced the phone on the hook and looked around. Nothing was different. People were still eating and laughing and sipping their water or their wine. Waiters still carried plates of food from the kitchen to their tables or heaved trays full of half-empty plates back in. The hostess was seating a young couple with a toddler in a booth nearby. Their worlds had not changed in the past few minutes. Not like hers anyway. She had the body. She knew where the body was. She didn't have the old man, but she had the DVD to support the theory that someone from the sheriff's department was involved, and that would, at least, mean that state police or the FBI would investigate.

Besides, this guy wasn't as anonymous as he'd like to believe. Someone at The Spoke & Wheel must know him by name, and they'd give it up if they knew his testimony would put Annette Baker's killer behind bars. He had to be getting Social Security and probably Medicare, too. He was traceable, much easier to find than he realized. With his testimony, the sheriff wouldn't have a prayer.

She was feeling lighter as she walked through the restaurant, despite the new information from Kevin, and she was anxious to get the night over with. She wanted to know that the sheriff was in handcuffs and that her daughter was safe. Really safe. She would look for the body first thing in the morning. Thankfully, things were slow on the news front. She would have plenty of downtime to map out her route and figure out how to get there without being followed. Lisa knew someone else must be helping the sheriff. He needed a supplier for the bodies, and he couldn't possibly keep tabs on her

134

himself at all hours. Whoever was in on it was probably taking turns with him, watching her too. But nothing was going on, and her feature story was finished. No editor would even touch it until tomorrow. She had some time, and her actions would probably bore them.

The sky had darkened in the time Lisa had been inside the restaurant, and the city had come alive with yellow streetlights, neon beer signs, red brake lights, and the occasional glow of a pedestrian's cigarette. In the distance, she could see blue and red emergency lights escaping from between the tall buildings of downtown, a sight that had become common since a new digital marquee had gone up on the Olympia Theater at that particular intersection this spring. Her story had just run in Sunday's paper, and the owners were furious, arguing that it wasn't their fault if drivers were idiots. As she walked down the hill toward the city square, Lisa was aware that the curbside parking spaces were filling up and that couples were spilling out of cars in single sets or in doubles, willing to risk red eyes with heavy bags beneath them at work the next day for a few flirtatious hours. Sometimes, she envied them and their freedom, but then she'd remember that freedom had a price. She had lost her freedom when she took on the weight of responsibility for Bridget, but that weight felt good. The thought of being without it, of being light and free, lost its appeal when she looked at it that way.

As she reached the bottom of the hill, the doors of the YMCA across the street flew open. Deep, hearty laughs and back slaps made it impossible to ignore the dozen or so men dressed in shorts and old T-shirts filtering out in small groups, sweat glistening on their faces in the street lights and basketballs under a few arms. Lisa recognized some of them. It was game night for the cops. One team was made up of deputies from local counties. The other consisted of cops from all over the place—the city, local villages, townships. It was the place to go when Lisa had to find a cop who was off duty.

She waved at a Salina Springs P.D. sergeant who had looked her way without breaking stride, eager to make a quick stop at the public safety building and get back to the newspaper so she could get this night over with.

Lisa had gone only a few steps when she heard the slap of sneakers behind her and felt a tap on her shoulder. It took her a moment to recognize the man. It was Deputy Donlin, the Mohawk County deputy with the limp. He was wearing dark blue basketball shorts, running shoes, and a faded T-shirt with an unzipped warm-up jacket over it. A duffle bag hung from his shoulder. He didn't have his cane, but he leaned heavily on his good leg and cocked his head slightly in the same direction.

"Lisa, isn't it?" the deputy said with a grin. She hadn't noticed his smile much before, but it was nice. Pleasant. With his thick, almost black hair in disarray and stubble casting a light shadow on his face, he looked like he belonged on some college campus instead of behind a desk at the sheriff's department. But the crow's feet gave him away. He had the same lines around his eyes as Lisa. He had to be close to her age.

"I couldn't play in the game, but I figured I'd work out the leg and then go show my guys a little support. You do know we beat the shorts off them tonight, right?" He shifted a bit, intentionally putting some pressure on the injured leg. "Ah. That's better. A couple more weeks, and I'll be back on patrol and on the court."

Deputy Donlin was good-looking in his own way and maybe even somewhat charming, but Lisa didn't date cops. She rarely dated at all, and she could tell this guy was interested. Cops didn't make idle chit-chat with reporters unless they had a shared history, a couple of homicides together, or a drowning or two. The kind of stuff that they both thought about all the time but never mentioned because it would eat away at them too much and prevent them from doing their jobs. Good relationships with cops, the ones who mattered anyway, had to be earned. This guy was too friendly too soon. She'd have to be obvious with her indifference.

"Glad to hear it," she said, taking a few backward steps and then turning fully away from him in hopes that he would see she was in a hurry and not take too much offense. She looked back over her shoulder as she walked, not wanting to leave him quite so abruptly. "It's good seeing you again. Don't overdo it."

"Wait," the deputy called. Lisa sighed. She should have kept those last words to herself. There was no good way out of this. Fortunately, the public safety building was only a block away. She wouldn't have to deal with him for long. "I'll walk you. My car's just down the street. Are you headed back to the paper?"

"No. I have to stop at the PSB."

"Good. That's where my car is parked. Right out front," he said, pulling up beside her. "Did you ever get everything you needed on that guy? Delano, I think his name was. You didn't look too happy when you left the sheriff's office. Why are you so interested in him, anyway? It seems like there must be a lot more intriguing cases in the city to investigate. Unless you're doing some drug exposé. I wouldn't recommend that. You probably ought to leave that to the DEA."

Lisa stopped and turned to face him.

"Every murder is worth looking into, okay? Why does everyone just want to write him off? The guy had no prior history or none to speak of, and everybody figures he just deserved to die. All because he had some meth in his pocket. Maybe that wasn't even his. Maybe someone else put it there."

Deputy Donlin raised his hands in mock defense.

"Whoa. Sorry. Didn't mean to upset you." Lisa started walking again, and he hurried to catch up with her. She slowed a bit when she remembered his leg. He wasn't such a bad guy, after all. Under normal circumstances, it wouldn't have bothered her so much. She just didn't need this tonight.

"I guess somebody has to balance us insensitive jerks," he said. "A few years of this line of work can color the way you see things, you know."

"I know," Lisa said. "I'm sorry I bit your head off. It's just been a long couple of days. When you're a reporter, nobody gives you a break. You hear it from the cops, the victims, and the bad guys, and you're always doing it wrong even when you know you're doing it right. I did get what I needed that day, and I appreciate that you were so nice about it."

They had reached the entrance to the public safety building, and Lisa stretched out her hand to shake his. "It really was good seeing you again. Thanks for walking with me and putting up with me."

"Well, you just be careful now," Deputy Donlin said with a laugh. "You never know when some old lady is going to back over your leg. You know, stuff like that." He reached in front of Lisa and pulled the door open. "I'm serious about this Delano guy, though. If he was into the drug business, you're stepping into some dangerous territory. I hope you'll let it go. It's a city case. These guys are pretty good. They'll find the killer."

"Thanks for the warning," Lisa said. "Take care of that leg."

The door shut behind her, and its latch echoed through the near-empty building. Without thinking, she turned and pushed it open again. Deputy Donlin was already halfway to his car. She hesitated, but only for a second.

"Just a minute," she yelled.

He stopped and looked at her with a smile, his eyebrows slightly raised. She walked toward him, suddenly realizing that he might just be taking this renewed attempt at conversation the wrong way.

"I'm sorry, but do you know a deputy named Phil Larsen? Worked for the department about four years ago? I interviewed him once, and he was a good guy, but the sheriff said he's not there anymore. I've been holding onto a photo of his forever, but I've never been able to track him down."

Deputy Donlin laughed.

"Larsen? Of course, I remember Larsen. He was a nice guy, but a bit of a flake. Not really cop material, you know. I think he went south somewhere, some kind of toy cop job. You've really held onto the photo for four years? I'm sure if he cared about it that badly, he would have gotten in touch with you."

The question had been an impulse, and so had the cover story, and now it did seem silly. Flirtatious, even. The expression on Deputy Donlin's face told her as much. He looked puzzled, doubtful, amused.

"Well, it was in my desk drawer, which I never clean anyway, and then, when I was out there in Mohawk County, I remembered him again. You wouldn't happen to have an address, would you?"

"I wasn't really close to the guy, but if you want to drop it off at the desk, I'm sure we can get it to him. The county must have a forwarding address somewhere. Give me a call before you come. Maybe we can have lunch."

"Yeah, I'll do that," Lisa said, thankful for the dark night sky and the dimness of the streetlights. She could feel her face reddening. She should have thought it out better. "Thanks again."

Lisa was overwhelmed with relief when the door closed once again, and she left the deputy behind. She watched as he walked unevenly toward his car, which was parked directly under a light. A newer-model, dark-red Nissan sedan. More practical than she would have suspected. He was a nice guy, but there was something about him that was almost smothering, claustrophobic. Or maybe she was the phobic one. She hadn't had a real relationship since Marty. First, there was school, then the new job. She'd had a few dates here and there, but nothing ever came of them. Nowadays, whenever the opportunity came along, she told herself that there would be plenty of time after Bridget graduated from high school. Lisa would still be young, in her mid-thirties. A lot of professional women weren't even married by then. And it wasn't like her biological clock was ticking.

The elevator opened at the push of the button. The building was quiet, and the elevator was empty as Lisa headed for the fourth floor to review the day's worth of arrests and incidents. She just wanted to get the night over with, to get tomorrow underway. As she was flipping through reports, her editor called, asking her to check up on a car fire. Apparently, it had happened while she was still in the restaurant on the payphone with her cell phone turned off. And he was angry. An intern was already on it. Lisa apologized and feigned illness, asking whether he wanted the details of the ailment that had kept her locked up in a bathroom stall. He declined and told her the intern would be thrilled to finish it up. He even offered to let her go early, if she'd just come back and type up her briefs.

Lisa got home around midnight, early for her. Dorothy was still up, trying hard to keep her eyes open with a crossword puzzle in her hand, but Lisa told her to go to bed. The doors were all locked, and so were the windows. Lisa rarely used the house alarm, but she had turned it on this time when she had come in. It would take a lot of effort and probably a good deal of noise to break in, and Lisa planned to stay awake for a while, anyway. Dorothy reluctantly agreed, but said she would sleep in the beanbag chair in Bridget's room. She would never be able to fall asleep anywhere else, she said, not until she knew this was over.

The first thing Lisa did was pour herself a glass of Merlot. The dry red wine felt soothing as it went down her throat, and it took the edge off. It was just what she needed. She re-corked the bottle and put it high up in the cupboard. With the stress she'd been under, it would be too tempting to refill her glass when it was empty, and she needed to be alert. She couldn't afford even the slightest hangover.

Next, she wrote a note for Bridget's teacher, explaining her absence that day. "Please excuse Bridget's absence from school Wednesday. We had a death in the family," Lisa wrote. Might as well tell it as it is. Maybe they'd be a little more lenient with her for the next day or two.

When that was done, Lisa reached into her pocket and pulled out the mini-cassette tape. Nowadays, she used a digital voice recorder or her phone for interviews, but she had an old microcassette player at home that she had used during college. She dug it out from her desk drawer along with a headset and put a new set of batteries in. It worked. She slipped the tape in, put the headset in place, and hit play. The quality was not the greatest. It sounded like he'd had it in his jacket or in a pocket, like some kind of fabric was rubbing against the microphone. But after a minute or two, she heard voices. One was Marty, but she couldn't identify the second voice. It wasn't the sheriff. Whoever this was, he was younger, and his voice had a higher quality to it.

"Look, I've been doing this for four years," Marty said. "Just let me take the transfer to Florida. You'll never hear from me again. I've turned it down twice already. There's got to be somebody who actually wants to run these bodies for you. Why can't you just hire somebody?"

"We told you before, Marty," the other voice said in a mocking tone, like he was talking to a child. "We can't trust anybody enough to hire him. See, we know you aren't going to try to cheat us out of money or start running for somebody else or blackmail us or go running to the cops. You have too much to lose and nothing to gain. This is perfect. It works out well for everybody, and you only have to work a couple of times a year. Look at all the money you've made. Can't make that running convenience stores."

The mystery voice laughed.

It definitely was not the sheriff, but Lisa had heard it somewhere before. She knew this guy, or had at least met him. He said "we." He had to be working with the sheriff. That would make sense. The sheriff couldn't do this by himself. The sheriff would need a partner, a supplier, a funeral director, or someone who worked in the crematorium. Lisa often got stuck taking obits in the middle of the afternoon when everyone else was off doing those final interviews and the editors were in meetings. Had she talked to him then? Was it one of the local funeral directors?

"This is it, and I mean it," Marty said. "This has got to be the last time. Haven't you made enough already, anyway? Don't you ever worry that you're going to get caught? Someday, you're going to take the wrong body. Then what? All that money won't do you any good in prison. Why don't you guys just quit while you're ahead?"

Next, Lisa heard what sounded like a lot of movement, more fabric moving against the microphone. A scuffle of some sort. A third voice, someone too far away to hear clearly, yelled something about being an idiot. Voices were talking over each other. It was getting harder to distinguish the words.

"Shit, man!" Marty said. "I didn't look. I didn't see a thing. It just slipped. That's all. Get the gun off my skull. Just put the damn thing away. I get your point. No Florida. Okay?"

"You keep that sack on your head, you hear me?" the voice said. "No reason you need to see anything or anybody. And don't ever pull that goody-two-shoes shit on me again unless you want this bullet right through your head. I never, ever want to hear that from you again. Do you understand?"

"Hey, calm down," a third voice said. It was muffled and hard to understand, but it was definitely a third voice.

"Calm down? You calm the hell down! This bastard thinks he's better than me. He thinks he walks on water. Well, you don't anymore, do you? You're a criminal just like me, just like my brother was. Just like we all are. Welcome to our world, you piece of shit. This is where you're going to stay. How does it feel to be one of the bad guys?"

He must have been right in Marty's face. It almost sounded like he was talking directly into the microphone, like he had it in his hand. His voice was frightening, even on a recording. "Think about how this bullet will feel going through your skull or your daughter's skull. Think about that, why don't you?"

A crash from the kitchen startled Lisa. She yanked the headset off and jumped up, grabbing the television remote, the nearest weapon she could find. Was this it? Was this how it would happen? She'd be found dead on her living room floor with a TV remote in her hand. Slowly, she crept toward the kitchen doorway. She had left the light on. It was bright as anything in there. She steeled herself and took another step forward, and another. Then she saw it. The dish rack, a frying pan, two forks and a knife on the kitchen floor. She had noticed that they were dangerously perched when she came in, but in her exhaustion, she'd forgotten to push the dish rack back.

"I'm the idiot," she muttered.

The man on the tape…he said something about Marty being a bad guy now. Something about his own brother and the fact that they were all criminals now. Maybe this wasn't so random, this business of recruiting Marty. Maybe this was personal. But what did Marty do to make someone so angry? Who would hate him enough to destroy his life like this and then kill him? At least now she had a motive, a likely one anyway. Marty wanted to quit. He wanted to move to Florida and leave it all behind him. He told them he would stay, but they knew he'd reached his limit.

Her nerves were shot. She would have to finish the tape in the morning, maybe in the car on the way to the burial site. Combined with everything else, the tape made for a solid case. Somebody would know who those voices belonged to, somebody in law enforcement. Then they could call in a voice recognition expert to verify it. Between the video, the body, the cassette tape, the old man's testimony, and Lisa's conversation with the sheriff, they'd have them nailed.

She knew she would have trouble sleeping, but she couldn't bring herself to take anything. She wanted to be alert. So, she grabbed her pillow and blanket, turned the TV on low, and curled up on the sofa. If anyone tried to break in, she wanted to be the first to confront him. Tomorrow it would all be over. She would dig up the body just enough to be sure that the guy wasn't some whacko—that Annette Baker was really there. Then she would call both the state police and the FBI. She had already entered the numbers into her contact.

She had thought about calling them sooner, letting the professionals find the body, but she wasn't comfortable with that just yet. If the old man did turn out to be crazy or just wrong, then she would still have nothing but the tape and the DVD, and she might have blown her credibility with the two other agencies. But if she didn't tell state police and the FBI about the tape and the evidence against the sheriff, they would decline to respond and would send the sheriff to the site of the body. It was, after all, his jurisdiction. So, she had to be sure. It was the only way. Lisa still hadn't figured out how she was going to get to Route 49 and the body in the morning without being followed, but she couldn't concentrate on that now, not while she was listening so critically to every noise, inside the house and out.

Lisa slept in fitful spurts, and each time she awoke, she jumped off the sofa, certain that someone was in the house. She was sure that her fears had been confirmed at five a.m. when a car slowed to a near stop in front of the house. There was no reason for anyone to pass by their home at that hour. It was a dead-end street, and they were the second-to-the-last house. She peered cautiously through the edge of the drapes and saw a rolled-up newspaper fly out of the open window. She took a deep breath and decided she should probably give up on sleep for the day. It wasn't worth it.

With coffee brewing, Lisa stepped outside in her bare feet to get the newspaper, looking for anything odd or out of place before she descended from the front stoop. It was still somewhat dark, but the sun was on the verge of rising, and the approaching daylight comforted her. Yes, bad things happened during the day, but even the stupidest of criminals would realize that at this hour, people are starting their days, getting their newspapers, letting their dogs out, checking the weather, and taking early morning walks or runs. It would be a really dumb time to murder a family of three.

She poured herself a cup of coffee and another for Dorothy, who had just gone into the bathroom. When she removed the rubber band from the newspaper and unrolled the pages, there it was: the front-page story about the crash with an intern's byline and a contributing line for Lisa. But this wasn't the story Lisa had envisioned. The crash had been fatal. An explosive had apparently been involved, and the cops were treating it as murder. The SUV had simply caught fire and then exploded right there in the street, less than a mile from the restaurant. Shit. She'd walked out on a murder. Not good.

But then her heart stopped, or she was pretty sure it had.

She couldn't breathe.

The victim was Kevin Donnelly.

Lisa nearly spilled her coffee. The room fogged, and her vision tunneled. She felt like she was going to faint. She carefully rested her mug on the counter and drew air deep into her lungs over and over. He was dead. The car seats. The Goldfish. The sippies. They were all burned. Melted and burned. He had kids and a wife, and he was dead. Murdered. His body would be charred, unrecognizable, with nothing left for his wife to cling to, no made-up face for his kids to kiss goodbye. And she was supposed to be in that car. Why not? She had ridden to the restaurant with Kevin. It would have made sense that she would ride back with him, too. It would have been too late when the sheriff or one of his buddies saw that she was not coming. She was supposed to die in that crash.

By now, the sheriff knew he had screwed up. This was more than photos on her windshield or dead dogs in the driveway. This was real. They killed Kevin, who had nothing to do with anything, and they had meant to kill Lisa. They could come back and finish the job any moment now, taking Bridget and Dorothy too. They would come back. She was sure of it. The house was not safe.

Lisa heard the screech and hiss of a school bus stopping to pick up kids on a neighboring street and immediately knew what she had to do. She grabbed a magnetic notepad from the refrigerator and, when Dorothy walked into the room, she was furiously scribbling away. She still didn't have enough to go to the police, and she knew it, but she had to do something, and she just needed time. Just a little time.

"Good morning," Dorothy said. "You're up early. Again."

"Yeah, I didn't feel well last night, so I left a little before deadline," Lisa said without looking up. "I'm just trying to write some notes on a story here before I forget. I'll be done in just a minute."

She passed the note to Dorothy across the table and quickly put her fingers to her lips. Then she pushed the newspaper in her direction, too, and pointed to the article on the front page.

Dorothy read the note: *The house is probably bugged. Say nothing about this. They killed Kevin last night. I was supposed to be in the car, but I walked back. I have a plan. Find a reason to ride to school with us. Throw a toothbrush, toothpaste, and a change of underwear in your purse.*

At first, Dorothy seemed confused. Then her face went white, and the hand holding the note began to shake. She steadied herself on the back of a kitchen chair, took a few deep breaths, and quickly regained her composure. She reached down and felt her ankle where the holster remained beneath her pajama pants. Lisa wondered whether she had worn the gun to bed. She was sure that she had.

"Thanks for the coffee," Dorothy said. "Hey, as long as you're up and dressed, how about coming to the grocery store with me after we drop Bridget off? I'll just ride with you. I'm always guessing about what you might need. It'd be nice to have you along for a change."

Lisa smiled the best she could. Dorothy was amazing.

"Sounds good," Lisa said. "We haven't done anything together in a while. Grocery shopping isn't my idea of fun, but it'll do."

Lisa took the notepad back, scribbled some more, and passed it back to Dorothy. *We'll talk in the car*, it read. Dorothy nodded. "I'll get Bridget up. She was so tired. I don't think she set her alarm last night."

"No," Lisa said, almost a little too quickly and loudly. "She had a rough day yesterday. Let's give her an extra fifteen minutes or so. As long as we get her there before the buses, she'll be okay."

"All right then," Dorothy said with a puzzled look. "I guess I'll just get myself dressed." She took the pencil from Lisa and wrote her own note: *I hope you know what you're doing. Maybe it's time to go to the police.*

Lisa answered by mouthing one word: *No.*

At eight a.m., fifteen minutes before school was to begin, and fifteen minutes later than Bridget's usual departure time, they all three climbed into Lisa's car. Lisa had slipped a few items into Bridget's backpack to get her through a night or two, including a photo of the two of them together on the ocean last year. Bridget was annoyed that Lisa had let her sleep in. She'd had to rush through her bathroom routine, and she hadn't had time to eat more than a few bites of toast. She was also annoyed by the excuse.

"Why did you have to write that?" Bridget complained from the back seat. "Why couldn't you just say I was sick? They are going to want to know who died. What am I going to tell them?"

Lisa ignored her and told them all to buckle up.

"Just hang on. This is going to be a heck of a ride," she said.

As she drove away from the house in the direction of the school, Lisa saw the car, just as she had suspected she would, in her rear-view mirror. It was a dark sedan, and it pulled into the road after the first intersection, staying a few car lengths behind them. She couldn't read the plates, and she couldn't see the face, but she didn't have to. She knew the car would be behind them all the way to the school and that the driver was waiting for a chance to get Lisa alone and kill her. The sheriff or his buddy, whoever it was, couldn't let Lisa out of his sight. He would have to kill her before she told somebody who mattered.

He wasn't very good at this stuff, Lisa thought. He was too obvious, following too closely, which meant he probably didn't stick a GPS device on her car. They didn't do much undercover detective work in Mohawk County, but that was to her advantage. She hadn't been sure that her plan would work, but now she was confident. She willed herself to remain calm and focus. Her timing had to be just right.

Dorothy said nothing, probably too nervous to talk, Lisa thought, especially with Bridget still in the car. But Dorothy had noticed the sedan, too. Lisa saw her look subtly behind them and then turn back quickly. As Lisa approached the semi-circle where she or Dorothy would normally drop Bridget off, it was starting to fill with long, yellow buses. Teachers and aides milled about, waiting to direct the kids getting off the bus inside the building. Lisa was late. Other parents were easing into the parking lot and leaving their kids at the gym doors. But Lisa pulled into the drive anyway, and the car followed. Idiot, she thought.

"Mom, you're going to get us in trouble," Bridget whined. "Look. There are buses behind us now, too. You're not supposed to pull in here when the buses come and, now we're going to get stuck. Why would you—"

"Don't get out," Lisa yelled.

She slammed her foot on the gas pedal and held it to the floor, flying between two buses just as an angry teacher's aide started toward the car, and the buses were settling into the angled positions that blocked the semi-circle completely, which would have trapped them for the next ten to fifteen minutes. She narrowly missed some walkers who were weaving between the buses to get into the building, but she kept driving as fast as she could until she was out of sight.

"Did he make it?" she yelled to Dorothy as she weaved through side streets, trying to go as fast as she could without violating the speed limit. She didn't want to attract any more attention than she already had—it would be a matter of minutes before the aide told somebody who she was and just a few more minutes until that somebody called the police. After all, she could have killed a student. "Did he?"

"He's a goner. Trapped like a bug. Just keep your eyes on the road," Dorothy said. "Do you have any idea where you're going?"

"Yes, I do, and we're almost there."

The school was on the edge of the city where the neighborhoods quickly went from small lots with public sewers and water to larger properties with leech fields and wells. Lisa left the city behind and drove past a few small developments to a more rural section, where the houses were scattered and unplanned. After a few turns, she pulled into the gravel driveway of a two-story house with blue vinyl siding, a good-sized red barn out back, a large garden to the side, and a few egg-producing chickens wandering the front yard.

"Aunt Winnie's?" Bridget gasped, finally able to speak. She leaned forward in the car, grabbing Lisa's headrest. "What did you do? What's going on? Why didn't you drop me off?"

"In a minute, Bridget," Lisa said, hitting the brakes just short of the barn. She felt bad, but Bridget would have to wait. First, they had to hide the car and get into the house. Quick. "Dorothy, jump out and open those barn doors, would you? Let's just hope Leo still takes his Mustang to the diner for breakfast every morning."

Dorothy flung open the tall, wide, double doors just as an attractive older woman with smooth, blunt-cut silver hair stepped onto the porch. The right side of the barn was empty. Lisa pulled in carefully and told Bridget to get out, take her backpack and go directly inside the house.

"Don't even talk to Aunt Winnie. I'll explain when we're inside," she said.

Bridget did as she was told, running from the car to the house without looking back. Lisa shut the barn doors, ran across the yard to the porch, and flew up the stairs, pulling Dorothy into the house with her. Winnie followed, too startled to stop them. Lisa took a quick look out the front window to be sure they hadn't been followed. The house was on a small rise. She could see clearly in both directions for a good stretch. Nothing.

"Thank God," she said, collapsing against the kitchen counter.

She turned toward her daughter, who was staring up at her with wide eyes from a stool in the corner, her backpack still in her hands. A few curls had fallen into her face, and her skin was slightly flushed. She was so beautiful. "Bridget, Dorothy will explain. But you need to know that I love you more than anything or anyone in the world. And you need to stay inside the house until I get back or call and tell you it's safe. I don't want to scare you. I really don't, but your life depends on it.

"Dorothy." Lisa stood up straight and reached into her jeans pocket. She tossed the cassette to Dorothy, wishing she'd grabbed the player too. "Take this and listen to it if you can find something to play it on. Call me on my cell phone if there is anything I need to know. You still have that gun, right?"

"Right here," Dorothy said, lifting her pants leg. Bridget drew back, clutching her backpack tightly to her chest. She looked so frightened. Lisa wished she didn't have to leave her. "Do you want it?"

"It'll be more dangerous if I try to use it," Lisa said. "No, I feel better knowing you have it here with Bridget and Winnie. I'm calling for help just as soon as I find what I'm looking for. He didn't follow us here, and he doesn't know where I'm going, so I should be safe." She paused and looked at Bridget, whose lips were now blue with fear. She walked up to the stool and wrapped her arms around her, holding her tight.

"It's going to be okay, honey," she said softly, taking in the scent of her freshly shampooed hair. "I wouldn't do this on my own if I thought I'd be in danger. All I have to do is drive to a spot where these idiots hid something, find it, and call the cops. They don't even know that I know about it. Once I find it, I'll call the police, and this whole thing will be over. Really, really over. But I have to find it first, or they might have a chance to get rid of it, and then we'll be afraid for the rest of lives."

"Lisa, I insist. Just take this," Dorothy said, already unstrapping the holster. "I'm sure Leo has a few shotguns around here, and nobody knows we're here, anyway. I'll feel better if you have it. And it's simple to use. If somebody threatens you, you just point it at him and pull the trigger. It's that easy."

Dorothy's face was hard as she held the gun and the holster out to Lisa. Lisa knew that look, and she knew there was no fighting it. Reluctantly, she released her hold on Bridget and took the gun from Dorothy's hands. Dorothy helped her strap the holster around her ankle. It felt surprisingly comfortable, and even her jeans, with their straight legs, slipped easily over it. Lisa practiced bending down to pull it out. Her fingers found the trigger which was more comfortable than she expected. Dorothy had her point the handgun toward the window and showed her how to hold it properly, how to aim. Lisa couldn't help thinking back to Brian. How did he hold that gun all those years ago? It was a little bigger than this one, probably heavier. He had played with it first, twirled it a bit by the handle, scaring Lisa so much that she took refuge behind Marty. Maybe, just maybe, he knew it was loaded. Maybe his accident was no accident after all.

"God, I hope I never have to do this for real," she said, returning it to the holster. "Thanks, Dorothy."

Lisa turned to Winnie, who was still standing by the door, looking bewildered, but wonderful in capris and a tailored, long-sleeved blouse. She was gorgeous, even after all these years. Her skin was smooth, and her creases were perfect, simple reminders of all the smiles and laughter that made her the kind of person people needed in their lives, the kind of person they wanted to know. She could relieve tension just by walking into a room. It occurred to Lisa that in all the time she had lived with them, after all Winnie and Leo had done for her and for Bridget, she had never thought to ask why they had never had children. She'd never even broached the subject. How selfish, Lisa thought. Was she that bad, that thoughtless? Lisa owed Winnie and Leo so much, and now here she was, taking advantage of them again. Maybe even putting their lives in danger. When all this was over, she would have to make up for it, really make up for it with more than just a few visits now and then. Leo and Winnie were family, or the closest she had to family besides Dorothy, and it was time Lisa started acting like a daughter, a good one.

"Winnie, I'm sorry to do this to you. So very, very sorry," Lisa said, "but we don't see each other enough for anyone to figure I'd come here, and you were my only hope. Dorothy will explain more, but right now, I have to get out of here. Can these guys stay with you awhile? Can you keep my car hidden and...?"

Lisa paused, praying that Winnie could forgive her for being such a jerk all those years, praying that she could forgive her now for bringing all this upon her with no warning and no explanation, praying that she would help her and trust her this one last time. "...And can I borrow a car?"

Winnie didn't hesitate.

"Take my Chevy," she said, reaching to grab the keys from a hook on the wall. "I just gassed it up. It's not fast, but it's in good shape. But where are you going and how safe is it? Are you sure it wouldn't be better just to call the police? I don't like this."

"The police are part of the problem," Lisa said. "Sheriff Weidenfeld killed Bridget's father, and he killed Annette Baker, that woman who disappeared four years ago. I know where she's buried, and it's in his jurisdiction. There might be a few other people involved, too. I just need to verify that she's there, and then I'm calling the state police. See, I even have a charged cell phone for a change."

Lisa took her cell phone out of her shirt pocket and held it up for Winnie to see.

"They have no way of knowing that I have connected them with Annette Baker, and no reason to believe anyone knows where her body is. As long as I don't get pulled over on the way, I'll be okay. By the way," she said. "Could I borrow a trowel too, and maybe some gardening gloves?"

Chapter Twenty-Two

The drive from Leo and Winnie's house to the grave on the riverbank would only have taken about twenty-five minutes if Lisa had taken the main roads, but she couldn't risk that. She decided on side roads instead, which would add another ten minutes. She had no idea who else might be involved. They couldn't know what car she was driving, but they might know what she looked like, and they just might recognize her behind the wheel. She tried to push the panic out of her head, the panic that might make her swerve or drive too fast or call attention to herself in any other way.

She'd barely gotten out of the suburbs and onto the country roads when her cell phone rang. Damn, she thought as soon as she heard his voice. It was Alex. Again. Lisa cut him off before he could say more than her name.

"Can't talk now," she said, clutching the wheel with her free hand as if that would get her there faster. She just needed to stall him for another hour or so. Maybe two hours, depending on how hard the dirt was packed.

"Lisa, time's up," Alex said. "Come on down, and we'll figure out what to do with this DVD, if anything at all. If you're nervous about it, I'll meet you somewhere, and we'll drive to the police station together."

"Look, Alex. I know the sheriff killed Marty, and I know he killed Annette Baker. Better yet, I think I know where the body is, Annette Baker's. I'm on my way there now. I'll call you when I find it."

"What are you talking about?" Alex's voice quickened. "Lisa, you can't just go around digging up corpses. Why do you think you've found her? Where are you headed? Have you told anyone? Have you called the police?"

"I can't call the police yet, and I haven't dared tell anyone else. If I do, they'll send the sheriff, or he'll try to get there first. I'm just going to go and dig a little. That's all. Dorothy and Bridget are in a safe place, and they don't know enough to be of importance to anyone. I want to keep it that way. So, no. Other than you, I haven't told anyone, and I'm not going to until I find her."

"Lisa—"

"I've got to go, Alex." With that, Lisa hung up and tried to focus once again on the road, which twisted through an apple orchard, crossing the main highway once or twice. When that ended, she took the old frontage road and then School House Road, which took her past a couple of farms and an old sawmill. Finally, she found herself on Route 49, just about two miles from the pull-off. She would have to find someplace to hide the car. If the sheriff just happened to pass by and see someone there, he might decide to check, especially with all that's been going on.

She drove up and down the same stretch, passing by the pull-off twice. There were no houses here. Just a few seasonal camps far off the main road down long, single-lane dirt drives, and they were too far away to risk parking halfway down them and walking to the site. The nearest one required her to cross the main road, and she didn't want to take that chance. So she kept driving. Finally, she saw it. The perfect spot. It was an abandoned hunting camp about half a mile from the trailhead and set back a few hundred yards from the road. The surrounding land was overgrown, though, camouflaging its worn wood siding. It was hard even to see where the driveway began. She'd checked each time she passed. There was no evidence that anyone was staying there, and despite the neglect, the driveway was passable. She could park behind the camp and work her way through the woods, out of sight of the road. Lisa hit the brakes just a little too hard and swerved into the rocky driveway. Branches and bushes scraped the car as she pulled in, no doubt damaging the paint on Winnie's car. The camp windows were boarded up, and the small front porch was in the midst of collapse. There was no way to see through the windows to the back. She pulled around the small building and parked beside an old woodshed, which would at least provide complete cover from one direction. The car wouldn't be entirely hidden from view, but someone would have to be looking hard to notice it even from the edge of the road.

It was when she stepped out of the car with the trowel in hand that it hit her. She was going on a hunt for a dead body. A murdered body. Alone in the woods. And she had left her daughter behind. Was Bridget really safe? Was someone holding a knife to her throat or a gun to her head right now, laughing at the thought of Lisa stabbing with a tiny trowel at a plot of dirt that held nothing more than stones and roots and slugs? Was there a body at all, or was this some kind of trick to get her out here, alone, to get her away from her daughter? She suddenly felt sick. Horribly, terribly sick.

She couldn't think this way. She was here, and she was here for good reasons, with good solid leads. She knew she was onto something because he had followed her, hadn't he? And she had left him behind, far behind, before she drove to Winnie's. She was sure of that. Bridget was safe for now, and no one had followed Lisa here. She had passed only one other car on the road, and it was a red MR2 driven by a couple in their fifties who really should have thought about the fact that driving such a sporty vehicle demands comparisons with the people in it. She saw no one behind her when she arrived near the pull-off or any of the times that she turned around and passed by looking for a good place to park.

She could feel the weight of the gun on her ankle. It didn't give her as much comfort as she had hoped. She'd read all the studies about how the majority of handguns are used against their owners, especially in the hands of incompetent owners. Dorothy's two-second lesson wasn't enough. Lisa slipped her cell phone into her back pocket and leaned on the car a moment, giving her legs a chance to stop shaking. At least Alex knew what she was up to. He didn't know where, but if she never returned, at least someone with authority would know that she had disappeared trying to prove that the sheriff was a killer. Some amount of serious suspicion would rest on him, more than just Dorothy's accusations or Marty's recordings. Despite her nerves, she smiled to herself. Alex had not tried to call back. He knew her well.

There were a few well-trodden trails leading from the old camp into the woods. Lisa wasn't the only person who had parked here for access to the riverbank over the years. At least her hike through the woods would be easy. She set off slowly, not daring to breathe as the canopy of autumn leaves—the brilliant reds, yellows, and oranges of the sugar maples—enveloped her. Just a few feet onto the trail, and already she was in another world, walking a path of rusty pine needles and decaying leaves, occasionally tripping over a tree root that bulged from the dark earth. Under other circumstances, it would have been comforting.

There was something familiar about these woods. Maybe not these particular woods, but about the smells, the sounds, the air. She was young—six, or maybe seven—and she was with her father. It was before the coke and the LSD and the heroin oil. Before cases of cheap beer had replaced the milk and juice that once filled the fridge and before the bottles of gin and vodka took over the snack cupboard. It was when her father had still noticed her, and her mother had still cooked meals and packed lunches, and her parents had come to conferences at school just like every other parent of every kid she knew back then.

Fishing. That was it. She and her father had gone fishing in this same river but a few miles further upstream. She had even put a worm on a hook, something she'd never thought she could do. Lisa had carried the bucket to the river, and her father had carried the tackle box and poles. It must have been summer because she wasn't in school that day, and he worked weekends until she was ten. He had sipped a beer while they fished, but it was just one beer, and there were no needles or lines or razor blades. Her mother had lectured them when they returned home. It was past dinner time, and Lisa's sneakers were full of mud. Did she lecture because she cared, because she worried about Lisa not eating, or had they just disrupted her schedule by showing up late? Did he take her fishing because he wanted to spend time with her, because he loved her, or because he was stuck with her and fishing was what he wanted to do that day? When had that part of it started, the not-caring part, the not-loving part? Before drugs or after?

Lisa stopped short as a squirrel skittered through a bush, sending three

155

birds scattering up through the leaves and into the sky, and she remembered again where she was and why. The trowel felt heavy in her grip, and her legs were reluctant to take her any further. She hadn't had time to think. What day was it anyway? How long had Marty been dead? What would Annette Baker look like after four years under the earth, four years of worms and maggots, and rain and snow? She could still call someone. The cell phone in her pocket was fully charged. It didn't have to be the police. She could call another reporter or a photographer. They'd be falling all over an assignment like this. But then she would have to explain and wait and then explain again, and she couldn't do that just now. She wasn't ready, and there wasn't enough time.

Lisa pushed herself forward and tried to ignore the morbid thoughts until finally, she could hear the river before her and then see the river. The trees gave way to sunlight over the tea-colored water, and Lisa felt just slightly less trapped. The river was wider than she remembered it, or at least it was wider here in this part. It was choked with smooth boulders, small waterfalls, and swirling currents. The rapids were at least level three, maybe four. No one could come straight across this section from the other side quickly. She could see a few yards in every direction. No sign of anyone. She stopped to listen. No footsteps. No cars. Nothing but birds, squirrels, the rustling of trees above, the rushing water, and her own rapid breathing.

She picked her way along the riverbank, losing her footing every now and then in the looser soil closer to the water, until she reached the spot the old man had described. The boulder was right where he said it would be, marked with "Me and TC" in red spray paint surrounded by a black heart and an arrow, just as he had said she would find it. The old man had come back a few times over the years, he said, just to check. Lisa walked fifteen paces diagonally away from the river and found a patch of earth that appeared to be more worn than the rest. The grass was newer and more sparse, like the ground here had trouble maintaining its covering. It would be easy to overlook, to attribute the baldness to an acid imbalance from the quilt of pine needles nearby; or from the sneakers and boots of teens gathering in this spot to drink and slipping away from their friends for a make-out session or more; or from the weight of the tackle boxes that fishermen had set far from the riverbank in hopes of making less noise near the fish when they re-baited their hooks.

But Lisa knew better. She knelt down, feeling the cool wetness of the ground seep through her jeans at the knees, and she started to dig. But the ground was harder than she expected. She sat back on her heels, tucked a few loose hairs behind her ears and looked around the forest, taking it all in. This was too much, too big for her. Not just the grave and the body, but the whole thing. She was just one small person. What could she really do? Why not just take Bridget and run far away from here to another state, where the sheriff couldn't be bothered to follow her?

She shook it off. This was fear possessing her, and she knew that fear could be destructive. She knew that only too well. If they tried to run, she would always be afraid, and she didn't want to live that way. She didn't want Bridget to live that way. So, she swallowed it and shoved the trowel back into the soil. Once she broke through the first layer, it became easier, softer, and she found that she couldn't stop. She jabbed the earth with her small, narrow shovel over and over, throwing the soil to the side, not bothering to look around her. Not bothering to give her hands, her shoulders, and her arms a rest. She just kept digging until she hit something that her trowel would not pass through.

That's when she stopped.

Lisa lifted her head and looked around. The sun was getting higher and brighter. It was a cloudless day so far and warm for late September. Temperatures would be in the low seventies, maybe, by mid-afternoon. The birds and squirrels were getting busier, and she guessed there were a few deer milling about, camouflaged with their brown fur. Leaves were falling from trees so fast that it was almost like a slow, soft, colorful rain. Still no one in sight. Still no strange sounds. Just peace. And soon, she would destroy that peace, and this place would become ugly.

The hole she had dug was long and wide, but only about a foot deep. Was he that stupid that he would bury her in such a shallow grave? If he was in a hurry, yes, she supposed, he could be that stupid. Weren't most criminals?

She scraped some of the dirt off the object she had hit. It was a tarp, a beige tarp with dark stains. Dark brown, almost ruby-like stains that Lisa recognized as dried blood. She uncovered a little more and tugged. Then she scraped and tugged again. And again. On the third try, a piece of the tarp broken away, releasing a stench that was unmistakable. Lisa turned away for a moment to take in some fresh air and then looked back at her discovery. What remained was mostly bone, but the tarp had preserved enough that Lisa barely had time to turn again before the bile rose from her stomach and she started retching. When she found the courage to peer once more at the corpse, she saw that the section she had uncovered was a shoulder and that it was, most certainly, human. The remains of a T-shirt clung to what remained of the body. Yellow. The T-shirt was yellow.

Lisa stumbled backward and wiped her mouth with her sleeve. Her arm and wrist ached, but that seemed irrelevant now. She'd seen plenty of dead bodies in the past eight years, but nothing like this. Never anything like this. Lisa reached for her cell phone, and just as she touched it, it rang. She let out a slight shriek that seemed to dissipate into the air, thinning until it made no sound at all. The phone's ring tone was out of place in these woods, and its disruption had shocked her. She took a deep breath and answered. The connection was mostly static, but she could hear Dorothy through it just well enough to make out her words. Her voice was shrill, high-pitched.

"He's in on it, Lisa! Do you hear me? Alex is in on it!"

"What?" Lisa felt the bile rising again. She stood and walked a few shaky steps away from the body, which was already attracting a small swarm of flies, and leaned against a young tree for balance. She must have heard wrong. Dorothy repeated her words, and Lisa was sure she heard her clearly this time. The reception had improved as she moved closer to the river.

"That's not...how do you know? That's impossible."

"He's on the tape. The tape of the exchange when Marty said he wanted out. He knows about Annette Baker. The sheriff might have killed her, but Alex knows. Winnie recognized his voice from TV, from the news conference on that murder-suicide last week. You didn't tell him where you were going, did you? Please tell me you didn't tell him."

CHAPTER TWENTY-TWO

Even through the phone, Lisa could feel Dorothy's fear.

"No. I didn't."

Lisa struggled to remain standing. Her head was spinning, and her chest felt like it would shatter if her heart beat one more time. She let her body slide down the tree trunk, resting her back against its rough bark. She was still too close to the body, to the smell of it. "No. I mean, I told him I knew where it was. I told him I was going to find it. I just talked to him on my way, but I didn't tell him—Oh, God. He knows. I didn't have to tell him where I was going. He knows."

"Yes," a voice behind her said. "He does."

Lisa dropped the phone and turned. Standing only about seven feet away was Deputy Donlin in a plaid shirt and worn blue jeans. He was leaning on his cane and pointing a gun at Lisa's head. Beside him was Alex. Good old Alex with his bangs covering his tired eyes as always. But this time it was far less endearing. His gun was at his side. It was Deputy Donlin that Lisa had heard before. The familiar voice. His was the voice she had heard on the microcassette tape.

"Get the phone and disconnect, Alex," the deputy said without taking his eyes off Lisa. "Ms. Jamison, I'm going to have to ask you to step into that clearing with your hands in view on top of your head. It stinks over here."

Chapter Twenty-Three

She didn't mean it. Any of it. Anything she'd ever said or done. She loved her mother so much, so very much, and she hadn't told her that today. Or yesterday. Why hadn't she told her? God, please take care of her, Bridget thought, as she curled her long body up tightly in the armchair near the fireplace in Winnie's home. Please, please, take care of her. Don't let her die.

Yes, Bridget was angry. She was very angry, and she knew she had a right to be. But she'd had time to think now. Things her mother had said when she was younger made more sense—that she was only fifteen when she'd gotten pregnant and that she didn't think about whether her baby would need a father as she grew up, only about how she would survive. Bridget hadn't known about the suicide she'd witnessed. Until now, her mother had left that out. How did she get through that? How could she have thought about anything else? Bridget was having enough trouble dealing with a dead dog.

Bridget thought about her own life a year ago, about her friends and soccer games and about the arguments with her mother over curfews and clothes. Those things all seemed so unimportant now, so small. Yet, she had accused her mother of not understanding over and over again. How would Bridget have handled it if she had gotten pregnant then, especially if she didn't have her mother to fall back on? What would she have done?

Abortion. That's what she would have done. That would have been the easy way out. But her mother didn't do that. Maybe she just couldn't afford it or didn't know where to get one. Whatever. It didn't matter. She did not abort Bridget. She did not give her up for adoption. Instead, she gave up being a teenager, and worked hard, and made a life for them, a life that wasn't much different from the lives of her friends. Maybe her mother had earned the right to be a bit paranoid.

Bridget could hear Winnie and Dorothy talking in the other room. The police were on their way. The state trooper they had spoken to thought they were crazy, but he said he'd send someone, anyway. He also agreed to call the medical examiner's office and try to locate Alex. Would that make them feel better, he had asked, to know the ME is in his office, doing his job? Dorothy was pacing. Winnie sounded like she might cry any minute. Bridget felt so helpless. So small and helpless. They'd killed her father, and now they were going to take her mother, too.

But then she remembered the map.

Bridget threw her feet to the floor and sat up straight in the armchair, suddenly alert and alive. She knew where her mother was going. It was on the map, the map that she had tossed into the back seat when they left this morning. The red circle had caught Bridget's attention. Right off Route 49, between the highway and the river. On the river, really. That's where her mother was going. That was where the body was. There wasn't time to argue with Dorothy and Winnie, to wait for the state trooper and show him the map, and to convince him to check it out. Her mother would be dead by then.

Bridget's mother always kept a spare key in a magnetic case under the rear bumper of her car, and Bridget had driven more than a dozen times already with her learner's permit. She wasn't helpless. Not at all. Slowly, quietly, she stood and eased her way out of the living room and into the den, and finally to the back door. She could still hear their voices. They were too preoccupied to hear her. Winnie was sobbing for real now, and Dorothy was trying to calm her down. Bridget turned the thick, steel knob and waited for the cover of another heavy sob before she pushed it open. Then she slipped out, closing the door softly behind her.

The back door to the barn was slightly ajar. Bridget found the key just where it always was. She got the car ready before she opened the barn doors, adjusting the seat and the mirrors and taking one last look at the map which, she was relieved to see, her mother had left behind. She wanted to be ready to go if Dorothy and Winnie heard her struggling with those large, heavy wooden doors, but they slid fairly easily. Once they were open, she ran and jumped into the driver's seat, not bothering to buckle up. She hit the gas too hard, pulling out of the barn, but it was too late for them to stop her. She was free, and she was on her way. Her mother needed her this time and she was going to be there for her.

Bridget drove fast, knowing that Dorothy and Winnie likely saw her peel away and would tell the state trooper that she was driving without a license and that she might be in danger. They'd be looking for the car soon after the trooper arrived. But that might be a good thing, she suddenly realized. She needed the state police. She would park the car in plain sight in hopes that they would find it. Maybe she would even park it illegally, partly in the road.

The route was simple, but the roads were unfamiliar to Bridget. Twice, she almost steered into ditches trying to get another look at the map, and once, she took a wrong turn. The GPS was useless without an address. But she found her way back and, finally, she saw the sign for Route 49. In her excitement, Bridget took the right-hand turn too fast and felt the two tires on the passenger-side lift off the asphalt. Then the car crashed down again as she landed, jolting her body. She clung to the steering wheel and tried to calm down. She couldn't afford to crash now. She was almost there.

Somewhere along here, about two miles down, she figured, was the site of the red circle, the site of the dead body that had something to do with her father, the place where her mother might die if she didn't get there fast. She didn't know what she would do once she got there. Grab a big stick, maybe? Sneak up on them from behind? Bridget pressed on the gas and glanced at her odometer—another mile or so. Faster. Faster. Come on. She looked up at the road again, and her eyes caught red lights flashing in her rearview mirror. A patrol car was approaching quickly. Relief washed over her. Winnie and Dorothy had done it. They had convinced the police that her mother was in danger. Thank God.

She pulled to the side to let the patrol car pass, but it didn't pass. It pulled up behind her, and an officer stepped out. He walked up to her car and demanded her license and registration as she rolled down her window. He was an older man, at least in his fifties or sixties, and his badge said "Lt. Hildebrandt." He didn't look happy or nice. He looked agitated, like she had just ruined his day. Bridget didn't have time for this. Panic seized her, and the words rushed from her mouth.

"Please, please, Officer. You have to help me. He's going to kill my mom," she shrieked. She couldn't control her voice, couldn't control her tone. He wasn't doing anything. He was just standing there, looking bewildered now. She had to make him listen. Bridget grabbed the map off the passenger seat and waved it at him. "Down there! Down in the woods. I have a map. It's the medical examiner and the sheriff. They killed my dad. She knows where some other body is. Annette Baker. She uncovered it. We heard them on the cell phone. They're going to kill her!"

The lieutenant just stared at her for a moment, saying nothing. Nothing at all. He probably thought she was crazy, that she was some idiot teenager trying to get out of a ticket, maybe. She had to do something. Her car was still running. She hadn't even put it into park. She was about to floor it, to peel out of there and leave him behind, when the lieutenant's expression changed, like he had decided something.

"Turn off the ignition, step out of the car, and come with me," he said.

He believed her. He was going to help. Bridget opened the door and followed the lieutenant back to his patrol car, a sheriff's department patrol car. Her heart sank. What had she done? He was one of them. She turned to run, but he grabbed her by the arm and squeezed it tight. She punched him in the chest as hard as she could and tried to hit his face with her free fist, but he dropped his notepad and grabbed that arm, too. Then he pushed her up against the patrol car, pulled both her hands behind her back, and cuffed her. He had to pry the map from her fingers because there was no way she was going to let go. Once he had it in his hands, he threw her into the back of the car and slammed the door shut.

"I hate you, you bastard," Bridget screamed when he opened the driver's side door and slid in behind the wheel. She kicked the seats and the doors as hard as she could. Nothing budged. "I hate you!"

"You don't know what you're getting into," the lieutenant said without turning to look at her. "It's for your own good."

Then he took the patrol car out of park and veered onto the road. Bridget fell backward with a jerk, hitting her head on the car door. She pushed herself up into a sitting position and stared ahead, no longer able to think, breathe or scream, feeling nothing but the tiny trickle of blood that weaved its way through the roots of her hair on her scalp.

Chapter Twenty-Four

Deputy Donlin motioned with his gun, and Lisa knew she had to think quickly. She pretended to stumble, and as she rose from a crouch, she reached for the gun in her ankle holster. Just as her fingers rested on the slim handle, she heard a shot fly past her ear and hit the dirt near her feet. She fell backward into the mound of soil she had removed from Annette Baker's grave, and the deputy laughed.

"What do you think you're doing?" he said. "Hey, now I don't even need to use this lousy gun. Took it from the evidence locker, you know. It was the only one with no serial number. It was so kind of you to bring your own weapon to kill yourself with. Now stand up like I asked and leave the gun where it is."

Lisa did as she was told. She stood up, raised her hands, and rested them on top of her head, unable to take her eyes off the weapon that he held with such confidence. She didn't know much about guns, but she knew this was not a Glock, the kind most police departments issued. She would have recognized that. This was small and black. Compact and powerful. Of course, he wouldn't use his own gun. He would leave no evidence. A deputy and a medical examiner. They would know better. And now he would have Dorothy's, too.

"Stop. Right there."

Deputy Donlin lifted his gun level with her head once more and moved a few steps himself. He was now about ten feet away from her. Far enough to avoid most of the splatters of blood, but close enough to get a good shot. Out of the corner of her eye, she could see Alex bending to pick up her phone.

He moved slowly, quietly.

"You look a little worried." The deputy smiled. A cocky, arrogant smile. "Don't be. I'm not going to shoot you now. We're just going to cuff you for a while and stash you someplace safe. Then we'll kill you. When the time is right."

Lisa's chest hurt even more than she thought possible, and she knew she was barely breathing. This was the way people she'd interviewed had described it, being threatened with death. Now she understood. Her mind was surprisingly clear and she could hear and see with unbelievable acuity, but her heart was working triple time. And all she could think of was Bridget. What had she done? Why couldn't she have heeded the sheriff's warnings and left this alone? And why had she trusted Alex? Lisa forced herself to look in his direction again. He hadn't stepped closer. He just stood where Lisa had been, staring at the mound of dirt with her phone in one hand and his gun in the other. He was staring at the spot where Lisa had exposed the decayed body.

"Alex," Lisa called, softly at first.

Then louder, shouting this time. "Alex, help me. Please."

The deputy laughed. "What'd you say, Alex?"

When Alex turned toward Lisa, she saw a face with no expression. It was dull, pale, worn out. His shoulders straightened as he drew in a deep breath—apparently unbothered by the stench of rotting flesh, of death, of murder that he pulled deep into his own body—and took one last look at the grave of Annette Baker. Then he walked slowly and carefully in their direction, stopping when he reached Deputy Donlin. He just stood there, looking at Lisa with that same blankness. Lisa used to think Alex was cute. Not her kind of guy, but handsome in his own childlike way. There was nothing childlike about him today. His skin was pasty and his face showed no emotion at all. Finally, he spoke.

"See, Lisa, this is the way it's going to go." He brushed the bangs out of his eyes with the back of the hand that held her phone. The phone rang, but he ignored it, like it didn't even register. It rang again, and then a third time.

"Shut that damned thing off, would you?" Deputy Donlin said. "And get her gun."

Alex pushed the power button on Lisa's cell phone. Then he shoved it into his own back pocket and stepped toward her. He reached down and gently lifted the leg of her jeans, taking the gun out of the holster. Lisa wanted so badly to kick him in the face right then, but she didn't dare move. She hated him with everything she had. Alex handed Dorothy's gun to Deputy Donlin and took his place beside him.

"This is the way it's going to go," Alex repeated in a voice that was flat. "We're going to cuff you, gag you, and throw you in the trunk of a car just like they do in the movies. For now, we'll park the car in Deputy Donlin's garage. He lives up on a big hill, far from anybody. His mailbox is at the base of it, and he's not expecting any packages or the meter reader. So, you can bang all you want, and no one will hear you. You won't die. We can't let that happen. It would be too early."

He looked down at his own gun and toyed with it as if seeing it for the first time. He caressed it, running his fingers over the barrel. Then he shifted his weight to one foot and turned his attention to Lisa again, squinting in the sunlight that blazed between the branches. "We have to wait until nightfall. Much later, really. We have to wait until everyone in Winnie's neighborhood is asleep."

Winnie? Lisa could barely stand. She was dizzy, and her legs wanted to collapse beneath her, but she wouldn't let them. She couldn't. Alex was her only chance. His behavior was different from that of the deputy, less calculating. Eerie in a way. He was doing as he was told, like some kind of puppet on strings. A puppet on drugs. Lisa needed to think clearly and figure out how to break through to him. They knew where Bridget was, where Dorothy was. And now Winnie and Leo. They were all in danger because of her. She had to keep him talking.

"But how—"

"How did we know? Lisa, you trusted me and I liked listening to you. I like you a lot. You told me about Winnie and Leo a long time ago when they sold their farm, remember? I knew you would go there. They're family to you. You said so. And we ran your plates. The plates on the car you drove here. Really, couldn't you do better? Hiding the car behind that old shack? Everybody parks there."

The smile had faded from Deputy Donlin's face. He was clearly getting anxious, his eyes darting around to identify every sound. He was like a wild animal, sensing a predator that he could not yet see. This is good, Lisa thought. This is good. If he's anxious, he might just make a mistake.

"That's enough," the deputy said in a loud and sharp voice. "We've got to get moving before somebody sees us here."

"No," Alex said, with his eyes still fixed on Lisa. "That's not enough. I want to explain a few things, and you're going to let me, Deputy Donlin. You need me, remember? Lisa is my friend. I want her to know why she should have listened to me and what's going to happen because she didn't. You should have listened to me, Lisa. You really should have because now a bunch of people have to die."

The deputy cursed aloud, his irritation obvious, but he didn't make a move.

"When it's good and dark, and everybody is asleep—though probably not Dorothy, Winnie, and Leo. They'll be wide awake worrying about you—that's when Deputy Donlin here will put on his black clothes, some gloves, and a wig with long hair like yours, take Winnie's car, and drive on up there. He'll get out of the car and shoot the first person who steps out to greet him with a silencer. Then he'll shoot the next and the next until they're all dead because they won't hear the shots, and the others will all still think it's you since he arrived in Winnie's car. He'll even track down Bridget, wherever she's sleeping, and shoot her, too."

Don't, Lisa said to herself, squeezing her eyes shut for just a moment. Don't let him get to you. Just listen. Keep your hands on your head, concentrate and keep listening. Every minute he talks is another chance that someone might see them. Alex said people park there at that camp all the time. Maybe someone will feel like hiking today. It's a beautiful day. He might even still feel something for her, maybe just a little obligation, enough to make him question what he was about to do and maybe argue with the deputy for a bit. If Lisa was going to die—if they were all going to die—she at least wanted evidence left behind. She needed something, or someone who saw something, like the old man who had led her here. A witness or a mistake. It was a gorgeous fall day. A great day for fishing.

"After that, he'll drag them all into the house, find your car keys, set the place on fire, and tear out of the barn in your car with the wig still on. See, the fire is sure to attract attention right away, so he has to make it look like you shot them all and then burned the place down. If they see anything, they'll see you speeding away in your own car. Then I'll meet him by a ditch off a dirt road we know of that gets no traffic at night and has no houses on it for a good three miles. I'll have his car...with you in the trunk."

Alex took another breath. He was calm. Too calm.

"We'll force you to hold the gun to your head. You'll be pretty weak by then, so it'll be easy. He'll just hold it there for you with his finger over your finger, and he'll help you pull the trigger so the residue is on your hands. Not that it matters because I'll do the autopsy, but just in case somebody else gets to you first, we have to be prepared. We don't know how long it'll take for someone to find your body. I might be having dinner or lunch when the call comes in. Anyway, we'll leave you in the ditch with the car, and it'll look like you killed everybody and then committed suicide. How's that?"

"Beautiful," Deputy Donlin said, his face reddening. "God damned beautiful. Now, let's get out of here. Grab the cuffs from the duffel bag and don't forget the cloth. We've got to make sure the cuffs don't leave any marks on her wrists and ankles." He motioned toward a small, gray bag that he had dropped to the ground when they'd first announced themselves to Lisa. But Alex didn't pick it up.

"Wait," Alex said, grinning. His grin was frightening. More frightening, in a way, than the deputy's gun. "I'm not done yet. Here's the best part. The comic relief. I got into this because I figured nobody would ever get hurt, and I'd make some extra cash. Lots of cash. I didn't really need it, but I'm greedy. And these were just bodies. They weren't even people anymore, and no one cared enough to even claim them. What a waste, you see? Those were the bodies we sold, you know, the unclaimed. Those were the parts and the bodies we sold. We pretended to cremate them and sold them to a clearinghouse of sorts, so we weren't always sure what they'd do with them, but we got more money for fresher, intact bodies and a whole lot less for bits of leg bones. The bones weren't always from unclaimed bodies. Sometimes, if the conditions were just right, if I was alone in the morgue and it was the right kind of family, and the body was going to the right kind of funeral home, I'd steal a bone here and there. I'd put something else in there, some PVC or a wooden rod. Once I even used part of an umbrella handle. I just sawed the hook off. Once in a while, I even took the bodies of people who were claimed, who were loved. But who did it hurt? The families had ashes. They believed those ashes were their loved ones. Ashes are ashes. Who cares?"

Deputy Donlin tried to interrupt again, but Alex put a hand up to hush him, and the deputy looked too perplexed to react. He couldn't stop looking around. Things were not going as planned, Lisa thought. Why was Alex telling her all this? She didn't even care as long as she gained another second, another minute, another breath.

"I'm getting off track here. Annette Baker...she was an old friend of Donlin's. She was in it from the start, but then she had that baby, and everything changed. She wanted out. The deputy here didn't even talk to me. It was a heat-of-the-moment kind of thing when he killed her, he said, and I was the one who was screwed. I didn't know until after the fact, but I was still screwed. Then he killed Marty, and I didn't know about that either. Not until a few minutes before I got a text, and the body was at my back door. He even slipped meth in his pocket after he shot him. How stupid is that? Ran to him in broad daylight and pretended to be a passerby. At least he was smart enough to split when the crowd formed, before the cops got there. And then your friend, that Donnelly guy. Then he did him in. See, he does that. He kills people without telling me. He tells me he had to. He had no choice. We couldn't even use the bodies. Too risky given the media attention. And now..."

Suddenly, Alex started laughing.

"And now," he said, nearly choking on a fit of giggles as he tried to speak, "and now, this whole plan, this plan to kill five more people, depends on me. On me. Can you believe that? He can't do this without me, especially with that lame leg of his, and if I don't do it, we'll get caught, and I'll spend the rest of my life in prison. I don't want to go to prison, Lisa."

He wiped his eyes, cleared his throat, and regained his composure.

"Shut up, Alex," Deputy Donlin said, keeping his gun trained on Lisa. He clearly wasn't that dumb. He seemed to know Lisa might take advantage of this fit of insanity, but at the same time, he was unsure what to do about Alex. His face was hard, his lips thin. "Shut up and grab the cuffs. You can talk to her all you want through the trunk of my car once we get her up to the house."

"I really don't want to go to prison because I'm not a bad person and those are bad people in there." Alex continued as if Deputy Donlin wasn't even there. He was entirely in his own world now. "There are people in there I testified against too, people who would like to do an autopsy on me. So, I'm afraid I can't save you, Lisa. I am really, really sorry. I am. Trouble is, I can't kill five people either, especially you. Like I said, I like you. The deputy here will have to figure something else out."

And with that, Alex raised his gun to his own head and fired, his body crumpling to the ground. Lisa screamed, or she thought she had, but she wasn't sure whether any sound came out. And she couldn't move. It was just like that night. He was here. He was talking. And now he was dead. She should have run, but she couldn't run now any more than she could sixteen years ago. Deputy Donlin looked unshaken, and he never took his gun off Lisa. Alex's shot was still echoing off the trees when he spoke. Lisa found it hard to listen to him, hard to hear or feel anything.

"Well, I guess I'll have to find me someplace else to get bodies," he said with a frightening chuckle. "But never mind that now. I have to come up with another plan. How about a lover's quarrel? You two thought you were so clever. Everyone knew he had eyes for you, and you used that, didn't you? You never had any intention of sleeping with him. You just wanted to string him along, flirting with him like an idiot, keeping him interested enough to give you what you needed. It won't be hard to make it believable."

Was he really alone in this now? Lisa had to know who she was up against. Were there funeral directors involved? Other deputies? Her throat was dry, and it took a few tries before the words came out.

"What about the sheriff? Isn't he working with you? Why did you need Alex?"

"Oh, the sheriff. Thanks for that," Deputy Donlin said, leaning a little more heavily on his cane now. He was getting tired. "I had no idea what that guy was up to until you relayed your little story to Alex, about him threatening you and all. I did a little poking around, watched him a bit, sneaked into his files, and guess what? He'd been investigating me all along, and Marty, too. He thought we were dealing drugs, that maybe I was stealing from the evidence locker, and Marty was running the drugs for me. He didn't have much evidence, but he had enough to make the right people suspicious. So, I had to do away with him, too."

He smirked.

"It's a shame, you know. I didn't get a chance to tell Alex about it. It was so clever of me. The medical examiner in him would have loved it. You see, the sheriff is severely allergic to nuts. So, I ground up some nuts really fine, so fine it looked like dust. Then I broke into his house yesterday afternoon when the boss and his wife were both working, and I mixed it into the coffee can. He always says how weird it is that his wife doesn't drink coffee, so I knew she wouldn't touch it. It'd be too late by the time he figured out that it tasted strange." He laughed and shrugged his shoulders.

"The thing is, Marty and I do have a history, and I couldn't let the sheriff find that out. The last time you had brains splattered on you, Lisa, do you remember that? You were new to the gang, so I suppose I can understand that you didn't know everyone's family history, their last names. Tyler, his last name was Donlin. He was my little brother, and Marty killed him. He didn't pull the trigger, but I know he killed him. I got a hold of the records, you see. It was Marty who told the cops there were drugs in the car, and now Marty is dead, too. And his legacy is drugs. Isn't that cool, the way these things come full circle?"

Lisa's arms were aching, and she was losing circulation. She would have to put them down soon or at least move them, but she didn't want to do anything that would stop him from talking. She forced herself to keep them up, anchoring her fingers in her scalp. It wasn't the sheriff. It was never the sheriff and now the sheriff, the one person who might actually have been able to help her, was dead.

"The sheriff should have taken his first sip of coffee around six a.m. He might have asked his wife for the EpiPen, or she might have noticed him struggling to breathe and tried to grab it, but what do you know? It isn't there. Somebody, somebody who wore gloves so he wouldn't leave fingerprints, stole it, and where they live, it would take an ambulance at least twenty minutes to reach him on a good day." He laughed again and squinted at her. "He would have been dead before they even got there."

Deputy Donlin suddenly grew serious again and moved a few steps closer. Lisa instinctively stepped back. Even with his cane, even with his limp and without a gun, he could easily overpower her.

"Ah, ah, ah. Don't do that. Don't move, or I'll have to kill you right here," he said. "You don't mind sharing a trunk with this guy, do you? Because I'd really like to move this tragedy elsewhere, and we could use Winnie's trunk instead. It's bigger than mine, and I have to get that car out of here."

He paused and then smiled. "How about this? You killed him, drove around with him in the trunk of your friend Winnie's car, and then you committed suicide. You could kill yourself a little way up the road, and then I'd never have to take his body out of the trunk. Just leave it there and make a dash back to my car. It won't be easy with this limp, but I'm getting stronger, and I'll put the car in the woods a ways so it won't be found right away. I probably won't be able to burn the house down, though. That won't work. I'll have to figure that one out while I clean up. Any ideas?"

He took a few more steps, walking directly at Lisa with the gun still aimed at her head. He stopped less than an arm's length away, so close that she could smell his sweat and see it forming at his hairline. He seemed calm, but he was nervous. She could tell now that he was closer. Alex had rattled him more than he cared to show.

"I'm sorry to do this," Deputy Donlin said, "but I can't cuff you all by myself when you're conscious. You might try to grab my gun or something, and who knows? Maybe you'll get lucky. When I blow your brains out, I'll just have to make sure I do it on the same side of your head. You know, to make the bruise a little messy. Hopefully, they'll think Alex hit you there when you two fought."

Before Lisa knew what was happening, she felt the crushing pain and the fire rushing through her head and the entire left side of her body. The forest darkened, and the deputy's face was gone. She felt her body falling, but she was powerless to stop it.

Chapter Twenty-Five

She wasn't sure how long she'd been out or if she had really been unconscious at all, but she couldn't seem to move. Her head was too heavy and throbbing too much. At first, she didn't know where she was. She tasted leaves and dirt in her mouth and blood, fresh blood that seemed to be coming from the side of her face. Then she saw him, and it sent her back into a panic again. The more she panicked, the more she hurt. Lisa was afraid she would slip away again. She couldn't do that, so she slowed her breathing: four counts in, eight counts out. Slowly, slowly, she began to calm down.

She didn't dare try to lift her limbs any more than she had. Deputy Donlin was just a few feet away, and he probably thought she was still unconscious. That was what he wanted, what he needed, so she would have to fake it. Though she could not tell whether the groans she heard were her own or whether they were even audible. She tried to stop them, but she couldn't. They were involuntary.

Lisa had opened her eyes just enough to see what was going on. Her vision was blurry at first, and one eye was worse than the other, but when she closed the bad eye and her sight adjusted, she saw him more clearly. He was wearing black rubber gloves, and he was picking something up from the grass. It was flesh, bits of Alex's head. He was putting them into the duffle bag. In a pile to her right, just a few feet away, sat the cuffs, some rope and strips of cloth.

He hadn't noticed her. He was too busy and too paranoid. Every few seconds, he would stop, stay perfectly still and listen. Then he would get back to work. She tried not to move. Not even a muscle. It was hard, so hard. He was moving closer to Alex's body now with the bag. He squatted down on the ground so near Lisa that she could have almost touched him. She noticed his sneakers and the fact that one was left loose and untied. The lame leg, she realized. It must be swollen. How would he get two bodies out of the woods on his own with an injured leg? He couldn't possibly do it. Maybe he would give up and just leave her there. Or she could crawl over and grab the cuffs when he was gone with Alex. She could cuff herself to a tree and, if the keys were in that pile, she could toss them far away. Then he would have to leave her, wouldn't he? But what if no one ever came? What if he did leave her there and coyotes found her first? What if he shot her arm off to get her apart from the tree?

Lisa's eyes wanted to close so badly. She wanted to sleep and just give in. She had to keep squinting in order to see him. It was getting harder to focus. The blood that had been dripping from her temple into the one eye was starting to spill over, and she didn't dare lift a hand to wipe it. She held her breath as best she could. While she watched, Deputy Donlin lifted what remained of Alex's head with one gloved hand and shoved the duffle bag beneath it with the other. Then he adjusted the bag a bit, pulled it over Alex's head, and yanked on the zipper. He was trying to keep himself clean, she realized, putting the bloodiest part of Alex into the bag. When it was all over and done, it would be easy enough just to burn the bag.

Then he disappeared. Deputy Donlin just left Alex's body and disappeared. Lisa couldn't see where he had gone without lifting her head, so she waited and fought to control her pain. She tried tensing muscles in her toes and fingers without really moving them just to see if they worked. They seemed to be okay. At least she wasn't paralyzed or anything like that. A few minutes later, or what seemed like minutes to Lisa, Deputy Donlin returned with two long, fresh tree limbs. She watched as he quickly trimmed the branches with a jackknife and then put the knife back into his pocket. He took the first limb and squatted again by Alex's body. He opened the neck of Alex's shirt with one hand and started shoving the limb down his sleeve with the other until it came out the other side. The limb was green and flexible. It bent easily without breaking. Then he unbuckled Alex's pants and forced the limb down the waist and into his pants leg a bit, and pulled out his jackknife again. Deputy Donlin cut a slit in Alex's pants and pulled the limb through a few inches. Then he did the same thing on the other side.

Lisa quickly closed her eyes as he turned and reached toward her. She heard his feet shuffling in the dirt close to her head, and then she heard a clinking that sounded like the handcuffs. She didn't dare try to look until she knew he was at Alex's side again. He had moved the cuffs slightly, but it was the rope he was after. His back faced her, but she could see it in his hands. He cut angled chunks out of the limbs where they emerged from Alex's pants and used them to hold the rope in place while he tied the limbs together, securing them across Alex's legs. Then he took the long tendrils that remained and wrapped the rope around the top of the limbs, tying them together to make a handle of sorts. He was going to drag Alex through the woods with the makeshift travois. Didn't he know what damage he would do to the body, Lisa thought? Alex would never have approved.

With each step that Deputy Donlin took away from her, dragging Alex's body, Lisa felt overwhelmed with both relief and fear. She was conscious, and this was her chance, but he was moving at a comfortable pace despite his leg. The stretcher was working. How much time did she really have? She would have to wait until he was far enough away before she even tried to move, and then she would have to be careful. Quiet and careful, making a dash away from him toward the main road without attracting his attention. Then she would have to hope that a car would pass by at the right moment and that it would actually stop. There were too many variables, but it was her only chance.

She watched as best she could as Deputy Donlin snaked through the woods on the trail that Lisa had hiked in, taking Alex to Winnie's car, where he would shove him in the trunk. And then she would be next—locked in a trunk with a dead man. She had to try. She couldn't die that way. Lisa lifted her head more, just enough to watch his figure disappear, but it took every ounce of her energy. Her head fell back to the ground. Oh God, no. She couldn't ride in that trunk. She couldn't listen as he shot all of them, as he shot Bridget. Instantly, her body heaved and shook, but nothing came out. She had nothing left. It wasn't possible. She couldn't run. She couldn't even sit up.

If only she had some control of her body, some confidence that it would do what she willed it to do. He had the cane and the limp. His leg was weakening with all this standing around and dragging a body so far through the woods couldn't have helped. She could feign unconsciousness and then fight him off when he tried to grab her. But she knew that wasn't possible. Her mind wasn't working right, and neither were her arms or legs. She'd never had a concussion before, but she guessed that this was what one felt like. At least she could still think right. She knew where she was and who she was and what was going on.

Alex's gun was still in the grass where he had fallen, but it was too far. She'd never make it, not without Deputy Donlin seeing her and pistol-whipping her again. She couldn't take that. Not again. She'd die, and she knew it. But maybe that wouldn't be so bad. She closed her eyes for a moment, just a moment. Her entire body ached: her head, her mind. She was cold. It felt good to close her eyes. She wanted to rest so badly. Just fall back into the darkness.

Lisa forced her eyes back open and lifted her hand just enough to wipe some of the blood away. The sunlight that poured through the branches was almost directly overhead now. It was getting late in the morning, and no one had come here since Lisa had arrived. No one but Alex and Deputy Donlin. Fishermen didn't typically start out this late in the morning, and most people were either at work or in school. It would be hours before anyone else hiked those trails to the river. No one was going to save her.

So Lisa made up her mind. She would make him hit her again. Hard. Harder than the last time. Make him kill her on the spot and try to dig him with her nails, taking some DNA evidence with her. At least that would screw up his plan. She'd be dead too early with a crush wound to her head and his DNA under her fingernails, and his "in" at the medical examiner's office was dead. Gone. He might be able to fake her cause of death with a bullet to her head, but not the time of death. It would be hours before he could kill the others. He'd already screwed up with Alex, anyway, bumping his body along the trail and marking it with the friction of the limbs.

She'd rather die than let Deputy Donlin put her in that trunk. He should be getting close now, she thought, with his rope, his gloves, and both guns—his stolen one and Dorothy's. Lisa steeled herself, preparing to use what energy she had left to appear threatening, worth fighting, worth hitting. But she'd have to wait until he was close enough that she could scratch him first. That was the most important thing. But then she heard a voice calling to the deputy from the edge of the woods in the opposite direction, where the main trail came in from the road.

"Hey, John," the voice shouted. "Thought that was you. Got a report of a shot fired back here. Anything going on?"

Who was it? She knew him. She lifted her head again just an inch or two and looked in his direction. She could make out only his shape. Large and round. He was too far away, and her eyes couldn't see straight even without the blood dripping in them. Then she remembered. It was the lieutenant from the Mohawk County Sheriff's Department, Hildebrandt, the guy who didn't want to give her the reports on Marty. Why was he here? Who might have heard the shot and reported it?

"Just a couple kids with a twenty-two-caliber rifle is all, aiming at the fish in the river. Threatened them with truancy, and they ran the hell out of here," the deputy called from the other trail. He was close now, almost back to the river, but he had started to bushwhack his way through the woods, cutting across toward the lieutenant, probably trying to head him off before he reached Lisa. He moved slowly, using his cane to break through. The gloves and rope were gone. He'd probably ditched them when he heard the voice. "Just came down here for a little peace myself when I found them."

"Thought you were sick today." Lt. Hildebrandt was getting nearer to them both. He was on the groomed trail, and Deputy Donlin was slowed by ruts, trees, shrubbery, and his leg. The deputy would have to do something soon. Lisa looked at the gun again and forced herself to focus. She put her head down low again and reached out one hand, grabbed at the grass and soil, and squirmed, pulling herself just a few inches. Then she reached the other arm out and gained a few more. It was getting harder to see. Harder to think. The pain in her head was overwhelming. She tried thinking of Bridget, imagining that she was reaching for Bridget and not for a gun and that it was Bridget he would be coming after any moment. She pulled herself some more.

"I don't know, John. Looks like we might have ourselves a poacher. Look at the grass over there coming up from the riverbank. Flattened in a trail almost, like somebody was dragging a deer," the lieutenant said. "You sure it wasn't a hunter getting a jump on the season? Were you here when they were firing, or did you come a while after? Doesn't seem like a twenty-two could be that loud."

"Might have been poachers earlier, but there's no one here now." The deputy's voice was growing impatient. Lisa could no longer hear footsteps. They had met up and stopped to talk. They were too far away for the lieutenant to notice Lisa, and she couldn't seem to get anything out of her throat, nothing more than a low groan. "Look. I'm not feeling too hot, and I shouldn't have come out here. I just thought a short hike might do me some good. Physical therapy, you know? Don't you have better things to do?"

"Where's your cane, anyway? You've got mud on your knees. Did you take a fall? Why don't I walk you to your car? You really don't look so good," the lieutenant said in a voice that was too concerned, too cheerful, too buddy-buddy. "You can lean on me if you have to. Come on."

It was clear now that the lieutenant was suspicious and a terrible actor. Something else had brought him out here. He knew something, and he was stalling. If Lisa could tell, then so could Deputy Donlin. She had to work harder. She continued to squirm and pull, digging in the dirt with her fingers and pushing with the toes and heels of her shoes. Finally, her hand rested on the cold metal. Her fingers felt for the trigger. She didn't know what she was supposed to do. Was she supposed to pull something else first? Was it even loaded? She couldn't lift it off the ground. After all that work, her arm was like lead. It was useless. She was useless. It was over.

"Just go along," Deputy Donlin said, trying to sound light-hearted. "I'm fine, and I want to be alone. I'm off duty, remember? Besides, I've got to walk without my cane once in a while. If I have to stay behind that desk and listen to you and the sheriff bicker much longer, I might go out of my mind."

A sharp pain traveled through Lisa's temple, down the back of her neck, and into her spine, making her wince. She must have moved too quickly or made some kind of loud sound because both the deputy and the lieutenant suddenly looked her way. Please see me, Lisa thought. Please see me. But the lieutenant simply turned back to Deputy Donlin and resumed the conversation.

"Tell you what. I've got me a Thermos of hot coffee in the car. I'd feel a lot better if I could leave that with you," Lt. Hildebrandt said. "Go sit down on that boulder over there. Just give me a minute, and I'll go get it. Maybe I'll even grab my lunch and join you for a few. It's a little early, but I started at six a.m."

Lisa turned her gaze back to the two men and lifted her head just slightly. The lieutenant had started walking down the path to the road toward his car. Deputy Donlin reached slowly behind his back and into his waistband. Then Lisa saw a flash of light, a glint of sun on black metal. She saw the deputy pull his gun out and around to the front of his body. And so Lisa lifted her body. She pushed herself up onto her knees, using energy she didn't know she had, raised the gun, and pointed it in his direction. Then she pulled. She pulled the trigger without thinking or aiming. She pulled hard. Her body crashed back to the ground as Alex's gun fired. Pain seared her hand and ripped through her arm. And, finally, finally, she succumbed to the darkness.

181

Chapter Twenty-Six

Strong fingers clenched Lisa's wrist, and something sharp pierced her upper arm. Lisa tried to pull away, but more hands held her down. She forced her eyes open, but everything was a blur. Voices, several of them, were talking to her. They were not yelling. They were talking softly, and one voice was female. Then three figures started to take shape, towering over her. Someone grabbed her other arm, and she screamed in pain. Then she felt relief. Incredible relief. The shapes slowly sharpened into people—two men and a woman. They were wearing firefighter jackets. Orange with reflective yellow stripes. They were paramedics.

"Sorry about that," the man on her right said. "Seems you blew your arm right out of the socket. You must have fallen on it pretty hard. It's best if we put it back in place as soon as possible. It should feel a lot better now, but I'm going to have to strap your arm in place. Can you talk?"

"What happened?" Lisa said, trying to sit up. "Where's my daughter? Where's Bridget?"

Another set of hands pushed her back down gently. It was the other man. Someone was checking her blood pressure. Then a penlight shone in her eyes. It was hard to tell who was who. Hard to remember where she was and what had happened. She was on the ground, lying on dirt and soft grass. The sun was bright between the branches. Why was she outside? Why was she afraid for Bridget?

"Everyone is fine," the paramedic reassured her. "Deputy Donlin is in custody. Your daughter is already sitting in the ambulance, waiting to see you. She bumped her head in the back of a patrol car, but it's just a scratch.

Right now, we need to get you to the hospital. We see that you dislocated your shoulder, but it looks like you took a nasty blow to your head, too. Can you tell us what happened? Just to your head? You can tell the troopers the rest later. Can you see all right?"

"I don't know," Lisa said. She tried to think. Why was she in the woods? Why did her head hurt so much? Why did she remember firing a gun? Why was Bridget here? Then she smelled it. Just faintly, but she smelled it. Annette Baker's body was just a few feet away. She turned her head and saw sheriff's deputies and state troopers gathered around the hole she had dug. Anita Ulman was there with them, down on her knees, peering into the grave. It all started to come back.

"No. I do remember." Lisa lifted her body slightly and heaved, feeling the acid burn her throat. The female paramedic held Lisa's head slightly off the ground and wiped her mouth with a tissue.

"He hit me," she said. "With his gun. The deputy hit me. He was going to put me in the trunk with Alex. Alex, the medical examiner. He's dead."

"We know." This was another voice, a familiar one.

Lisa looked up to see Lt. Hildebrandt, whole and unharmed, standing above her. "I heard the shot, but I couldn't get in the woods fast enough. Then I saw the gun at your head, and I couldn't risk it. I figured your chances were better if I hiked back and got these guys, especially after I heard him say he needed you alive. The guy's an idiot. He was practically shouting at you. You saved my life, you know. The other units were just arriving. I'm just sorry I couldn't stop him before he hit you. That looks nasty."

"But how did you know I was here?" Lisa was still having trouble putting it all together. Two paramedics lifted her body, and the third slipped a board underneath her. She winced with pain at the movement and felt the straps coming across her chest and legs. "I didn't tell anyone. I thought I was dead. He was going to kill my daughter. And Dorothy and Winnie and Leo. He killed Annette Baker. That's her."

She motioned toward the body with her chin.

"That's Annette Baker."

The lieutenant raised his thick, bulky eyebrows and called over one of the deputies who had been standing near the grave. He relayed the information and told him to pass it on to the state police investigator, who was among the group, and to Anita Ulman. With a Mohawk County deputy involved, state police would have to take both murders, he said. Then he turned back to Lisa, who was being moved, backboard and all, onto a gurney.

"I didn't know you were here," Lt. Hildebrandt said. "The sheriff's been investigating Donlin for years. Got nothing. The guy was good at covering his tracks. Then Delano was killed, and we thought we might finally get something on him. The sheriff suspected Delano was running drugs for him. He just couldn't prove it. That's why he was such a jerk to you. He didn't want you poking around, stirring things up. He should have just let me handle it, not given you the reports in the first place. We have different ways of doing things, you know."

The Lieutenant took off his hat and looked up at the trees, like he was noticing the sun and the warm breeze for the first time. Then he placed his hat back on his head and turned his attention to Lisa again. He looked much kinder when he wasn't angry, Lisa noticed.

"Then this morning, I get this call from Phil Larsen. He's all upset. Says you've been trying to talk to him about a murder and that you claimed the killer was a deputy who worked a traffic stop with him. You told Larsen they stopped a guy named Martin Delano. He remembered that one because the guy got in a fight with Deputy Donlin after Donlin found pot in the car. Then Donlin said he'd take him to the ER, but he didn't. Donlin never booked the guy, and the ER had no record of him. Larsen checked. The pot disappeared too. When Larsen tried to talk to Donlin about it, he told Larsen to leave him out of it and just file his own reports. He told him the DEA was involved and that it would probably never go to court and that he should keep Donlin's name out of it. Had Larsen believing that even the sheriff didn't know anything about the DEA investigation and that they had to keep it quiet or they'd blow it. Larsen wasn't very bright, you know. We fired him a few weeks later."

The female paramedic put an oxygen mask over Lisa's mouth and nose, telling her it would help with her nausea. At the very least, she said, she wouldn't have to breathe in that horrid smell anymore. Lisa wanted to fight it at first, but the paramedic was right. Her stomach instantly felt better. She could concentrate a little better on what Lt. Hildebrandt was saying.

"So, I pulled out the reports to review them myself and took a trip down the hall to relieve myself and what do I see? There's Donlin coming out of the room where the evidence locker is. That room is all storage. Not much reason to go in there. A few minutes later, he claimed he was sick and headed home. He didn't look sick," Lt. Hildebrandt said. "Just nervous."

"I checked the locker while he was getting ready to leave. In a hurry, too, he was. I knew everything that was in that locker, and a gun was missing. Did he think I was an idiot? I log all that stuff. I grabbed the keys to the unmarked car and followed him. I had to hang back, though."

The paramedics were talking with each other now, clearly hanging back to give the lieutenant a minute with Lisa. They were packing up their things and smiling at her whenever they looked her way. Smiling. People were smiling, and Bridget was fine. That was all that mattered. The paramedic had said she was fine. Lisa tried to focus on Lt. Hildebrandt's words. She could relax now, she told herself. Donlin was in custody, and Bridget was fine.

Since the roads were rural and clear of traffic, the lieutenant said, he tried to stay out of sight, catching up once in a while just enough to get a peek and see which way Donlin was turning. Then he came to a stretch of Route 49 where he couldn't seem to catch up anymore. He realized he'd lost him, so he backtracked, slowly checking every road and driveway he had passed. That's when he saw the girl in the Ford Taurus. She was speeding like a bullet and swerving, too, and she wasn't wearing a seatbelt. He'd already lost Donlin, and he couldn't let this kid go. She looked too young to drive and like she might be on drugs or drunk, so he pulled her over.

"She started screaming something about her mother and the sheriff and her dead father and shoving a map at me. Then she said the medical examiner was going to kill her mother down by the river where her mother uncovered a body. That's when I noticed the skid marks. They were just a few yards down the road, blacker than tar. Can't believe I didn't see them before. I'm afraid I was a little rough with your daughter, but she was going to get herself killed. I had to cuff her and lock her in the car."

The marks pointed at the road leading to the old hunting camp, like somebody had slammed on the brakes and turned in there fast. Then he saw the rear end of Donlin's car jutting out from behind the building. When he looked more closely, he was pretty sure he saw three cars. He knew where those trails led. They busted parties down there all the time. So he left Bridget locked in the back of the patrol car and parked in the pull-off near the main trail. From the river, he could take the trails to the camp and get a better view. He'd just gotten out of the car when he heard the shot.

"I thought I'd find a drug deal, maybe you lurking in the woods trying to be a big shot reporter," he said, "but I found you with a gun aimed at your head, Donlin and a dead medical examiner."

Lisa struggled to speak through the mask. She couldn't reach it with her arms strapped down, and it hurt too much to move, anyway. Finally, one of the paramedics came forward and moved it for her. The nausea returned immediately.

"It wasn't drugs," Lisa said. "And Marty didn't want to do it. They blackmailed him. There's a DVD and a tape. I gave one of them to Alex. He had it at the office. It was a DVD. Dorothy has the tape, the microcassette."

Then she remembered the rest. The nuts. The allergy. She tried to sit up, but the straps held her down. She couldn't raise her voice. The pain in her head was unbearable. "The sheriff. He killed him. Donlin killed him. He poisoned his coffee at home. Something about nuts. Nut powder. Nut dust. He mixed it in. Broke into the house yesterday. He said the sheriff would be dead after the first sip. He took his EpiPen. Somebody has to go see—"

"Calm down," Lt. Hildebrandt placed a gentle hand on her good arm. He laughed, a thick, stout kind of laugh. "Deputy Donlin should have paid more attention when he was working the desk. The sheriff's daughter went into labor before dawn. Probably never even thought about coffee. First grandkid, you know. He's at the hospital now. I just talked to him a few minutes ago on my radio. I'll get someone out to house right away."

Just then, someone stuck a needle in the back of Lisa's hand and held an IV bag full of fluid above her. The oxygen mask came back over her face and Lisa's body relaxed as the Lieutenant motioned to another state police investigator and called him over. He was with forensics. Lieutenant Hildebrandt explained what Lisa told him, and the investigator said he would send a team over to the sheriff's house immediately. Another state trooper came over. This time it was a captain. Anita was with him.

"Sorry, Lieutenant," the captain said, putting a hand on the Lieutenant's shoulder. "But I'm going to have to ask you to stop talking to the victim. You know how it goes. This is our case now, and we don't want some defense attorney saying we screwed it up by letting you influence her."

"Good. Then you can have the reporters, too," Lieutenant Hildebrandt laughed. "They're already gathering."

He turned to Lisa.

"You take care of yourself now. Work on getting better. Maybe we can talk again sometime when this is all over."

Lt. Hildebrandt and the captain walked off together, already deep in conversation as they headed up the trail toward the car trunk that held Alex's body. But Anita lingered, watching them go. When they were several yards away, the chief assistant medical examiner leaned over and whispered in Lisa's ear.

"I never trusted Alex, and because I never trusted him, I never trusted you," she said. Her tone was firm and curt as always, but there was a hint of softness in her voice this time, a bit of amusement maybe. "I knew he was up to something, and I tried to warn you, but you just wouldn't listen. You did well today, though. I've got to give you that."

Then she left Lisa to follow them.

As the paramedics wheeled Lisa toward the ambulance, she could see the television reporters, too well dressed for the woods, standing at the edge of the road with their microphones and cameramen. Among them were the newspaper's own photographer and Jacob, who was wearing his usual shirt and tie and trying hard to chat with an uncooperative trooper.

She thought she saw Jacob look her way, but he never tried to approach her. She was grateful, but, at the same time, she found it odd. She had the story. She was part of the story and obviously incapable of writing it. She could tell him everything he needed to know in great detail, and he could have an exclusive. Even if he didn't care about Lisa and her well-being, any good reporter would want to know what happened from a source who was actually there. Knowing Jacob, she thought, he would probably find his way to her the moment she finally got some peace and quiet. For now, she was grateful for the reprieve.

As Lisa's gurney reached the ambulance, she felt a familiar hand slip over her own. Bridget's face was stained with tears, but these were happy tears. She was grinning wide, and she laid her head on her mother's chest. Lisa finally let her head sink into the small pillow the paramedics had placed under her. Bridget was safe, safe forever from Deputy Donlin, and so were Dorothy and Winnie and Leo. Her family was safe. All she wanted now, she thought as Bridget climbed in with her and the ambulance doors closed, was to be with Bridget. To hold her hand and to hear her voice. To smell her skin. That was all.

Chapter Twenty-Seven

O vernight, they told Lisa. One night in the hospital and, if everything came back normal, she could go home with lots of restrictions. Her concussion was not severe, but the doctor wanted to run a few tests to make sure she had no bleeding in her brain from when Deputy Donlin had pistol-whipped her. When Lisa had protested, the doctor suggested that she sleep. Take advantage of the night on her own, with no responsibilities, no pressure. But how could she possibly sleep? Whenever the voices and the clanging and the footfalls in the hallways finally stopped for a moment, a nurse would barge in to check her blood pressure. Whenever her eyes did finally start to close, fear overwhelmed her. She'd forget where she was, forget that it was over. She just wanted to go home.

Bridget had stayed by her side the entire day, even when she was giving her statements. The investigators thought it best that Bridget leave, but Lisa didn't want to hide anything from her ever again. She wanted her to know everything. Bridget was a mess. Her face was all swollen again, and her skin was blotchy and red. Her nose was running, and she alternated between laughing and crying, hugging Lisa and pushing her away. Bridget needed her mother, and Lisa needed Bridget. Dorothy finally forced them apart at nine p.m. They would never rest this way, she argued, and then Lisa would never recover and be released.

The pills the nurse gave Lisa made her feel loopy, but not loopy enough to push her daughter and that image of her out of her mind. What would have happened if Lt. Hildebrandt had not pulled her over? What would Bridget have done? She was proud of Bridget, so proud, but at the same time, she wanted to ground her for the rest of her life. She tried closing her eyes again, hoping that at home, Bridget was doing the same thing. Bridget needed sleep—peaceful, restful sleep. She was the one who needed a night without worries. Lisa was supposed to worry. She was a mom.

It was strange to be alone in the room. It was a private room with a view of the parking lot from one window, a view of the hallway from the other, and a view of wallpaper with tiny, faint rosebuds everywhere else. She hadn't really been alone since she had regained consciousness down by the river. Investigator after investigator had questioned her in the ER, in the hallway, in the elevator, in her room. They had easily found the DVD in the morgue, they said. Alex hadn't tried to destroy it. He'd simply tossed it into a garbage can marked "biologically hazardous material." The janitor pulled it out and left it beside the garbage, thinking it must have been a mistake. Why would anybody put a DVD in that garbage can?

Dorothy had given the state police investigators the microcassette tape, and they were working on tracking down the old man who had tipped Lisa off. Sheriff Weidenfeld had stopped by to thank her for immediately telling the lieutenant about the tainted coffee, though, he said, Donlin was an idiot for thinking he kept only one EpiPen in the house. Apparently, the sheriff was severely allergic to lots of things—cats, eggs, bees. He had EpiPens in the kitchen, both bathrooms, and in his bedroom. The sheriff was in a good mood. He even showed her a photo on his phone of his new grandson, who was in another wing of the same hospital. Sheriff Weidenfeld wasn't so bad, Lisa decided, though he still struck her as shallow. Lisa had commented that the baby was cute, and he'd almost seemed offended.

"Cute is not a word you use to describe a boy," he said, pulling the picture out of her hands. "My grandson is not cute."

Sheriff Weidenfeld apologized if his mention of Bridget had upset Lisa that day in his office but, he said, it wasn't hard to figure out the relationship, and he felt it was necessary for both her safety and for the integrity of the investigation. He'd been investigating Marty for a few years, and he'd done some research, he said. Marty's name had appeared as the father on the birth announcement, so Lisa's name was right there in the file. Then Lisa came around wanting information and the sheriff realized that she would probably not let it go, not if this was her daughter's father.

"If he had been dealing drugs and somebody caught you poking around, you'd have ended up right there in the ground with him, and my investigation would have been over," the sheriff said. "Deputy Donlin was pretty clever and careful as it was, but I didn't know who he might have been working for. There are plenty of markets for drug dealers. They would have just backed out, and we never would have gotten anywhere."

The sheriff ran a hand through his thick hair. His face was covered with stubble. He looked like he hadn't even been home yet and, with all that was going on, Lisa was sure he wouldn't get the chance to shave for quite a while. "Body parts. I still can't believe they were dealing in body parts and corpses. No wonder I could never catch them with the drugs. All I needed was a little solid evidence to take it to the DEA. I was never going to get it, was I?"

Birth announcement. He had said it so casually. Lisa hadn't even known there was a birth announcement. How stupid could she be? Of course, there was. It was public record, and her own newspaper ran the local list of births, complete with the sex of the baby and the names of the mother and father, every Sunday back then. Maybe that was how Marty's mother knew. Maybe Marty never did tell her. It would have been in the *Sun Times* and in the local weekly.

Whenever Lisa got a break from the investigators, she talked with her editor. She had promised the district attorney that she would strike a balance between her journalistic loyalties and the need for secrecy about some of the facts in the case, so she filtered the details she passed on to the newspaper, something she had never imagined she would do. Unfortunately, the DA warned her that he would still probably seek a gag order, preventing her from talking about the case with any journalist at all or writing about it until after the trial. So, she spent her spare time passing on all the information she could and answering questions for other reporters while it was still legal to do so.

Lisa was so tired, but she was still too overwhelmed and distracted to fall asleep. She had been lying there in her room for what seemed like hours with her bed partially reclined, staring at nothing in particular in the darkened room, and thinking about how strange this whole thing must be for the others in the newsroom, when her eye caught an odd movement in the hallway. Someone had moved quickly, almost too quietly, near the window to her room, unlike the nurses who walked with purpose regardless of the hour. Seconds later, her door opened and closed, and a figure stood there, silhouetted by the lights that seeped in from the hallway through the blinds. A male figure.

"Who is it?" Lisa squinted for a better look.

"Shhh," the figure said, stepping closer. "It's me. Jacob. I wanted to come earlier, but I was stuck on deadline, and they weren't letting anyone in here, anyway. Then, when I got off work, visiting hours were over. I figured I'd just sneak in."

Lisa sat up a little more, leaning on her good elbow for support, and scanning the room for a digital clock. There was none. "But it's got to be at least two in the morning. I appreciate your visit, but I really don't feel like talking right now. I've been on the phone with the newsroom all day, and they gave me some drugs for the pain. I'm a little out of it right now."

Jacob moved closer until he was beside her bed. She could see his face now. Even in the dark, she could tell that he was tired. His skin was darker around his eyes, his lips were pale and dry, and he had loosened his tie and rolled up his sleeves. Sweat had seeped through his shirt under his arms, leaving wet stains. He definitely looked like a reporter coming off deadline on a big news day.

"Relax," he said, gently pushing her back down on the bed. "I didn't come here for a scoop. I came here to see you."

This was strange, Lisa thought. She and Jacob were not friends. They were co-workers who merely tolerated each other. It would not ever have occurred to her to sneak into a hospital room in the early morning hours for a social visit if Jacob had been the patient. Lisa looked at his face again. There was something about him. His eyes were not focusing right. He was a little jumpy. Something was wrong here. Very wrong. She kept watch on Jacob while she carefully reached down beside her bed with her good arm,

192

feeling for the call button that she knew was there somewhere, but he leaned across her and took her hand in his. His grip was firm. Painful.

"I wouldn't do that," he said, revealing a small pearl-handled knife in his other hand that he quickly placed on her throat. Lisa wanted to scream, but she didn't dare to even swallow. She could sense the cold sharpness of the blade. She could feel it slicing her skin just a little, just enough that she would know it really was there. And she could feel the warmth of her own blood as it began to roll in a thin stream down her neck.

"I just want to talk. That's all. You see, that's what Deputy Donlin is doing right now. He told me he would do that when he gave me the money to keep my mouth shut about Annette Baker. He gave me the cash and talked the sheriff into giving me the interview, but he said that if ever he went down, I would go down too. So, I'm going down. Tonight. Tomorrow. I don't know when."

He pushed just a little bit harder with the blade.

"I didn't figure it was that big a deal," he said. "She was scum. I didn't know why he killed her or if he really did it himself, but I knew there were no witnesses in Texas. He was in charge of that part of the investigation, you know. No one ever bothered to double-check, nobody within the department. They trusted him. Even the sheriff trusted him back then. Did he tell you he was an investigator before that injury landed him on desk duty? They're a small department. Since he couldn't go on the road, they made him work the desk and work on investigations at the same time, whatever he could do by phone. Nobody does just one thing in that department.

"Somebody would have killed that woman sometime if she didn't kill herself, anyway. Did you know that she dropped out of high school senior year? What kind of job could she get? A drain on society. A lazy, welfare bitch. That's what those people are like, and that's what I don't get," Jacob said, leaning so close into Lisa's face that she could feel the heat of his breath. "You're one of those people."

It was getting harder to stay still. Lisa's head still hurt, and her neck was slightly arched. It ached. Her back ached, her spine ached. Her temple hurt, and her right shoulder was too weak to give her much support, but she couldn't give in. After all that she'd been through, she couldn't die like this. Her throat was dry, and she feared that any movement would force the knife through her skin, but she made herself get the words out.

"Why, Jacob? Why am I one of those people, and how would this make anything better?" she asked. Her voice cracked. She couldn't help it. "You're looking at a misdemeanor at most, obstruction maybe. Why make it murder? If you keep that knife on my throat, you're going to kill me."

"Why? Why? Lisa, do you honestly believe anyone will hire me after this? I'm done. My life is over, and I can't let you keep going, sitting there in that newsroom, eating your whole wheat bagel, pecking away at your computer with your stupid, sorry-assed stories. I'm not a dirt-bag like you. I went to Syracuse University, to the Newhouse School of Journalism, on scholarship. I was the editor of my high school newspaper. My dad was the managing editor at the Chicago paper before he died. I am better than you, and nobody's going to get that. They are going to fire me when I didn't even hurt anybody. It was just money. She was already dead. I didn't kill anybody."

Jacob smirked and rocked the knife blade, pushing the point into her skin just a bit more. The pain, the shock to her body, was unbearable. He looked directly into her eyes. "Did you really think I just wanted to talk?"

Think. Think. She could not let the pain, her panic, take over. She had to think. Three more people were dead because of him, because he took that money and didn't report the story, but he would never get that. He would never understand that he was an accomplice because those people didn't count in his mind. Guilt wouldn't work with him. Even now, he was drawing that line, that insane line of his. Killing her wouldn't make it visible, but he seemed to think it would. She had to think like him. What was he thinking? He didn't know exactly what happened in the woods. She had promised she wouldn't give the newspaper specific details. She could use that. But, oh God, what if it backfired?

Jacob put a little more pressure on the blade. Lisa winced and felt the trickle of blood on her neck grow wider, thicker. She was bleeding more and bleeding faster, and his blade was near her jugular. Had he pierced it?

194

Was that what he was trying to do? Was he going to make a slow leak and keep the knife there, watching her die? The nurse had just been in before he came. It would be another two hours before she came back. How long would it take to bleed to death? Already, she could feel it running down her breasts.

"What if...what if I said I did it? Record me right now. Use your phone app. I'll tell you I'm sorry you're taking the fall, but that Donlin and I made an agreement in the woods when I got hold of that gun. I could have blown his brains out, but I said I'd just fire a random shot to get attention if he promised to take you down with him. You know, because I couldn't stand to compete with you anymore. You were too good. He can't prove that he paid you, can he?"

Jacob's arm stiffened, and he shoved the blade a little harder. Then he pulled back slightly, just a bit, but it was enough that Lisa could feel the difference. Still, her throat was bleeding even more, almost gushing now. It was flowing down her neck and chest, soaking her hospital gown and her sheets. She didn't have much time. She was starting to feel dizzy, but she didn't know whether it was from the loss of blood or just because she was scared. Horribly, terribly scared.

"Yeah. Yeah. We could do that. I'll bet he can't prove it. Why would he keep a receipt? That'd be stupid. And he gave me cash."

He started to pull his phone from his shirt pocket with his free hand.

"Jacob, you've got to stop the bleeding. I'm not going to do this if I'm going to die, anyway. Just let me put pressure on it. Let me put my hand up there. Please." Lisa started to lift her good arm, but he knocked it back with his phone.

"No! First the recording. Then you can put your hand on it."

Shit. He was going to record her, and then he was going to kill her, anyway. There was no way out. She just made it more satisfying for him. But he wasn't watching her as closely anymore, and he knew she was getting weak. He was fiddling with the app, alternating his gaze between her and his phone while still trying to keep the knife at her throat. Slowly, Lisa felt about with the fingers of her left hand. The rail, there was the rail. She traced the bed rail, feeling for the wire that led to the button. She found it. Then she stopped when he looked at her again.

"Got it," he said with a casual sort of enthusiasm, as if they were back in the newsroom reporting a story together, like they were working on a co-byline. He even smiled. "Now start talking."

She just needed a second. Just long enough to press the button, but she would have to get a little leverage to push down, and he might see the movement. She needed to distract him one last time. Just one second.

"Why don't you give some kind of introduction," she said between breaths, trying to sound as if it were a struggle just to get the words out. "So it makes sense? I'm really losing it here. Just ask me questions, like in an interview. Lead me through it. I can't think straight."

"Don't do that!" Jacob said, pushing the knife closer again.

Lisa's hand froze. How did he know? "Don't start talking about what we're doing here while I am recording. You ruined it. Now I've got to erase it and start over. I'll ask you questions, but no more talking like this is pretend, got it? This has to stand up in court."

"Sorry," Lisa said. "Got it."

No more waiting. This was it. While Jacob fiddled with his phone, trying to erase with one hand and keep her under his knife, Lisa lifted her left arm just slightly and pushed the button, triggering a quiet buzz. She'd forgotten about that. The buzz. That and the fact that sometimes it took the nurses a while to respond. It would be worse at night when there were fewer on duty. Jacob threw down his phone. He was mad. Very, very mad.

"You bitch."

He raised the knife above her with both hands, and Lisa watched him, as if in slow motion, plunging it downward, tip-first, toward her throat. It was like that moment in the woods when her heart beat so fast, she felt sure her chest would explode. But, once again, her mind was perfectly calm. Perfectly sane. Calculating, even. She was in control, and this time, she knew it. The rail was down on that side. The nurse had forgotten to raise it after she took her blood pressure the last time. That gave Lisa more room to move.

She threw her left fist up as fast as she could and knocked the knife off its path, screaming as it pierced her right shoulder. Jacob jerked the blade out of her and prepared to plunge again. But this time, she threw one leg off the bed for leverage, pushed up with her good arm, and rammed her entire body into his, ignoring the pain that ripped through her injured arm and shoulder, and knocking both Jacob and the knife to the floor. Her own body rolled off the bed and crashed onto the floor beside him. She screamed more and more, as loudly as she could, while he scrambled to his feet with the knife again in his hands, and within seconds the door flew open, and the lights were on.

"Run!" Lisa yelled to the nurse as Jacob lunged for the door.

The nurse backed out and screamed into the hall. Lisa dragged herself along the floor and into the hallway, trying not to faint. She was getting weaker, and blood covered the tiles now. Men in security uniforms appeared on either end of the long hall. They didn't have guns, but they had nightsticks. Jacob had no choice. There was nowhere else to go. Lisa watched as the guard Jacob headed for pulled his stick out and, in one graceful movement, brought it down on Jacob's head. Jacob lay sprawled on the floor, and this time, the screams and moans were coming from him. The knife had slid out of his hands, and the guard grabbed it. The other guard rushed past Lisa to help, stepping over her legs.

Lisa immediately felt hands putting pressure on her throat and shoulder, and within minutes, she was on a gurney and back down in the emergency room getting blood and stitches. Once again, investigators arrived, asking questions. All kinds of questions. When she was returned to her room—a different room on another floor—a police officer was stationed outside. There was no struggle this time. As soon as the nurses transferred Lisa into her bed, she closed her eyes and fell asleep.

Chapter Twenty-Eight

It turned out that Jacob had a history. But as often happens in the media business, editors and HR departments who worked for his former employers agreed to keep it quiet in exchange for a silent exit on his part. Owners of news outlets are more afraid of scandals than most of the people and organizations they report on. Scandals and lawsuits can cost them credibility. Without credibility, they lose readers. Without readers or listeners, they lose advertisers and revenue. So, no one told anyone that Jacob had been fired (allowed to quit, really) from a major news magazine for stalking and threatening another reporter or from an entertainment magazine for making up quotes and sources. He never even told his wife why he left the magazines. In both cases, he blamed it on disagreements with the way things were done and his desire to do daily reporting newspaper-style.

* * *

The weather had cooled considerably, and Lisa pulled her jacket tightly around her body as she stepped out of her car and waited for Bridget to do the same. She was four weeks into six weeks of disability leave from the newspaper. She had fought it at first, but, after consulting with their lawyers, all the high-ups had insisted on it—her editors, the publisher, and the director of human resources. She'd been through an awful lot of trauma, they said. She needed time and counseling before she returned. Lisa agreed that she needed time, but not counseling. She went anyway and ended up bringing Bridget and was surprised by how good it felt to talk to someone, someone who didn't know her or any of the people in her life. Bridget needed it even more, and the two of them, she now realized, needed it together. They had been to only two sessions, but they were two very good sessions. And because they had talked openly and honestly, they had both agreed that this trip was necessary.

Lisa walked around to the passenger side of the car, draped her arm around her daughter's shoulder, and pulled her close as they walked along the broken sidewalk to the front door. They had not called ahead of time, and Lisa hesitated before she knocked. She had to push the negative thoughts out of her head and accept her right to be here. This was her home once. This was where she grew up. Her departure was partly her own fault—there were other places she could have gone, people she could have asked for help—but mostly, it was their fault, her parents. She was learning to accept the blame and to give some of it away. Giving it away without adopting anger in return was the hard part. That was why she had come.

Bridget had her own reasons, and Lisa accepted that, too. Bridget needed to experience her mother's family for herself. She was almost an adult now, and adulthood gave her the right to choose. Lisa could let her pursue it on her own, or she could guide her through it. As painful as it was for Lisa, she wanted to be there. She wanted to catch her daughter if she fell or if her grandparents pushed her down. She just didn't trust them.

Lisa and Bridget said nothing as they stood there in front of the door. There wasn't much more to say. It was strange. She'd never knocked on her own front door before. She'd never even taken much notice of the worn gold knocker engraved with the name Jamison. Had that always been there? Thinking back, she supposed it had. Had the door always been beige? Had they ever hung a Christmas wreath on it or put out a "Welcome" mat for friends, family, and strangers? Those were the little things she couldn't remember, and that bothered her. It seemed she'd always been too busy, too stressed to store those kinds of details in her mind.

Finally, Lisa raised her hand and tapped the wood with her knuckles, gently at first and then harder. The door flung open and, as Lisa had expected, the new woman who she had seen a few weeks earlier getting the mail answered, the woman with the spiky hair. She could see the back of her father's head over the sofa where she was certain he was either smoking a cigarette or drinking a beer or both. The TV was on, loud and large. He was watching some talk show, where two people screamed at each other, barely able to contain themselves in their chairs, while the host leaned back and watched.

"Who the hell is it?" he yelled, without turning.

"I don't know," the woman said in a husky voice that indicated a long history with tobacco. "Some lady and a kid."

The woman gave Lisa an inpatient nod.

"What do you want?"

Lisa looked at Bridget, who nearly pushed her over the threshold with her eyes. The woman was tapping on the door with her fingernails as she held it open. Her hair was clearly bleached, almost white, and she wore jeans this time with a baggy, pink sweatshirt and baby-blue slippers. Her face was heavily made up, but the creases were impossible to hide. She was probably younger than she appeared, but she had that tough, leathery look. She was worn out, at least on the outside.

"I'm here to see my father," Lisa said, her hands shoved in her jacket pockets. "My name is Lisa Jamison. It's been a while. I'm not sure whether he ever told you about me. This is my daughter, Bridget. She's sixteen, almost seventeen."

Instantly, the television clicked off, and her father stood, putting his beer down on the end table. When he turned to look at her, Lisa's heart did all kinds of strange things. It wasn't love, and it wasn't longing. It was simply the familiarity of it all and the memories that flooded back when she saw his face. She remembered, suddenly, her life, her childhood. The good stuff and the bad. Things she had pushed deep down because she had thought they would be uncomfortable, potentially damaging. There might have been good reason for that years ago, but now they were nothing but memories. Harmless memories. She looked at him and felt nothing greater than nostalgia.

"What do you know," he said, tossing the remote onto the sofa. "Look who's decided to come home."

Her father hadn't shaved that morning. He probably hadn't been up more than an hour or so. It was eleven a.m. The house smelled of fried bologna, a favorite of his before and during the drug years, cigarettes and stale beer. He looked good, though, compared to the last time she'd seen him up close. He no longer looked like a drug addict. Just unhealthy. Skinny, frail, leathery, and old. The house looked as unkempt as he did with piles of magazines along the walls, clutter on the dining room table pushed back just enough to allow room for two plates, empty glasses, and bottles scattered about here and there. Not dirty, really. Just a mess.

"Suppose we've got to let you in." He didn't move from his spot beside the sofa. "Hurry up now. Shut the damned door. You're letting the cold in."

The woman rolled her eyes, stepped back, let them in, and closed the door behind them. Lisa took a better look around. She could see everything now from where she stood—the living room, the small kitchen that was separated from the rest of the house by a long, narrow counter, the dining nook that filled the space between the kitchen and the living room, the sliding glass doors that led to the deck out back. The place hadn't changed much. It had been seventeen years since she'd stood in this foyer and, really, seventeen years wasn't that long. People lived in their houses for thirty, sometimes forty years, with few changes. Why should her father be any different?

The drapes and carpeting were the same—antique gold on the windows and light brown shag on the floor. The furniture was different, or at least most of it. He had the same dining room table from what she could see of its surface with the same set of chairs, and the countertop was still covered with the same moss-green Formica. The house had always been at least somewhat cluttered. It was different clutter now.

Lisa's eyes rested on the door to her former bedroom, which was close to the top of the short flight of stairs and visible through the railing. The door was open, and she could see the corner of her old queen-sized bed, covered with an unfamiliar, blue, white, and red, knitted afghan. Open boxes and dark green garbage bags were strewn about on the floor and the bed, like someone had thrown a life's worth of junk in there. She guessed those things belonged to the woman. Lisa wondered whether her belongings were still there: her jewelry box, her posters, her CDs. She hadn't bothered to take much of anything when she left. She was too tired back then, too worn out to care, and she had no idea where she was going. Even now, she had no real desire to gather them up and take them home. They reminded her of times and feelings that she still preferred to leave behind.

"Well, at least you didn't bring any suitcases with you," her father said, finally moving a little closer. "This must be the kid that lady from social services mentioned. She's not staying with us. She's yours. Not my responsibility. So, if that's what you're here for, forget it."

Lisa wished she could have covered Bridget's ears just for that moment. Her young face had gone pale, and she looked stunned. But then Lisa saw the color beginning to return, too much color and too fast. Her face was reddening. Her hands were clenched in fists beside her body. Her lips had thinned, and her jaw tightened. All in less than a minute. Lisa reached over and gently took her daughter's arm, pulling her close. Bridget pulled away and yanked her arm back.

"You were right, Mom. This was a mistake," Bridget said, in a hard voice without taking her eyes off her grandfather. "Why did I ever want to meet him?"

"Because you had to find out for yourself, sweetheart," Lisa said, turning her attention to her father. "And I needed to remember. Dad, we don't want anything from you. Bridget wanted to meet her grandparents, despite my objections, and I wanted to make sure that I'd done the right thing all those years ago. Thanks for the reassurance. Now, where's Mom?"

"Hey, I gave you a house with a bed. A warm house with hot water and whatever else you needed. That wasn't enough for you. Even when I was using, I still gave you a safe place to be. So, don't give me any of that guilt crap. You left, and we weren't about to go dragging you back, kicking and screaming, not if you didn't want to be here. You were old enough, and you made your choice."

He looked at the floor.

"I got coffee if you want it, but that's about all."

Lisa let out a sigh and looked at Bridget. She had cooled down a little, and she shrugged. They'd come this far. Why not have a cup of coffee. Besides, he looked so pitiful. It was an odd feeling. She didn't feel any obligation toward him, any love. But he was family, and he was her father. She was starting to realize that without expectations, she was also free of judgment. She could have a cup of coffee with this man, get what she needed from him and leave. Her father couldn't hurt her anymore, not if she didn't let him.

The woman, whose name was Marie, managed to find a warm Sprite for Bridget, which Bridget pretended to sip while Lisa and her father talked at the table. Her mother had left long ago, not long after Lisa. She was heavily addicted, and she hooked up with some guy who had a lot of crack. They were headed to Boston, last her dad knew. When she left, he just stopped using. Cold turkey. It was tough, but he didn't have the money or the energy to keep going.

When he came out of it, he looked around and saw the mess. That was when he met Marie. She saved him, he said with a tired smile. She stood behind his chair with her hand resting on the back and took a long draw from a cigarette. Then she turned her head and blew the smoke in the air, clearly reveling in her hero status. Marie worked for an insurance agency as an underwriter. She helped him pull himself back together and get a job before the bank could foreclose on the house. They married a couple years later after he filed for divorce and placed the required legal notices in an attempt to locate her mother.

The house was his now. Her mother was probably dead, he said.

"That crack is nasty stuff. Beer and cigarettes might kill me, but at least they won't make me crazy," he said. "That stuff made her crazy. It made me crazy. We had some fun times, though. Got to give her that."

Marie gave Lisa's father a slap across the back of his head for his comment. "She still gets a little jealous of the old lady now and then," he said, rubbing his scalp. "Afraid she's going to show up someday and take me back."

Lisa had always felt that she had been right, that her parents had stopped caring for her when they fell in love with drugs and alcohol. Her father still did not love her, not really, even though he had given up the drugs long ago and now clung only to his beer and cigarettes. She didn't know why, and that hurt. That hurt deeply. But this time, Lisa left her father's home with a new kind of confidence. She left knowing their inability to love her was not at all her fault, not even a little bit, something that she had not realized she'd been questioning until now. She was not unlovable. Rather, they were incapable of love. But she worried about Bridget. Her grandfather had taken no interest in her at all. The only thing he'd noticed about her was her skin color, and that elicited a look that Lisa hoped Bridget had not noticed. Bridget had spent most of her time while they talked intensely scanning the house with her eyes while she toyed with her Sprite can.

Lisa felt no pull when they finally stepped outside, none of that allure that had brought her here time after time to stare at her childhood home from a parked car in the road, fighting that sick feeling in her stomach. The attraction was gone. The power that part of her past had over her was gone. Lisa's father was pitiful, and he was right—her mother was probably dead. And it was okay that she didn't much care. Lisa could see the young girl that she once was from a distance now and forgive her for her choices and actions. My God, she was only fifteen. Just a kid. She was even a little proud of her teen-aged self. Look what she had become despite all this. She was not like her parents, and Bridget would not be like her. Bridget was surrounded by people who set good examples for her, who made good choices in their own lives every day. She would make mistakes, but her mistakes would be her own.

After they had left the house and before she started the car, Lisa turned toward her daughter, who was quieter than usual. Calmer. She seemed so lost in thought that Lisa wished she could dig down in there, pull her out and cradle her in her arms. "I'm sorry," she said, noticing for the first time the features Bridget shared with her grandfather—the nose, the high cheekbones, the large eyes. Lisa couldn't remember her mother's features well enough to recognize them, but she probably inherited a few of those, too.

"He's kind of a jerk," she said.

Bridget surprised her mother by throwing her head back and releasing a long, loud laugh. A sweet, childish, contagious laugh that pulled Lisa along with it. They laughed so hard and so long that Lisa's stomach hurt, and she could feel the heat in her cheeks. She let the tears stream down because, for once, they were welcome tears. It was so good, so very good, to see Bridget this way.

"You think?" Bridget said when she caught her breath. "Screw him. Let's get pizza. I'm hungry."

Lisa found a small Italian restaurant just off the highway, halfway between her past and her future. It seemed like the right place to tell Bridget her news—that Marty's toxicology reports had come back negative for recent drug use. It was the final evidence Lisa had sought for her daughter's peace of mind. Bridget's father was definitely no user and no dealer. Anita, who had been promoted to chief medical examiner, called Lisa herself when the results came in. Deputy Donlin had already admitted to investigators he had planted the methamphetamine. He told them he crossed the street after the shooting with his gun under his jacket, pretending he had just seen Marty fall. He slipped the meth into his pocket and then simply walked away as other passersby took over and the sirens wailed.

Deputy Donlin was proud of it, proud that he knew patrols were several blocks away when he shot Marty, and proud that he knew he would have time to plant the drugs. They had found it easy to get a full confession from him. He loved to brag, especially when he believed he was among his own kind. Despite the fact that he would probably never again be a free man, he still seemed to think he was cleverer than all of them.

Chapter Twenty-Nine

Bridget had spent all afternoon with Grandma Celeste, getting to know her new Delano aunts, uncles and cousins over hamburgers and hot dogs, cooked over a backyard grill. She barely had time left to get ready. She pulled her red dress on, and it fell perfectly, the silken fabric slipping gently over her curves. It stopped just above her knees and was held up by thin straps. Her mother had offered to pay for an up-do, but Bridget didn't want it. They'd had their nails done together the day before—fingers and toes—and that was enough. Instead, she loosely clipped her curls behind her head and let the rest fall over her shoulders and into her face. Looking into the mirror, she was satisfied. Dressy but comfortable. Made-up, but natural. She didn't want to hide the person she was.

The doorbell rang, and she heard her mother invite Benjamin inside.

"Down in a minute," Bridget hollered.

After all she'd been through, Bridget had decided that she needed to be honest with Mandy, Benjamin, and herself. So, she had called Benjamin a few weeks ago, and he agreed to meet her for hot chocolate at Starbucks. She told him why she had broken up with him and why she had shut him out completely afterward, and about the emotions and reasons that she had denied at the time. She wasn't sure what would happen, but she needed to let him know that she loved him, or had loved him anyway, but that she had been too scared to keep seeing him. She told him she wasn't trying to break up his relationship with Mandy and that she wished the best for them, but that she was sorry. For everything.

He didn't say much. He drank his hot chocolate and listened. He offered his sympathies for all that she and her mother and Dorothy had been through. They talked for a bit about his family and about the jazz band that he had started playing with at some local clubs. He couldn't play in bars, only in the places that served food too, but he was making good money with his saxophone and learning a lot. He didn't have as much free time as he used to, and Mandy didn't like that, he said. They had different tastes in music, anyway.

Bridget quickly changed the subject and told him about her job at the vet's office, how she was beginning to think about becoming a vet herself. She was drawn to animals, even the mange-covered, flea-bitten ones. Something about them, about their nature, made her feel at peace. Benjamin had seemed distracted when they parted, and Bridget began to wonder whether what she had done was unfair. He was with Mandy, and they seemed happy enough. Sort of. She didn't want to be the reason they broke up...if they did.

Later that night, Bridget sat on Mandy's lime-green comforter in her room full of bright make-up, loud jewelry, and posters of half-naked men and confessed. She told Mandy about her feelings for Benjamin and about her conversation with him earlier that day. Then she apologized if she had overstepped her bounds and assured her that she wasn't trying to get him back. Mandy simply laughed and told her not to worry about it. She said that Drew McNeil in the eleventh grade was into sophomores. Maybe Bridget could nab him, and then they could double date. Mandy added that she was thinking about sleeping with Benjamin on prom night and asked whether Bridget would come with her to Planned Parenthood to get on the pill. She didn't want to end up like Bridget's mother. Didn't her mother know about Planned Parenthood when she was a kid, she asked. It's practically free, and you don't have to tell your parents.

That was when Bridget decided that she didn't need Mandy anymore.

Two weeks later, Benjamin showed up at the vet's office as she was leaving work and asked to walk her home. They were so engrossed in conversation that it seemed like the walk was over before it began. Her mother's car was in the driveway at six p.m. when they arrived, which was not unusual anymore. After the incident, she had been offered a position on a newly formed projects desk. Her hours over the past month since she returned from leave were odd sometimes, but she was often home for dinner, and she was almost always home when Bridget went to bed for the night. It was close to normal, but not too close. Bridget was proud of her mother and her career. She couldn't imagine her in some nine-to-five job. Normal wasn't her thing. She hoped that someday she would find a career that she would be just as passionate about.

Bridget wanted badly to invite Benjamin in, but she knew that dinner would be waiting, and the rule about her job was clear: she had to tackle her homework right after dinner if she wanted to keep it. Any drop in grades, and she was done. She thanked Benjamin for walking with her and was about to turn the doorknob when he stopped her. "Would you mind stepping back," he asked.

She looked at him, and he simply smiled, so she did as he asked, too curious to protest. Benjamin cleared his throat, stood on the top step directly before the door, and rang the doorbell. Dorothy answered and, after a brief introduction, Benjamin asked to have a word with "Mrs. Jamison."

Bridget's mom seemed a bit surprised to see him, but she shook the hand that he extended and asked him whether he would like to come inside. Then she looked at Bridget. Bridget raised her eyebrows and shrugged her shoulders. She had no idea what Benjamin was up to.

"Thank you, Mrs. Jamison. But I have something important to ask you, and I need to do it before I lose my nerve. With your permission, I'd like to ask Bridget to the junior prom. I promise we'll stay away from the parties, but I would like to take her to dinner beforehand. Just her and me. If she wants to. I mean, if she'll go. I mean…"

Without thinking, Bridget put her hand on Benjamin's shoulder and, when he turned around, she pulled him into a long, tight hug. She laid her head on his shoulder, like she used to when they were dating, and he held her just as tight. For a moment, she forgot that her mother was watching, and that Dorothy was likely peering through the living room drapes. She let him go and stepped back, slightly embarrassed, and his hand followed her arm to her hand, taking it in his.

"Hmm," her mother said. "Under one condition."

Bridget caught Benjamin's eye. He was a wreck.

"I have to approve of the dress. Now get in here and eat and do your homework. Benjamin, you're welcome to come by tomorrow when Bridget has more time, and I hope you'll stay for dinner. If you're going to spend a bunch of time with my daughter, I want to get to know you better."

And now here he was, waiting for her. Bridget pulled on her red, sling-back heels and started down the stairs. Benjamin was laughing about something as he talked with her mother, who seemed to be listening intently. Bridget stopped and stood there for a moment, watching them from above. They seemed so comfortable together. They both lifted their eyes as she descended, and the looks on their faces was something Bridget knew she would never forget. Dorothy came running in from the living room, camera in hand. Bridget was happy. Happier than she had ever been.

Chapter Thirty

Green blades of grass had overwhelmed the brown of last season, giving Lisa hope that this fall and winter would soon be behind her. She was fully recovered now. Well, almost. She still had a long, purple scar on the side of her head and a tiny triangular mark where the knife had pierced her throat as reminders, and her shoulder still ached if she overworked it or lay on her right side in bed. She still had dreams sometimes, horrible dreams. But the good nights were more frequent now, and the dreams less intense.

Her new job was an adjustment. She had always had to work extra hours to fit in the kind of investigative journalism that she loved, and she had always kept those stories quiet until she was almost done for fear that some anxious editor would want to run them too soon. But now that was her job, her only job, and she had an editor who was her sounding board, her advisor, and her protector from those who were more interested in filling that day's twelve-inch gap than in the quality of the story itself.

She had a daughter who was happier than she'd ever seen her and who finally had more than Lisa and Dorothy, more than just a few close friends who were labeled "relatives." She had a flesh-and-blood grandmother with aunts and uncles and cousins, and they were not all from Marty's side. Two months after the killings, Lisa wrote a column in which she reflected on the events and on her life. Calls, letters, and emails poured in after that—consolations from people who had lived similar lives, messages from those who just wanted to let her know how much her story had touched them, and requests for speaking engagements.

But the most important was the phone call from the uncle she never knew she had. Her mother had a younger brother. They were never close, and they grew further apart after her mother married. Then, when she changed—when she became rougher, more distant, more selfish—the rift became permanent. He didn't know his sister had been doing drugs, he said, or he would have fought for Lisa. He had held her as a baby and had taken her swimming a few times when she was five and six years old, though Lisa had never called him "Uncle." Her mother wouldn't allow that. Did she remember him, he wondered? And Lisa was surprised to realize that she did.

When she reached deep into her memory, she found two paddleboats spinning in the water and laughter echoing off the lake's surface. She found tall Cokes and French fries drenched in ketchup at a concession stand. She found a little girl, holding a firm hand as she waded in the part of Lake Tioga that was roped off for younger kids, for non-swimmers. She remembered his kind, excitable face, his long skinny legs, and his boyish chest. She remembered feeling safe and happy. Lee Vickery was, no doubt, her uncle. And when they met again, it was like they had never parted. She didn't know how much she needed family until she wrapped her arms around him and hugged him tight, and he hugged her back.

Lisa took off her jacket and threw it over her shoulder. They had been hiking through the old hayfield and up the hill along deer paths and old tractor roads for twenty-five minutes, and she was getting hot under the warm late May sun. Dorothy was in the lead with more energy than Lisa would ever have at her age. She stopped where the hill plateaued, spread her arms wide, and grinned.

"This is it," she said. "This is the front door."

With a burst of speed, Lisa caught up, stood beside Dorothy, and looked around. It was breathtaking. From their perch, they could see deep into the valley and over the lower hills. They could see rivers, ponds, and slices of lakes. Yet they were protected from the wind by the remainder of the hill that rose behind them. Lisa could imagine sipping coffee on this porch at sunrise on a summer morning, watching deer graze near the edges of the field where the trees formed a natural border. She could understand why Dorothy wanted to build here and why Dorothy had avoided the land entirely since her son and husband died. The house Dorothy had shared with her family was about three-quarters of a mile below as the crow flies, just a few hundred feet back from the stone-and-oil road. The couple who had rented it from her had two children now. A large wooden swing set and a trampoline occupied the side yard. They had built a treehouse in the back with Dorothy's permission. They were shocked and thrilled when Dorothy offered to sell it to them along with two acres at far less than market value. But Dorothy was finally ready to let it go, and she couldn't imagine passing it on to anyone else.

"This will be the living quarters," Dorothy said, turning to gesture behind and around her, "and the fireplace will be over there. I've already started gathering stones. I want that tall, cozy kind of stone hearth. The study will be a little larger than usual because I'm guessing that's where people will gather in the evenings. I'll have a wet bar over there in case anyone wants to relax with a drink. You know artists. They like their wine and gin. The kitchen will be good-sized too, and the dining room table will seat twelve. Everybody will have to help with either cooking or clean up."

The workshop with all of its studios would be a separate building with a covered breezeway attaching it to the main house. She wanted her guests to fully concentrate when they were working and to socialize with all of their energy when they weren't. Friendships that might form are part of the allure of artist retreats, and Dorothy wanted her guests to have the kind of experience that made them return year after year. An architect who specializes in Adirondack design was drawing up the plans. Dorothy had always loved the camps of the Adirondack Mountains with their cedar siding, forest-green trim, swinging screen doors, and porch swings. She wanted hardwood throughout the main house and Native American rugs. She described a huge porch that wrapped around the east side. Part of it will be screened in for the buggy days of early spring and late summer, Dorothy explained, hardly taking a breath. Though she planned to stay with Lisa and Bridget until Bridget left for college, work on the road would begin this summer. It would take time to landscape the lawn after the house was finished, at least a season or two, she figured. Dorothy wanted everything completed down to the last detail before she opened.

While Dorothy waited for construction to begin and end, she intended to keep painting and to start working on her business plan. She was more practical than most artists, and she knew how to manage money. Thanks to Lisa and her refusal to accept rent long after Bridget stopped needing a daily nanny, Dorothy had saved enough to pay for the house and workshop, but she still needed to earn a living. She would not fail, she said. She could not. And Lisa believed her.

"Bridget will have a job here whenever she wants it—summers, holidays, whenever," Dorothy said. "I know she has a whole lot more people in her life now, but I adore that girl, and I'm not letting her go."

"Oh, Dorothy," Lisa said. "You know how Bridget feels about you. None of that will ever change. You have been a second mother to her throughout her life. Sometimes you were the first mother. I couldn't have raised her without you, not the way that I did. We would both be different people, and it wouldn't be very pleasant."

Dorothy smiled and then surprised Lisa when she pulled her into her arms and gave her a quick, strong hug. She was full of life, full of excitement, full of energy that needed release. Her own artists retreat with classes for both residents and local folks. It was a dream that she had never imagined having the enthusiasm to make real. But Lisa's experience had taught her a thing or two, she said. She was tired of mourning what she'd lost and then pretending to be more than okay. She still had herself, and that was a pretty valuable commodity.

Lisa had noticed that in the past few months, Dorothy's color pallet had changed. The brightness was gone, replaced with more subtle, more warming colors. The earth tones remained, so beautifully integrated with that warmth, that Lisa sometimes just wanted to wrap herself in Dorothy's paintings. She was selling more and for higher prices. Her work was in demand, but she continued to pace herself like she always had, never tempted by money or success enough to burn out.

Lisa slid her pack from her back and pulled out a cold bottle of dry champagne along with a small tarp and two plastic cups. She spread the tarp over the grass where the front porch would someday be and gave Dorothy the honor of popping the cork into the air. Then they sat and toasted to Dorothy's dream. They drank their champagne without another word, comfortable with their silent thoughts, and then refilled their glasses, emptying the bottle.

"What about you, Lisa? What's your dream?" Dorothy said as she sipped. "You never talk about the future. You're young. A lot of women your age aren't even married yet. What are you going to do when Bridget is gone?"

"Me?" Lisa raised her eyebrows and stared across the hills. "I haven't thought much about it, but I think I plan to relax. Sleep as late as I want to, stay in my PJs all day once in a while, go out to dinner in a hot, red dress with some good-looking, rich guy just for fun, run a marathon. When I'm not doing that, I'll be worrying about Bridget, which means I probably won't do much of the other stuff."

A cool, gentle breeze passed over them, giving Lisa a chill and reminding her that summer was not yet here. It was spring. Buttercups, daisies, and phlox were everywhere, stretching up through the hay, reaching for the sun. Small, white butterflies alighted on their petals, sucking their nectar. Birds sang, cawed, and hooted from the nearby trees, probably chatting as they built their nests. Spring surrounded her. Spring should mean new beginnings, but that wasn't what Lisa wanted. Not anymore.

"I used to think I would leave here as soon as Bridget graduated, apply to some big-city paper like the *Boston Globe* or the *New York Times*. But that seems so silly now. I think I just wanted to be noticed, to be somebody, you know. And I believed that being somebody meant being well-known, maybe publishing a book or two."

Lisa looked down into her near-empty glass and shook her head. She had a slight buzz, a pleasant one. It'd been a long time since she'd had champagne. "I have so much here. Why did I ever think I wanted to give that up?"

"Well," Dorothy said, standing up and stretching. "We're all stupid once in a while."

Lisa stood, too, and finished her drink. She packed up their cups, the bottle, and the tarp and slipped her pack over her shoulders. Then she took one last look at the view that stretched out before her. She had promised Bridget a movie tonight, and she wanted to get cleaned up first. Her feet were unsteady as they made their way back down the trail, but Lisa didn't care. She knew that if she fell, there were people who would pick her up, and she would do the same for them. That's what it meant to really be somebody.

Acknowledgements

A novice writer once asked members of a writing group how many novels each author had written before getting published for the first time. I scoffed at the question, certain my first novel would sell immediately and launch my full-time fiction writing career. Here I am a decade later, a debut author with five completed manuscripts in hand.

Writing is tough and the publishing world is even tougher. What I failed to understand then is that the road to publishing requires a complicated support system built on the selflessness of others. The people who have buoyed me throughout this journey come from all walks of life. They are family, friends, former colleagues, fellow writers, literary agents, and even near-strangers, people with whom I have had only one conversation or one exchange.

I would like to extend my gratitude, first and foremost, to my publisher, Level Best Books, led by The Dames of Detection—Shawn Reilly Simmons, Verena Rose, and Harriette Sackler. You had faith in me and gave this novel life. Your expertise, guidance and unlimited support made *A Dead's Man's Eyes* stronger and gave me much needed confidence. I am fortunate to be working with all three of you.

So many people have supported my writing journey, beginning with three professors who profoundly affected me during my academic career: Michael Martone, Leigh Allison Wilson and Charles Wyatt. All three inspired me at different stages and in different ways. Amanda Avutu, Dee Garretson and Bill McFarland were my first fiction-writing colleagues and my first true beta readers. We came together as strangers forming a writing group in Cincinnati, but we emerged as lifelong friends. It was during my six years in Cincinnati that I met author Beth Hoffman as well. Thank you for always being there, Beth.

I would also like to thank the members of the Cozy Café, especially Savannah Thorne, Judy Walters, Karyne Corum, Laurie Will, Sara Backer, Lina Forrester and Jenny Milchman, for keeping me accountable, sharing so much terrific advice and supporting me through all the ups and downs. I owe tremendous thanks to Hank Phillippi Ryan and Mark Pryor for words of praise for *A Dead's Man's Eyes.* Your writing has inspired me, and your support and friendship have been invaluable.

Elizabeth Trupin-Pulli of JET Literary was my agent for four years. Though we eventually parted ways, she had a tremendous influence on me and on my work. Liz taught me patience and persistence, important skills for success in this business. Thank you, Liz.

And where would I be without beta readers? I would like to thank my sister Kathy Riley, who left this world before I could tell her about my book contract. She read all my novels and was among my greatest supporters. Also, thanks to my book-savvy sister Angela Bader; my cousin, Kelly O'Leary; my good friend and avid reader Tina Sabourin; and Patricia Monroe, my childhood friend, who is both well-read and a fantastic pediatrician.

Thanks to those who have always remained interested and invested in my work. The list is long. It begins with my stepdaughter, Kelly Foster, and my other siblings and their spouses—Patricia Bardua; David and Jean Duffy; Ed and Linda Duffy; James Duffy; and Andrew Duffy. Thank you to my mother-in-law Ava Foster; my aunts Kathy (Biddie) Lahue, Dolores Martin and Anna O'Leary, who has since passed; and my good friend Georganna Doran.

My children—Riley, Kiersten, Matthew and Jonathan—have been my cheerleaders from the moment they could understand what exactly I do. Their pride in me props me up whenever I feel overwhelmed or tempted to give up. I could never bear to let them down. All four have creative souls, which melts my heart. They have had an interesting childhood with a mother who sees murder plots in deep ravines, old warehouses and stormy nights, but they love me anyway.

I reserve my deepest thanks for my husband and fellow author, Tom Foster, who never stopped believing in me and supporting me even when that meant making do with less so I could find time to write. Tom has read every piece of my work. He is my greatest critic and my greatest supporter. I couldn't ask for more.

Last, but not least, I would like to acknowledge the writing organizations I have leaned on all these years. We all need our tribes and they have been mine. Thanks to the people of Pennwriters, Mystery Writers of America, Sisters in Crime, International Thriller Writers and The Historical Novel Society for the comradery, advice and support. It is invaluable.

I am sure I have failed to mention some people. It's inevitable. I never expected to write five novels before my first was published, so I was not as meticulous about keeping track of who read what as I should have been. You might not be listed here, but please know you are in my heart.

About the Author

Lori Duffy Foster is a former crime reporter who writes from the hills of Northern Pennsylvania, where she lives with her husband and four children. She was born and raised in the Adirondack Mountains of New York State, where a part of her heart remains. Her short fiction has appeared in the journal *Aethlon*, and in the anthologies *Short Story America* and *Childhood Regained*. Her nonfiction has appeared in *Healthy Living, Running Times, Literary Mama, Crimespree* and *Mountain Home* magazines. *A Dead Man's Eyes*, the first in the Lisa Jamison mystery/suspense series, is her debut novel. Look for book two in the series, *Never Broken*, in April of 2022. She is also author of *Raising Identical Twins: The Unique Challenges and Joys of the Early Years*. Lori is a member of Mystery Writers of America, Sisters in Crime, The Historical Novel Society and Pennwriters She also sits on the board of the Knoxville (PA) Public Library.

CPSIA information can be obtained
at www.ICGtesting.com
Printed in the USA
BVHW031915190821
614798BV00007B/86